This is a work of fiction. All of the characters, organizations, and events portrayed in this novel are either products of the author's imagination or are used fictitiously.

For information, address

Write 2 Eat Concepts, LLC

P.O. Box 2228

1965A Morris Ave

Union, NJ 07083

www.kwanfoye.com

ISBN 978-099810611?

'ARD

D0080052

Write 2 Eat Concepts

Hoodlum II: The Good Son @2017 by Kwan Foye
Printed in the United States of America
All Rights Reserved, including the rights to reproduce this book or portions thereof in any form whatsoever. For information address Write 2 Eat Concepts, Rights Department,
P.O. Box 2228 1965A Morris Ave. Union, NJ 07083

First Edition

Book and Jacket Design: PiXiLL Designs

Cataloging in Publication data is on file with the library of Congress

ISBN 978-0998106113 (trade paperback)
Printed in USA

HOODLUM II:

THE GOOD SON

KWAN

Other Novels by K'wan

Gangsta

Road Dawgz

Street Dreams

Hoodlum

Hoodlum II: The Good Son

Eve

Gutter (Gangsta Sequel)

Blow

Diamonds & Pearl

The Diamond Empire

Hood Rat Series in order:

1. Hood Rat

2. Still Hood

3. Section 8

4. Welfare Wifeys

5. Eviction Notice

6. No Shade

Little Nikki Grind (Vol 2: Purple City Tales)

The Life & Times of Slim Goodie (Season 1)

First & Fifteenth (A Hood Rat Short)

Black Lotus

PROLOGUE

Thick gray clouds hung over Staten Island, occasionally opening up for the sun to make brief cameos or pour down another heavy wave of rain. Even with the patches of sun, it did little to fight off the chill brought on by the damp air. Still, Carmen had made the trip as she had many times no matter the weather. The heaviness of her heart seemed to make the ground where she walked sink a bit deeper, but her back remained perfectly straight and proud with each step.

A handsome young man with rich black hair and evenly tanned skin walked a few paces behind her. He played her close enough to be able to protect her if necessary, but not close enough to invade her personal space. More than once he had been tempted to reach out to comfort her, but he held his position like the soldier he had been raised to be.
Enzo had grown up as one of New York's many forgotten children of Coney Island, Brooklyn in a single

parent home. His mother had taken off with a second- rate lounge singer when he was eleven years old, and it was him and his dad ever since. His father was a decent enough fellow who had made a bit of a name for himself around the neighborhood, but could never quite get a handle on the workings of the underworld. They had been a hard luck pair, but all that changed the night young Enzo had saved an older woman from being robbed by some crackheads when her car had broken down on Coney Island.

The next morning, Enzo found two very serious-looking men standing in front of his apartment door. They informed him that a Mr. Tessio had requested his presence, but knowing an order when he heard one, Enzo went along without struggle. His first impression of Michael Tessio was, "This is one fat son of a bitch," but he kept the thought to himself. He was both nervous and clueless as to why the fat man had asked to see him, but when Carmen entered the room, he made the connection.

"I want you to recount for me, word for word, how you came to know my wife," Mike ordered.

Enzo swallowed hard, before doing as he was told and repeated the events as best he could remember. When his story was done, his mouth was extremely dry and he couldn't help but to think how badly he needed a glass of water, but was too terrified to ask for one. Mike just glared at him as if he was searching for any hint of a lie in his words. Enzo became nervous. Had his story not matched up, and did the mobster think he was somehow involved? The young man was just weighing his chances of escape when the big man finally moved. It was a simple nod of approval, but it felt like a weight had just been lifted off of Enzo's shoulders.

Enzo waited for Mike to speak, but he simply got up and walked out of the room without so much as a thank you. One of Mike's men gave Enzo a ride back to the neighborhood and when they dropped him off, he was one thousand dollars richer. He guessed it was Mike's way of thanking him. By that point, Enzo figured his brief association with the mafia was over, but it would be a week later when he found out otherwise.

One early morning, Enzo's father had woken him to

announce that he was finally going to get help for his addiction. He was to check into an in-patient program the following day and Enzo would be left in the care of a friend during his recovery. That friend ended up being Mike Tessio. To repay the debt for saving his wife's life, Mike was going to change his. That was the beginning of an education that would span several years.

There were hundreds of tombstones lining the cemetery lawn, but Carmen paid them no mind, keeping her eyes fixed on the plot she had come to visit; the same one she had visited once a month for the past five years. It was a great marble sculpture of an angel with its arms and wings outstretched to the east to receive the sun every morning.

Wearily, Carmen approached the sculpture and knelt at the base. The damp ground soaked through her cotton dress, but she hardly felt it. She hadn't felt much of anything over the last few years except grief. Carmen's delicate fingers traced the groves that spelled out her husband's name and felt her heart clinch as she tried to find the words.

"My dear husband," she whispered. "I can't tell you how much I've missed you these years since..," she paused to compose herself.

"Michael," she sobbed, "You were a lousy husband, and a half-assed father, but you were all we had. Every year since your death, I have taken my request to Mr. Cissaro, and four times he has denied me my justice, saying only to be patient. One year ago, when the FEDS dragged him away, I cried tears of joy! But now Genaro Giovanni is head of the family, and his fear of our enemies and his greed for the money they bring in has him complacent and happy to co-exist. Instead of spitting in the faces of our enemies, Genaro allows them to eat at our table! I fear I will never have my justice."

A wave of sobs washed over Carmen and she went down on her hands and knees. Enzo took a step towards her, but she waved him away.

"My love, from the moment I saw him, I knew that the shadow of death walked with him and it was his children that walked death into our home. I tried to warn you, but you wouldn't hear me. Now, I find myself a widow with a bleeding heart," Carmen bowed her head as if she were deep in thought before popping up and continuing.

"Thankfully I have found a way to bring my heart peace. When they find out what I have done, I will probably soon join you in whatever hell you occupy, but it's a risk I'm willing to take at this point to see our enemies destroyed. I have even swallowed my pride and incorporated the source of this family's greatest shame into my plot. It would seem that not everyone is content to lap at the feet of that nigger lover, Gee-Gee. Soon all this will be made right."

Carmen rubbed a pinch of dirt between her hands and let the flakes fall at the foot of the headstone.

"If I can promise you nothing else, I can promise you this: Shai Clark is living on borrowed time."

PART I
"MEN OF RESPECT"

Hoodlum II: The Good Son

CHAPTER 1

Wally tugged at the neckline of what had once been a fresh white tee, and his fingers came away damp. He was sweating like a runaway slave with "Massa" hot on his heels. It was ninety-three degrees outside, and the heat trapped in the two-bedroom project apartment made it feel like the temperature was on hell. The air conditioner was busted and all they had to work with were two dollar-store fans that only circulated the hot air. Between the heat and the fumes coming from the kitchen, Wally felt like he was going to fall out, but he reasoned it was all a part of the job.

In the kitchen, Melinda stood over the stove, whipping two pots like she was making Sunday dinner. She was auditioning for a job with the new crew who had set up shop, so she knew she had to bring her best whip game. A bead of sweat rolled down her butter-flavored cheek, and splashed on the mural she had tatted on her forearm in memory of her deceased brother, True. Ambidextrously, she worked the water around in both pots at the same time, watching the cocaine and baking soda take their marital vows before the drug gods and forge a union known as crack. When she was satisfied with the consistency, she whipped the pots around once more for good measure before taking them from the heat and sitting them on the dining room table.

One of the fiends they had at the spot to test the finished product danced too close to the pots and Melinda met him with a forearm the chest.

"You can't taste the meal until it's done. When it cools, you'll get your blast."

"C'mon shorty, I can take my steak rare. Just let me wet my beak right quick."

The fiend shuffled in place, scratching his arm and sucking up the drips hitting the back of his throat. There was no way to say for sure when he'd last fixed, but his extreme thirst suggested it had been a while.

Melinda didn't like the desperate look in the fiend's eyes. Her hand swept across the table and inconspicuously picked up one of the razors they'd

bought to cut the crack up. She hoped to God she
wouldn't have to use it, but she was prepared to.

"Yo, why don't you be the fuck easy?" A slender light
skinned dude stepped into the living room. He was
dressed in a Nike jogging suit, with a gold chain and
cross hanging down his chest. From the way everyone in
the room perked up, you could tell he was the man in
charge.

"How we looking?" he asked Melinda.

"I just whipped the last two," Melinda nodded to the
two pots.

The slim kid picked one of the pots up and examined
it. Floating in the bottom of the cloudy water was a
perfectly round cookie.

"You got skills, kid," he told Melinda.

"Shit, I been in the kitchen since I was a kid. I told
you I had the god-hand with it. Y'all need to stop fronting
and put me on the payroll," Melinda said.

"Yeah, we might have a position to you," the slim kid
cracked a smile. "Yo Wally, go find them other two

young boys and have them come up here and help you cut this shit up. We about to flood the hood."

"I'm on it," Wally moved for the door. He had just undone the lock when the door burst open. He never got a good look at the person who had kicked the door open, but he had a great view of the stars that danced in front of his eyes when the baseball bat made contact with his head.

Two men rushed the pad, holding automatic weapons and wearing masks and ordering everyone to freeze. They were led by the young boy who swung the bat. He wore his hair in box braids with a red bandana tied around his head. He opted not to cover his face, because he wanted his victims to know exactly whom they were dealing with. He saw Wally trying to get up and gave him another whack with the bat. He hit him over and over, and continued hitting Wally long after he'd stopped moving. Everyone in the room was horrified about Tech's display of brutality, which was just what he was shooting for. He wanted to leave no doubt in anyone's mind how far he was willing to go in the streets.

Hoodlum II: The Good Son

"I think he's dead, so you can stop hitting him," Swann entered the apartment. He was a light-skinned kid who looked more Hispanic than black. His sandy hair was neatly braided into cornrows that hung to his shoulders. Physically, Swann was a pretty boy, but mentally he was as ugly as they came. His exploits in the streets had earned him a reputation as a killer, and a seat at the table of one of the most notorious crime families in the eastern United States, the Clarks.

"What the fuck is this about?" the slim kid asked as if he didn't already know what was up. He thought he would be able to fly under the radar and get his weight up a bit before he had to deal with the problem that he knew would come from opening up a crack spot in a hood that was claimed as property of the Clark family.

Swann looked at Tech, who stepped forward and smacked the slim kid. "Nigga, you know what it is. You been warned about this bullshit, but you still trying to violate so now you gonna get violated," Tech barked.

The slim kid looked like he wanted to try Tech, but he knew better. Tech was the alpha male in the Dog Pound, a crew of young hitters who were about the business of mayhem. None of them were old enough to drink, but they were old enough to kill. The slim kid figured he could probably take Tech in a fistfight, but whether he won or lost, the end result would be the same. He would die.

The slim kid finally found his voice and addressed Swann. "I know you said we couldn't pump around here unless it was y'all work, so I was just trying to sell off what lil' bit I had left so I can get up out your way."

Swann looked at the two fresh brewed pots on the counter. "And this is why you still cooking and bagging?"

The slim kid looked at the paraphernalia on the table. His lie was a weak one, and he knew it before he'd told it, but it didn't stop him. He had a feeling this was about to go poorly, so he tried to appeal to Swann's nostalgic side. "Swann, you know what it is to be a young nigga struggling, you been there. Every kid in the hood has heard the stories of how you gave it up as a young outlaw trying to get to the top."

Swann's lips twisted into a scowl. "The fact that you know my history and you still tried this dumb shit only makes me feel more disrespected." Swann picked up one

6

of the coffee pots with the crack cookies floating in them. "You lil' niggas always wanna throw

that shit out there about how you like us, but you ain't like us. Y'all punks, out here stepping on toes, because you so thirsty to get noticed. Well guess what, we see you now homie!"

He smashed the coffee pot against the slim kid's head. He looked at the slim kid, now on the floor crying, and shook his head in disgust. He turned to Tech. "Earn yo stripes, Blood, but leave nothing to chance. Everybody is aboard on this flight."

"Swann, you gotta be kidding leaving this young boy to clean up this mess. He ain't ready," one of the masked men said. He was the burlier of the two.

Swann looked at him. "And I was how old when you and the OG used to give me guns to play with?" he asked. The burly masked man didn't have an answer. "Exactly," Swann said, and turned back to Tech. "When you done, toss the pad. All you find, all you keep. Consider it a bonus."

"Say no more," Tech dropped the bat and drew a 9mm from his waistband.

"Wait, you gonna kill me over a few sales?" the slim kid asked in a frantic tone.

"Nah, I'm gonna kill you so the rest of these muthafuckas know what happens to clown ass niggas who go against the grain," Tech told him before pulling the trigger. The bullet took the slim kid off his feet and slammed him into the window. Tech shot him twice more, painting the wall and table with blood. When he was done with the slim kid, he turned his attention to Melinda.

Melinda threw her hands up defensively. "Wait, wait, wait, I ain't got nothing to do with this. I was just trying to make some extra money cooking up for some work. I don't even know these dudes like that."

"Next time, be smarter with the company you keep," Tech said and prepared to finish her.

"Hold on, youngster," Swann said. He was examining the remaining coffee pot. He turned his eyes to Melinda. "You got some skills, ma. You want a job?"

Melinda hesitated; making sure it wasn't a trick question. "Ah...yeah," she stammered.

"Cool, come see me tomorrow morning and I'm

gonna put you to work. I don't think I have to tell you what'll happen if you ever breathe a word of what happened here, right?" Swann asked.

"Hell no, I ain't seen shit and I don't know shit," Melinda assured him.

Swann nodded. "Good answer. You start tomorrow morning at eleven."

"But wait, how will I find you?" Melinda asked. "You won't have to, I'll send somebody to pick you up," Swann told her.

"But you don't even know where I live."

"I will by tomorrow morning," Swann winked. "Just some food for thought in case you get any big ideas, ma. The name is Swann. Ask anybody in the hood how I give it up." Swann turned and addressed his crew. "Let's make moves. Shai's function starts in a few hours and it'd be in poor taste for us to show up late."

CHAPTER 2

Ghost pushed the Rolls Royce through Central New Jersey with no regard for the posted speed limit. When he bent the corner of Raritan Road, he made sure to cut it extra sharp, causing the older couple in the back to slide from one side to the other. Sparing a quick glance in the rearview mirror, he silently chuckled at the looks on both of their faces. From the way his mother, Maureen, was clinging to her seatbelt, he knew that she was nervous, but she wouldn't give him the satisfaction of saying so. His father, Chance, on the other hand looked like a powder keg waiting to explode. In the passenger seat, his sister, Lolli, did a poor job of hiding her amusement. She knew what Ghost was doing and why he was doing it.

"Ghost, why don't you slow down? This ride costs more than some of the houses out here and you're driving it like a hooptie!" Chance finally snapped.

"Sorry, Daddy. I was just making sure we weren't late. I know how important it is for us to stay in favor with the prince," Ghost replied sarcastically.

Hoodlum II: The Good Son

Seeing anger flash across her husband's face at his eldest son's defiance, Maureen interjected before the situation got worse. "Junior," was all that she needed to say, and just like that, the tension between the two men was drained away and Ghost eased his foot off the pedal. Maureen had always had that effect on all of her boys, including her husband. Chance King might've been the head of their family, but Maureen was the law that governed them.

The next mile or so of winding New Jersey roads were spent with Lolli and her mother making small talk, but the men were relatively silent. Chance could tell from the tightening of his son's jaw that he was still holding onto his anger. He leaned forward and flicked Ghost's ear like he used to do when he was a child. "I know you ain't sitting up there salty because I asked you to fill in for Joe and drive us today?"

"Nah, I'm good, dad," Ghost said without taking his eyes off the road.

"You come from me, so you can't lie to me, C.J." Ghost cut his eyes at his father. "You know I hate it when you call me that."

"Why? I named you after me, Chancellor King Junior, and you should wear it with pride," Chance told him.

"I do, Daddy, and I didn't mean no disrespect by it. It's not the fact that I gotta play driver, instead of sitting to your right where I belong. I'm cool with that. It's everything else about this little outing that's got me irked. Why the hell do we have to come all the way out here to kiss the back of this nigga's hand like we ain't royalty too?" Ghost fumed.

"First, let's get something straight, son. We have been Kings of Five-Points in name and power for over one hundred years. From great granddaddy on down, we were born gangsters and have never, nor will we ever, kiss the hand of another muthafucka. This trip isn't about a pissing contest, but a gesture of good faith. Our two families have been doing business together for decades and it'd have been looked upon poorly for us not to show up in person to deliver our congratulations."

Ghost snorted. "And when was the last time they been south of Lafayette? Listen, Daddy, I get what you're trying to say. This is a respect thing, and I get it. I had no problems with it when the old man was running things. I was even cool when it looked like the eldest boy was in charge, because he had earned his stripes in the streets, but what has this kid done to earn the respect of a real gangster?"

"Stepped up and kept his father's legacy intact when his number was called!" Maureen interjected, tiring of Ghost's belligerence. "Son, regardless of how anyone feels about the present state of things, there isn't much any of us can do to change it, at least not presently. Politics are a part of the game. Now if spending an hour or so of your time to help solidify this new relationship is too much to ask of you, then you can drop us off and come back to pick us up when we're ready to leave. If not, stand as your father's strong right hand like I raised you to be and stop crying like a damn girl!"

*

"Damn, look at all these cars!" Belle squealed with her face pressed against the glass of the Range Rover she was riding in. She was a petite young thing with rich brown skin and large doe eyes. There were luxury cars and limos stretching nearly an entire block, all waiting to be granted access to the same place. Several valets scrambled back and forth trying to accommodate the guests and their cars, but they were having a rough time of it with all the traffic.

"Gotta be at least a dozen of them, at least that I can see." Brianna adjusted her glasses, taking a quick mental count of the vehicles. She was a light-skinned, unassuming girl with zero fashion sense, but the mind of a genius. This is how she got the nickname Brain.

"And we're stuck at the back of this shit," Natalia huffed, flashing traces of the accent she had been trying to shake since arriving in the United States two years prior. She was a Nordic-looking blonde with cold blue eyes and thick pouty lips. For as beautiful Natalia might've been, she was also incredibly dangerous. Before coming to stay with Ruby, she had been an orphan on the streets of Belarus. Those days in Russia were dark ones and Natalia was forced to do some things she wasn't proud of in the name of survival.

Hoodlum II: The Good Son

"Language!" Ruby snapped from the backseat, tapping her cane on the floor of the truck for emphasis. She was swathed in the shadows of the vehicle, face hidden under a large church hat and eyes masked by sunglasses. Ruby had been so quiet that the girls had almost forgotten she was with them. That's how the old woman was, rarely seen but she was always heard when it mattered.

"Sorry, Ms. Ruby," Natalia said, sounding like a child who had just been scolded.

Belle cupped her hand over her mouth to try and hide her snicker. Natalia was always picking on her so she got a kick out of Ms. Ruby humbling the white girl.

"And you," Ruby whacked the back of the driver seat to get Belle's attention, "When we get inside, you be sure to keep those sticky fingers to yourself. I don't want you embarrassing us in front of our hosts. Do you understand me, Lulabelle?"

"Yes, ma'am." Belle seemed to curl in on herself. "Dag, why y'all always act like I steal stuff wherever I go?" she pouted.

"Because you do!" Natalia slipped in.

Belle and Natalia went back and forth, with Brain trying to defuse the situation to no avail.

Ruby sat in the back shaking her head in disappointment while the girls bickered. Belle had Natalia so mad that her face had turned as red as a tomato. From the frightened look in Brain's eyes, she probably thought Natalia was about to hit Belle, but Ruby knew better. In Ms. Ruby's house, most offenses could be forgiven, but harming each other would get you exiled or worse. Ruby instilled a sense of sisterhood into all the young women who came under her wing. No matter what race or background you came from, all were family in her house.

Of her three charges riding with Ruby, Belle had been with them the shortest time. She had a knack for rubbing most of the girls the wrong way, but got under Natalia's skin the most; probably because of the circumstances under which Belle had come to them.

Belle had made the mistake of picking the home Ms. Ruby and the girls stayed in to burglarize. Natalia had been on guard duty that night and didn't even notice the little girl slip into the house. Had it not been for Brain's

Hoodlum II: The Good Son

weak bladder ruining the heist, Belle would've made off with all Ms. Ruby's good jewelry and half the silverware. Natalia wanted to bury Belle in the backyard, but Ms. Ruby had something else in mind. Anyone skilled enough to get past the blue-eyed wolf would make a welcome addition to their little family of misfits. So, against Natalia's protests, Ruby welcomed Belle into her home for wayward girls. Belle would one day go on to become a master burglar... if she didn't manage to get herself killed first.

Ruby spotted a handsome man wearing a black suit and ear-piece making his way towards their vehicle. He had rich chocolate skin and curly black hair that was freshly cut and blended into his smooth black beard. To women who laid eyes on him, he looked downright edible, but Ms. Ruby recognized the killer glint in his eyes. "Moment of truth," she tapped her cane on the floorboard. "Be sure to mind your manners and don't speak unless spoken to. Most importantly, remember who you represent," she warned, adjusting her big hat.

"Invitations?" The man in the black suit requested in an easy tone. This was Brutus; he handled security for the property. He was as dangerous as he was easy on the eyes.

Ruby removed a laminated card from her purse and handed it to him. He eyeballed it for a few seconds before pulling what looked like a supermarket price-checker from his jacket. He scanned the card, and only when the LED light flashed green did he motion for the other valets to come open the doors. He reserved the pleasure of helping Ruby out of the car for himself. Ruby remained poised, while the other girls looked over the property, starstruck. Even the normally stoic Natalia seemed impressed, but it was Belle who put into words what they were all thinking.

"Holy shit!"

Brutus smirked. It wasn't the first time he had seen that response when people visited for the first time, but no matter how many times he saw it, his heart always filled with pride knowing that he was the guardian.

After letting Ms. Ruby and her girls bask in it for a few seconds, Brutus spoke up. "Welcome, honored guests, to the Clark Estate."

CHAPTER 3

Shai Clark sat in his office, hunkered down in his favorite chair. It was a large leather wing-backed number, lined with metal studs. If you looked closely, you could see that the studs were crafted to resemble small golden crowns. It had been commissioned by his late father, handcrafted and imported from Italy. Shai could still remember the first time he had climbed into the beautiful chair. With his thin legs hanging over the edge, feet barely able to touch the ground, it was like sitting on a cloud and looking down at the world. Years later when the leather had begun to crack and some of the crowns had fallen away, the effect it had on Shai hadn't changed. It was then he realized that it wasn't how the chair was built that made him feel powerful when he sat in it, but what it was built for - to seat kings.

On the desk in front of him, his laptop sat flipped open. An old college basketball game was playing on the

screen; NC State vs. Kentucky. The television was
muted, but Shai didn't need to hear the play-by-

play to know what was happening in the game; he had
relived it more times than he could count. The match had
been promoted as The Battle of the Backcourts, with a
future NBA draft pick out of Kentucky trying to knock
the chip from the shoulder of a second-year point guard
from New York City who had nearly singlehandedly
carried N.C. State to within a win of a tournament berth.
The stands inside Rupp Arena were packed for the
nationally-televised event. Most expected it to be a good
game, but none were quite ready for the ensuing duel.
Kentucky's NBA prospect hung thirty points on N.C.
state, with twenty coming in the first half, but the cocky
sophomore's game-winning three-pointer is what
everyone remembered. Shai Clark carrying his team to
the tournament was amongst the sweetest of his life, and
then the other shoe dropped and life as Shai knew it had
been ripped to pieces.

In addition to being the school's star point guard, Shai
was also the campus bookie. However disgruntled loser
blew the whistle about Shai taking bets on the games he

played in, and got him bounced out of school and a lifetime ban by the NCAA. His father putting a good lawyer on the case saved Shai from being brought up on charges, but his career and reputation had been ruined. With his academic and sports career dashed, Shai returned home and got involved in the family business.

A soft knock on the door drew Shai's attention from the game. "Come," he said, closing the laptop.

A heartbeat later, Swann walked in the room. He had traded his street clothes for a button-up shirt, jeans and Timberlands. "I thought I'd find you hiding in here, Slim," he called Shai by his nickname.

"Man, I wasn't hiding."

"I don't know what else I'd call it when you've got about three hundred guests on the property, but your ass is tucked away in here instead of mingling. You were probably in here watching that damn game again," Swann turned the laptop towards him and flipped it open

"You think you know me, don't you?"

"Better than most. We've been running tough since the seventh grade," Swann reminded him.

21

Swann and Shai had a history that went back to before Poppa was boss of bosses and the Clarks were still living in the hood. Back then, Swann was just a snot-nosed kid selling dime bags on the block for whoever would allow him to eat. In the beginning, Poppa didn't like the fact that Shai and Swann were so tight, because Swann was what his father called "street poisoned" and he didn't want it rubbing off on his middle child. He had a plan for Shai, and getting caught up in the things Swann was doing wasn't a part of that plan. Even when he tried to forbid Shai from running around with Swann, the two would sneak and hook up anyhow. After a while, Poppa realized that there was nothing he could do about the bond between the two boys, so instead of pushing Swann away, he pulled him in closer. He pulled Swann in off the corners and gave him a position as a part of Tommy's crew. While Shai was getting his education in the classroom, Swann was getting his on the block. Tommy's new protégée proved to be not only loyal, and it didn't take him long to climb the criminal ladder. By the time Shai had come home from college, Swann had risen from Tommy's pupil to his right hand.

Hoodlum II: The Good Son

Shai had been around the streets all his life, but never truly in them. After Poppa was murdered, it was Swann who Shai leaned on heaviest to help put things back in order. Shai Swann became both his confidant as well as his enforcer. Swann played a major role in holding the family together when things were falling apart and in truth, Shai doubted that he'd have been able to hold onto what his father had built without his best friend. When Shai's ascension to the throne became official, it was only right that Swann stand as his right hand and second in command. Some of the other capos had frowned on the move, thinking it should've went to Big Doc, or maybe even Angelo. Both of them had served faithfully under Poppa Clark for many years, which was the exact reason Shai didn't offer the position to either of them. They were Poppa's friends, but Swann was his. The old ways were gone and he was ushering in a new era for the Clark family as he saw fit.

"How did that thing go?" Shai asked.

"For the most part things got a little messy, but that's to be expected when Tech is involved," Swann told him

Shai shook his head. "That little muthafucka is all bite and no bark."

"That's why I fucks with him," Swann said proudly. "By the way, I appreciate you inviting Tech today. I know you really don't care for him or the Dog Pound."

"It wasn't an easy decision, believe that. I figure if you insist on grooming that little maniac then we might as well begin the process of teaching him some table manners. You just make sure you keep that dog on a short leash while he's here."

"You ain't gotta worry about that, Shai. I made it clear to Tech how important this day is so he ain't gonna fuck it up," Swann assured him.

"You better make sure he damn well doesn't, because if he does then it's your ass!" Shai warned.

"Knock it off, Shai. You act like you forgot that we were once young and wild too."

"Wild is one thing, but Tech and his crew are only a step up from rabid dogs," Shai said in disgust.

"That's the same thing they said about Gator, but Poppa gave him an opportunity to prove otherwise. When the time came, Gator laid down his life so you could sit in that chair!" Swann shot back.

Gator was Shai's wild ass cousin. He was on the run for a murder in Florida and had been hiding in New York. Shai had met a lot of gangsters over the years, but none were quite like his cousin. Gator was down for whatever, whenever and had proven it more than a few occasions during his short time in the service of Poppa Clark. Shai and Gator had always been close, but the blood they had spilled in the streets together strengthened that bond. He was a one-man kill squad and had singlehandedly turned the tide in the Clark war against the Italians. He lived for the Clark cause and had ultimately died for it having given his own life in a fire-fight with the police so that his comrades could escape. There was not a day that went by that Shai didn't think of his cousin and what might have been had he lived.

"You can't compare Gator to Tech," Shai told him.

"Why? Because Gator had us to turn to and Tech is out here all alone? That plus a few years is the only difference between them," Swann said. "Look Shai, I'm not asking you to take the kid to the park and play catch with him, just don't be so quick to condemn the youngster. Give him a chance."

"I'll think about it," Shai finally relented.

"Fair enough, but while you're thinking, just remember that this empire was built on the bullets and blood of men like Gator and Tech."

"You seen Tommy?" Shai asked.

"Not since this morning. He's probably in that little private library of his, brooding and shit," Swann joked.

"Seems like that's all he ever does lately. Since he came home from prison, Tommy has been acting different and I'm starting to worry about it," Shai admitted.

"You'd be a little sour too if you had to sit up in a wheelchair for the rest of your days, not to mention the two years he had to lay down while fighting those murders," Swann pointed out.

Poppa Clark's murder affected the lives of everyone around him, good or bad, especially his children. It had changed them all mentally, but Tommy was the only one forced to make physical adjustments. He had been first on the scene the evening Poppa was hit. They had Shai to thank for discovering Fat Mike's treacherous plot. Tommy showed up, guns blazing and murder in his heart. He laid down several of the assassins, but was too late to save his father. Shortly after Tommy showed, so did the police. All it took was for them to see a reputed killer, armed and standing in a ring of dead bodies, and it wasn't even up for debate. The police put a dozen slugs into Tommy without giving it a second thought. They had failed in their attempt to kill Tommy, but succeeded in breaking the foundation of the Clark family.

Tommy hadn't been given a chance to mourn his father let alone recover from his injuries before he found himself locked up on a slew of charges, including multiple homicides. They were charging him with the bodies he had dropped trying to save Poppa.

To make matters worse, because of Tommy's reputation, the D.A. moved to have him held without bond. They stated that because of the Clark's vast resources he represented a flight risk, which was laughable. The bullets Tommy took had made him a quadriplegic and he needed round the clock medical attention, which made fleeing unlikely, but the judge went for it anyhow and honored the district attorney's request. The Clark lawyer, Martin Scott, had filed several appeals, but the ruling stuck and Tommy had to fight the case from the prison infirmary. It was obvious to all of them that someone very well connected was pulling the strings that kept Tommy locked up. With Poppa dead and Tommy caged, the streets reasoned the Clark empire would be easy pickings, but Shai had other ideas about what would become of his father's legacy. It took close to three million dollars in bribes and backdoor deals for Shai to get the charges reduced to manslaughter and Tommy's bail reinstated so that they could bring him home, but Shai had already been crowned king and the war was dying out. The battle in the streets was over, but the one to heal Tommy's broken body was just beginning.

"After all that bullshit and being crippled to boot, I might be sour at the world too, Slim," Swann continued.

"Had I known the big chair would come between me and my brother, I'd have never accepted it," Shai said honestly.

Hoodlum II: The Good Son

"And that's probably what stings the most. You've got something that Tommy has craved all his life and you don't even want it."

Shai slunk in his seat, seeming to shrink under the weight he was carrying. "I never asked for the crown, Swann."

Swann shrugged. "Yet on your head it sits. Ain't much left you can do about it at this point except wear it as best you can."

Shai didn't reply; he simply nodded. Swann was right, as he usually was when it came to those matters. Whether he wanted it or not, the mantle of leadership had fallen to him and he had a responsibility to his father's legacy.

"Oh, before I forget, I saw old man Chance and his family out on the lawn."

"Really? I wasn't sure they'd attend," Shai admitted.

"C'mon, Slim. Everybody who received an invitation knows it would've been taken as a personal insult not to attend. Old man Chance is a lot of things, but a fool isn't one of them. Besides, you and I both know why he made it his business to show up."

"To butter me up about this expansion," Shai sighed. "The King family has been content to rule over Five-Points for decades and now all of a sudden they wanna stretch their legs into Brooklyn. This sudden change of heart is puzzling."

"Ain't too much of a puzzle if you really think about it. Chance is a politician, but his bread and butter has always been real estate. Brooklyn is on the come-up. The same run down tenements they were selling for under a hundred grand ten years ago are being priced at close to a million dollars now. If I'd been smart, I'd have invested some of my bread into real estate when Poppa tried to get me to. The old man is probably trying to score one last big payday before he turns everything over to his son, Ghost."

The mention of the eldest King male made Shai shiver. Ghost King's exploits in the streets were the stuff of legend. He moved like a shadow, snuffing out life wherever he went. Rumor had it that Ghost's body count in New York City alone was somewhere in the double digits. It was all speculation because no one could ever positively I.D. him as the killer. He moved as silently as the grave, which is how he had earned the nickname Ghost.

"I ain't never been no big fan of Ghost or his people, but his little sister Lolli can get it," Swann said thirstily. "I hope she takes advantage of all this free liquor you setting out so I can try my hand with her tonight."

"Nigga, you playing with fire trying to push up on that girl with Giselle out there," Shai warned him.

Swann sucked his teeth. "Man, you know wifey a square. By seven o'clock she'll be on my nerves to take her home. I'll drop her off and double back, telling her you need me for something tonight."

"Oh hell nah. If I get caught up in your bullshit, she's gonna tell Honey and set off her paranoia meter and I'll be stuck arguing about shit I did two years ago all night. I love you my nigga, but you better find another scapegoat."

Swann gave Shai a funny look. "After all the bullets I took, and still take, for your ass? My G, you can't be serious."

"That was the old me, Swann. Lately I been trying to keep my spoon out of hoe soup," Shai said honestly. It

31

was common knowledge that Shai was a player. Before and during his time with Honey, Shai had knocked down women from all across the globe. He was young, fly and powerful, which drew females to him like flies to shit. Shai played modest, but he loved the attention. Adoration from women fed his ego more than being rich or running the empire could have. He'd slowed down after he met Honey, but his tipping out hadn't stopped all together. Honey was a good woman who held him down and kept his secrets, but Shai was used to having a variety in his life. With age came wisdom and Shai had purged all the side-chicks from his life, but he'd be lying if he said his craving for new pussy wasn't still lingering.

"So, if you ain't gonna help me fuck Lolli, are you at least gonna grant her old man's request?" Swann asked.

"I haven't decided yet. There are other things to factor into his expansion, like the Wongs. I gave them a little patch of land out there to play with and the King expansion might step on their toes," Shai said. The Wongs, Billy and Max, were a pair of Chinese brothers who the Clarks did business with. Tommy's decision to start buying heroin from them instead of Fat Mike was what had inadvertently sparked the war with the Italians.

"Fuck them sneaky ass slants!" Swann spat. "For as much as we sacrificed for them, you'd think at the very least they could've shown up today."

"Be cool, Swann. You know Billy has had his hands full trying to get his brother back into the country after his deportation. Besides, Billy sent a gift with his apologies days ago."

"Well if he couldn't make it himself, at the very least they could've sent a representative," Swann countered.

"Billy gets a pass, and let's leave it at that," Shai said, letting him know it wasn't up for discussion. "Where's Sol? I'd like to bounce this Chance King thing off him before I make a ruling."

"Lansky called ahead earlier and said he'd be late. He had to take care of something before coming out," Swann told him.

"I wonder what was more important than coming here and standing as my left hand, as you're my right?" Sol was one of the Clark family's oldest and dearest friends.

He had been a business partner and advisor to Poppa, and now he lent counsel to Shai.

Swann shrugged. "Who knows? You know he plays his hand close to his chest. He assured me that he'd be here though. As far as this thing with the Kings, I'm sure me and you can put our heads together and figure it out."

Shai smirked. "I love you for always being there for me, Swann, but this isn't your area of expertise. I come to you in matter of war, but it's Sol who I consult in matters of finance. Just keep an eye out for him and have him find me when he arrives. On another note, did Louie get here yet?"

"So far, no meatball sightings, but you know he ain't gonna pass up no free food or drink. Why'd you even invite that cat when the Italians don't really fuck with us like that and we sure as hell don't fuck with them?"

"I didn't invite him; he reached out through a friend. It has something to do with Gee-Gee and he wouldn't talk about it on the phone."

"Sounds like some heavy shit needs to be hashed out. You need me to put a few of the boys on standby in case this nigga comes in here talking crazy?" Swann asked eagerly.

"I doubt if it'll be all that. Our families really don't care for each other, but my arrangement with Gee-Gee keeps everybody at least civil."

Swann shook his head. "I still can't believe you got that sour old bastard to play nice. So you ever gonna tell me what went on in that meeting?"

"I've already told you, at least as much as you need to know. Trust me Swann, it's better this way," Shai said honestly. "Leave it at that."

"You got it, boss." Swann stood to leave. "So you gonna keep hiding in here reliving your past, or put your crown on and come embrace your future?"

"I'll be along in a few." Shai grabbed his autumn-colored tie from the arm of the chair and began looping it around his collar. "Keep the party going until I get there."

"Well don't take too long. I hear the guest of honor is getting antsy."

Shai ran his hands over the five o'clock shadow growing over his cheeks and sighed. "When is she not? Her ass will be okay for a few more minutes."

"If you say so, Slim. I'm a tough muthafucka, but I'd sooner take on one hundred Italians than an angry pregnant woman," Swann capped before leaving Shai to his thoughts.

After Swann had left, Shai went to stand in front of the full-length wall mirror to finish tying his tie. As he stared at the image, he couldn't help but to think how much different he looked than the gangly, doe-eyed kid who had carried N.C. State to the Division 1 tournament. He had put on ten pounds (mostly fat,) was sprouting the first signs of a beard on his cheeks and the youthful glint that once danced in his eyes was gone. The boy had become a man. Once he was satisfied with his appearance, he headed for the door. Before making his exit, he stopped short, eyes landing on a large oil painting that hung over the loveseat. It was a portrait of him, Poppa, Tommy and Hope. "Heavy is the head," he whispered before slipping from the room.

CHAPTER 4

"Where the hell is he?" Honey mumbled to no one in particular. She was in the master bedroom, peeking through the curtains of her picture window that looked out over the rear of the property. No matter how many times she saw the rolling green hills beneath the mid¬day sun, it was always like the first time. Growing up as a poor little girl in Harlem, the closest she had ever come to something like that was the class trip to the Great Meadow in Central Park. Now she had only but to step off her back porch.

The normally quiet backyard was now abuzz with activity. At least two-dozen tables, and four times as many chairs, were scattered across the manicured lawn. Between the furniture and all the people trampling through her prized backyard, she would need to call the landscapers when it was all said and done. Power players dressed in all their finery helped themselves to the buffet tables and open bar. She could imagine the phony conversations being had about how happy they were for her, but it was bullshit. Had it been a few years ago, some of the people in attendance wouldn't have pissed on her if she was on fire, so to see them now going out of their way to earn her favor made her smile. Whether the love was genuine or not, they all had to pay homage to the new queen. Not bad for a girl who once had to sell pussy to put food on the table.

Melissa, affectionately known as Honey, had been a hard luck story. Poor choices and an even poorer upbringing had made Honey a teenage mother to a little girl that she would do whatever she had to in order to make sure she didn't go hungry. She made no apologies for being way too young doing way too much, and lived her life according to how she saw fit, but that all changed when she met the man who would be her salvation, Shai Clark. Back then, he was still a semi-square dude trying to figure out how to become a circle, but he had an undeniable swagger about him that intrigued her. What had started out as just some good dick on the side evolved into a ring on her finger and the sole heir to a multimillion-dollar enterprise growing in her belly. Everyone in attendance that day had come to pay homage

38

to the new prince or princess of the Clark family. It was Honey's baby shower.

"Yo, it's hella people out there," Paula said coming to stand next to Honey. She wasn't quite as discrete as Honey had been in her guest-watching. Paula was one of her oldest and dearest friends and had been with her through all her lows, so it was only right that Honey kept her close during her highs.

"I know, right? From the turnout, you'd think a celebrity wedding was about to go down," Honey said.

"Shit, you and your man are celebrities and this is better than a wedding. All these people have come to pay homage to the young king of kings growing in your belly." Paula rubbed her stomach.

"You're worse than Shai," Honey swatted Paula's hand away. "For all the two of you know, this could very well be a girl."

"Nah, you're not carrying high enough for it to be a girl."

"So you're a doctor all of a sudden?" Honey asked sarcastically.

"No, but I've been pregnant enough times to know. Besides, I don't think it'll too much matter the sex of the life growing inside you; that baby is going to inherit the earth," Paula motioned to the crowded backyard.

"Yeah, and hopefully not the bullshit that comes with it." Honey's eyes landed on one of the guests on the lawn. He was tall with long dreads that touched his back. The man slithered through the crowd seemingly invisible to the rest of the guests. Something about the way he carried himself rang familiar to Honey, but she was sure she had never seen him before that day. He must've felt her eyes on him because he looked up at the window. His lips parted into a half smile that made her shiver.

"You okay?" Paula asked, noticing her tense.

"Yeah, I'm cool," she answered her friend. When she turned her attention back to the lawn, the man was nowhere to be found.

"So now that we got the baby shower in full swing, when are we gonna start planning your bridal shower?"

Honey sucked her teeth. "Bitch, we ain't even set a wedding date yet."

Hoodlum II: The Good Son

"Then you need to!" Paula shot back. "You and Shai been engaged almost two years already. What the hell is he waiting for?"

"With all that's going on with his transition, it just isn't the right time," Honey said, repeating what Shai had told her the last two times she pressed him about setting a date.

"And you bought that shit?" Paula shook her head. "These niggas is all the same. They want the milk for free but drag their feet about buying the cow. You been riding with this nigga since he was still wet behind the ears, and now that he's sitting in the big chair he wanna act funny about giving you your just reward? Couldn't be me."

"This coming from a single chick with three baby daddies," Honey snorted.

"You got that, but it beats throwing stones at the penitentiary on a promise," Paula shot back. The response was reflexive, and the minute the words left her mouth and she saw the hurt flash in Honey's eyes, she regretted it. "Look, boo," she took her hand, "You and me go back too far for me to start sugar-coating shit now. You've got a dream life, but don't act like you don't know what this dream was built on. If things ever went sour, as the girlfriend you wouldn't be entitled to any of this, but the wife gotta be taken care of."

"You know I ain't in this for the money," Honey insisted.

Paula waved her off. "Tell yourself whatever you like that helps you sleep at night, but don't overlook the point I'm trying to make. It ain't about the money, ma. It's about insurance. If you can hold his secrets, then you can hold his last name."

Honey wanted to argue with Paula, but she knew that she was right. Granted, Shai had given her a life greater than she could have ever dreamed of having, but at the end of the day, none of it was hers. The house, the cars, the trips, their entire lifestyle had been provided by Shai. Honey had a reputation for being a hustler and was never without her own money, but becoming Shai's girl had put an end to her hustling days. He had promised to always take care of her, and she believed him when he said it, but what if the choice was stripped from him? The Clark family made millions off their legitimate businesses, but their foundation was built off drug money and they still maintained heavy ties to the streets. Shai was now far removed from the dirty side of the business, but the threat of prison would always linger. If the rug were ever snatched out from under them, Honey would find herself without a pot to piss in. She couldn't do that to herself or her kids. After the baby shower, she and Shai were going to revisit their conversation about a wedding date.

There was a soft knock on the door that seemed to irritate Honey. "I swear if one more muthafucka comes in here asking me where Shai is, I'm going to shoot them!" she stormed towards the door.

As if on cue, Shai poked his head in the door. "I heard someone speak the king's name," he said jokingly.

"Boy, where the hell have you been? Did you forget we've got a backyard full of people waiting for us?" Honey snapped.

"They've waited this long, I don't think a few more minutes will kill them. Besides," he stepped into the room, "I had to stop and pick up some precious cargo." He turned to reveal the little girl clinging to his back. It was Honey's daughter, Star.

"Hi mommy! Shai was giving me a piggy-back ride!" Star squealed.

"Girl, quit horsing around before you ruin your dress!" Honey pulled her down and smoothed over the green satin fabric. "We paid too much money for this dress for you to ruin it before you get a chance to show it off."

"Leave that girl alone," Shai shooed Honey away and pulled Star to him protectively. "It ain't nothing but some fabric and thread. If she messes it up, we'll replace it. Ain't that right, baby girl?"

"Umm hmm," Star agreed, hugging Shai's waist protectively and smirking at her mother.

"You keep thinking that hiding behind Shai is gonna save you from an ass whipping and you're going to learn a very painful lesson, young lady," Honey warned the little girl.

"My teacher says parents can get in trouble for whipping their kids. They got laws against that," Star sassed.

"Well you tell that bi..."

Hoodlum II: The Good Son

"Honey!" Shai cut her off. "Paula, can you take Star out to the lawn to get a snack? Honey and me will be down in a few minutes."

"I don't wanna go down with, Paula. I wanna walk in with you and mommy like we practiced!" Star started doing her princess wave. She had been working on it for days.

"We can do it later, sweetie. I gotta talk to your mom for a sec. Grown up stuff." Shai pinched her cheek.

"Y'all always gotta talk grown up stuff," Star huffed and folded her arms.

Paula seeing anger flash in Honey's eyes interjected. "Star, come on with Auntie P. We'll go find Mikey, Mark and Mercedes. I brought them a big stash of blow pops and sour patch before we came. I'm sure they'll share it with you."

"Yes, hood candy!" Star pumped her fist. "Come on before they eat it all, Auntie P!" Star grabbed Paula by the hand and nearly dragged her out of the room.

"That little girl and her mouth are gonna make me catch a case!" Honey fumed.

"She got it honest," Shai teased.

"You need to stop that."

"Stop what?" Shai asked, confused.

"Stop acting like everything she does is so fucking cute. Ain't nothing cute about a disrespectful kid!" Honey snapped.

"Honey, Star isn't disrespectful. She's mischievous. There's a difference. Now if you wanna see disrespectful, look at Paula's bad ass kids. You ever hear how she lets them talk to her?" Shai was only kidding, but Honey didn't take it that way.

"So what, you judging my friends now like yours are any better? Hmph, I'd rather have a bunch of babies than a bunch of bodies, but you and yours wouldn't know anything about that, right?" Honey said slyly. The minute the remark left her mouth she wished she could have it back. She hadn't even realized that Shai had moved until he was looming over here, with her arm clutched tightly in his hand.

"First of all," he sneered, "I was only joking, trying to make you laugh. And second of all, you watch your fucking mouth when it comes to things you don't know shit about."

Hoodlum II: The Good Son

"Get off me. You're hurting my arm!" Honey tried to hide the panic in her voice.

"Better a bruise to your arm rather than a bullet to the back of your head if the wrong person hears you talking outta your ass. There is power in words!" Shai hissed. "Baby girl, you ain't been a square long enough to forget who I am and how this life we've chosen works."

"You've made your point, now get your damn hands off me!" Honey jerked away from Shai and went to stand by the window.

Shai saw the tears dancing in the corner of her eyes and felt like a world-class dickhead. "I'm sorry, ma," he moved to comfort her. She was resistant, but didn't stop him from embracing her. "I'm not sorry for checking you, because you do need to watch your mouth, but it could've came out a little better. I got a bunch of shit on my brain, so I been kinda short with everybody."

"Well I'm not everybody, I'm your fiancé." Honey shot back. "I know you got a lot on your plate, Shai, but you're not the only one going through something. Look at me," she gestured at her body. "I'm fat, pregnant and ugly. You think this shit is easy for me?"

"Don't say that about yourself, Melissa," he called her by her real name. "Pregnancy got you a little thick, but it's all in the right places." He ran his hands over her curves. "As a matter of fact, we got a few minutes before we make our entrance, so how about you let me show you just how much I appreciate that pregnancy weight?" He began fumbling with Honey's dress, but she pushed him away.

"Boy you must be crazy. I spent too much time getting this hair done to let you sweat it out." Honey fluffed the curls of her sandy blonde weave. "But on a serious note, I'm over this pregnancy shit, Shai. I don't know what I was thinking about by letting you gas me to get pregnant again after ten years since my last kid."

"Didn't take no gassing; you just saw my vision." Shai got down on one knee and kissed Honey's stomach. "This life growing inside you is one of four little kings you're going to bless me with. When my sons become men, I'll send each one of them to a different corner of the world to claim as their own, and by the time I die, the Clarks will have inherited the earth."

Hoodlum II: The Good Son

Honey smiled down at him lovingly. "You always were the dreamer."

"This ain't dreams, baby. They're prophecies," Shai said seriously.

"Well while I got you in the proper position, you think about a wedding date yet?" Honey asked.

"Here we go with this again," Shai stood up and dusted his knees off. "I thought we talked about this already? Shit is crazy right now because everybody is still getting used to the shift in power. We're in transitioning right now, but as soon as things get settled we can talk about it."

"Shai, you've been at the head of your father's organization for three years. How much transitioning you need to do?" Honey looked him up and down.

"Melissa..."

"Melissa my ass," she cut him off. "Shai, these are the kinds of word games you play with one of your side bitches, not the woman you profess to love. I've carried your secrets and your seed, haven't I proven myself worthy yet?"

"Baby you know it ain't like that," Shai said sincerely.

"Then help me to understand what it's like, Shai. From where I'm standing, it looks like I'm just another dumb bitch waiting on an empty promise." Honey's voice was heavy with emotion. "You think I don't see it, Shai? Being the boss is slowly stripping away the sweet and honorable kid I fell in love with, and I don't know if this new you has the same set of values. If I'm chasing a dream, then keep it one hundred with me and let me go. Don't hold me hostage on false hope."

Shai scooped Honey in his arms and tilted her chin so that they were looking into each other's eyes. "Baby, you must have an incredibly low opinion of me if you think I'd let go of my rib because the stakes got a little higher and the money is a little longer. Everybody else loves me because I got it together, but you loved me when I was still trying to figure all this shit out. The fact that I gotta tell you this and you don't already know means I'm slacking."

"Never that, Shai. You take good care of me, Star, and everybody else who needs a blessing. That pure heart of yours," she tapped his chest, "is what made you stand out amongst the rest. It ain't never been about titles or finances between us, Shai. I just wanna make sure I'm protected."

"And you are, babe. You and Star will never have to worry about money again another day in your life. I'll see to that."

"I believe you, Shai, never doubt that, but what happens to us if you go away and all this goes up in smoke? Two people shacking up don't hold no weight in court when assets are being seized, and the girlfriend is the first one the FEDS attack when they're trying to bring somebody down, but a wife can't be forced to testify against her husband."

"You must've been binge watching Law & Order reruns again," Shai joked.

"You're laughing, but I'm serious, Shai. This ain't corner-boy shit you're handling. You've got more enemies than just the ones on the streets, and I'm more worried about the gangsters waving indictments than I am about the ones waving guns. This life you inherited brings a lot of time with it. If we're gonna play," she took his hand in hers, "we need to be playing to win."

Shai mustered a smile. "You're always three steps ahead, aren't you?"

"And that's why you're with me. The queen protects the king at all costs." Honey kissed him. "We can finish talking about this later. I don't want to keep our guests waiting any longer."

CHAPTER 5

Tech sat on a folding chair in the backyard trying his best not to look uncomfortable. He had donned a white button-up shirt, black jeans and a pair of white Air Force Ones. Swann had told him to dress up, but he didn't own any dress clothes outside of two white button-up shirts that he kept on standby for funerals. He was a street nigga, and nearly his entire wardrobe consisted of hug-the-block attire.

He was seated at a table in the rear of the yard, just off the driveway that lead to the main house, with some of the other soldiers and a few lieutenants. Whoever did the seating arrangements made sure to keep the undesirables as far away from the regular guests as possible, because Swann would've probably needed binoculars to even see what kind of food they were serving at the heart of the yard. When Swann invited Tech to attend the baby shower, he didn't exactly expect to be welcome into Shai's inner circle, but he didn't expect to be stranded in no-man's land either. It was probably for the best.

Amongst the high profile guests, he would've stuck out like a sore thumb. They were sheep and Tech was a wolf.

"This shit is hella boring," Jewels said, reminding Tech that he was sitting at the table. He was a brown skinned cat, with a handsome young dude of about Tech's age who had a thing for jewelry, especially bracelets. His signature gold Bengal bracelets looped up his right arm from wrist to nearly elbow. Like Tech, he was a budding soldier trying to prove his worth to the Clark clan.

"It ain't that bad," Tech told him, snatching a glass of champagne from the platter of a passing waitress. He sipped it and frowned at the lack of the kind of punch he was used to when attempting to get faded.

"Spoken like a nigga who ain't never been to a real Clark party," Jewels cracked.

Tech looked at him. "Jewels, you ain't been down that much longer than me, but you stay talking shit like you a part of Shai's inner circle."

"I might not be now, but I will be in a minute." Jewels assured him. "Unlike the rest of y'all lil' niggas,

Hoodlum II: The Good Son

I got the memo that it's a new day for the Clarks, and I aim to prove that I'm fit to get money under the new regime."

"Speak for yourself, but I kinda like the freedom of being an independent. One source of income is as good as another, so long as the numbers make sense," Tech replied.

"I hear you, but that's small time thinking." Jewels leaned in so that only he and Tech could hear what was being said. "I did that independent shit for a while, and got my marbles from it, but that cash is sporadic. You gotta go out and chase your business. When you fucking with the Clarks, business comes to you. Having this shit on your resume is like having gone to M.I.T!"

"So, you say." Tech brushed Jewels' speech off.

"So I know," Jewels retorted. "My nigga, let me give you some real spit: Shai got at least one thousand niggas who'll move in a wave when he gives the say-so, and that means only a few stand out. You wanna get on Shai's radar then you gotta set yourself apart from the rest, and that means doing what the rest of these muthafuckas won't!"

"You talking like you 'bout it," Tech teased him, knowing it would only get Jewels more riled up.

"Fucking right I am! You think you the only shooter the Clarks got on payroll?"

"I ain't a shooter, I'm a killer." Tech corrected him.

"Same shit! Bottom line is that my gun go off too!"

"We'll see," Tech dismissed him. He was just giving Jewels a hard time. Tech actually liked the young dude. He was a little chattier than Tech was used to, but if he walked it like he talked it, Jewels would make a welcome addition to the Dog Pound.

Jewels continued to chatter, but Tech only half listened. He was too busy doing recon. He watched from a distance as actors, athletes and politicians mingled in the same circles as criminals, and a chuckle escaped him. Outside those gates he doubted if some of those people would have even spit on each other if they were on fire, let alone be eating hors d'oeuvres and laughing like everything was all good. Yet here they were with their false faces and plastic smiles, waiting to kiss Shai's ass.

"Fuck y'all two little criminals over here scheming on?" A brutish looking man with a salt and pepper afro

and a goatee to match approached Tech. This was Big
Doc. He had been one of Poppa Clark's enforcers and
now busted heads for Shai. Big Doc was one of the few
of Shai's inner circle that didn't treat Tech like trash.

"Ain't nothing, just shooting the shit with my man."
Jewels flashed a toothy grin.

"Seems like that's the only thing you ever shoot is the
shit," Big Doc teased him. "Take a walk, while I wrap
with Tech for a sec."

"You got it, B.D." Jewels got up and went to harass
one of the waitresses for another drink.

"You straight, lil' homie?" Big Doc asked Tech when
Jewels had gone.

"I'm straight," Tech told him.

"No you're not." Big Doc sat in the chair next to his.
"You look about as comfortable as a hooker in church.
Drink this." He placed the glass he was carrying on the
table. "It'll ease your nerves."

Tech looked at the brown liquid suspiciously.

"Hennessey," Big Doc answered the question on his
face. "Don't act like you don't drink it, because that's all
you corner boys drink these days."

"Man, I ain't no corner-boy. I'm a shooter," Tech said proudly.

"I ain't talking about what you do professionally. I was referencing where you spend most of your time. I be seeing you and your crew all times of the night, skulking like some damn vampires. Y'all might wanna stay out that building on Eighth Ave, though. I hear it's getting hot on that block."

Tech was surprised by Big Doc's familiarity with his routines. "What, you been following me or something?"

"Only for the first few months you started hanging around," Big Doc admitted. "Once I seen you had the potential to be about something, I cut it back to the occasional ride by just to check up."

"Man, you're one suspicious old dude," Tech smirked.

"You don't live long enough to get gray hairs by being trusting," Big Doc capped.

"Well, now that you've let me in on your secret, what's to stop me from changing my routine?" Tech asked slyly.

"I should hope you would. When you play like we play, you should never be that easy to find. You do too

much of the same thing twice, and that's dangerous, kid.
But even if you do get yourself some sense and decide to
change up how you do things, trust and believe I'll
always be able to find you. Wherever you are, no matter
how deep in the cut you think you are, for as long as
you're standing next to Shai, I'll always be able to lay
hands on you."

"Damn, if I didn't know any better I'd say that
sounded like a threat."

Big Doc chuckled. "Lil' buddy, you ain't did enough
in your life to use them kinds of words with a man like
me. No disrespect. I ain't threatening you, Tech. I'm just
being upfront."

Tech nodded. "I can respect that."

"As I knew you would." Big Doc reached into his
pocket and pulled out a pack of cigarettes. He tapped one
out for himself, then offered the pack to Tech. The youth
gratefully accepted. "You see that cat right there?" He
pointed to Shai, who had just appeared on the lawn from
the rear of the house with his lady on his arm. "I love that
lil' nigga - love him enough to smoke a hundred dudes in

broad daylight and happily go to prison for it. Do you know why?"

"Because he keeps your pockets fat." Tech chose the obvious answer.

"Nah, man. I came up under his dad, so I had bread before he stepped up. The only reason I ain't retired yet is because I know Shai still needs good people around him to keep his head on straight. Like I said; hustled with Poppa Clark so I been knowing Shai since he was knee-high, and before any of us lived in a big house. When you got roots like that with someone, it's not a friendship anymore; you're family. Contrary to what any of y'all on the lower rungs may think of the new king, I happen to know how he was bred, so I can speak on what's in his heart."

"So you're saying you'd throw your life away for him because y'all got history?" Swann asked, starting to catch on.

"No, because Shai represents the future. We need him to win or we all lose."

"That's some heavy shit," Tech said.

"And it only gets heavier."

Hoodlum II: The Good Son

"What up, fellas?" Swann walked over and joined them. He gave dap to some of the soldiers who were lingering about before taking a seat with Tech and Big Doc.

"Ain't shit, just giving fresh fish a crash course on what's expected of him," Big Doc told him.

"Oh word? If that's the case then you should consider yourself lucky, Tech. Next to Tommy, Big Doc is the best teacher in the game," Swann said.

"Next to Tommy?" Big Doc drew his head back. "Young nigga, who you think it was that gave him that killer edge? Poppa taught Tommy how to boss up, but it was me who showed him the art of laying niggas down. Quiet as kept, I gave him his first gun long before Poppa did, but had it ever got out the O.G. would've had me killed," he laughed.

"You're right about that. Poppa didn't fuck around when it came to niggas trying to corrupt his kids, especially Shai," Swann agreed.

"Then how the fuck did he end up a kingpin?" Tech asked. It was an innocent enough question, but he had obviously struck a nerve.

61

"I'll leave Swann to fill in those blanks. Get with you later, youngster." Big Doc got up and left the table.

"I'm sorry, Swann. I didn't mean no disrespect." Tech said sincerely.

"Nah, that ain't about nothing." Swann assured him. "Big Doc was close to Poppa. He knew the old man had a plan for his youngest son, and inheriting this bullshit wasn't part of it. We can talk about history, but right now I need you with me." He got up.

"Where we going?" Tech asked.

"To give you a glimpse into your future."

CHAPTER 6

The minute Honey stepped through the glass doors, the worried fiancé fell away, and the queen of the rose in her place. She was wearing a cream dress, trimmed around the sleeves and hems in autumn to match Shai's tie and shoes. The dress hugged her swollen breasts but flared out over her stomach, ending in a train that barely dusted the ground. She could have gone with a more over-the-top outfit, but she wanted to kill them without looking like she was trying to. The men standing around tried to act like they weren't staring at Shai's lady, but she could feel their eyes on her. She smiled inwardly knowing that even pregnant, she still had it.

The photographers sprang to attention when they saw the couple finally arrive. They had been waiting for over an hour, but for what Shai was paying them, nobody complained. They had some trouble getting through the wave of guests who had moved to pay homage to the royal couple, but Brutus was on it. He moved like a black barrier, keeping the guests at a fair distance until the photographers got the shots they needed. The couple

walked arm in arm into the yard, immediately drawing a
crowd of people wanting to congratulate them or kiss
their asses. Brutus, Shai's new watchdog, formed a
wedge between them and their guests, keeping them at a
fair distance until the photographers got the shots they
needed. The camera loved Honey and she loved it right
back, striking all the necessary poses to best capture her
in all her radiance. Of course, she would have to approve
every single photo before anyone was able to see them.
While she and Shai took pictures, Honey was also
assessing the crowd. Her eyes swept the lawn making
mental notes of who had shown up and who hadn't. She
was petty like that. Off in the cut she spotted a few of the
wives and girlfriends of Shai's inner circle. In their eyes,
she saw a range of things; from adoration, to sadness,
with a touch of envy sprinkled in for good measure. For
the most part she got along with the counterparts of
Shai's friends, but there were a few of them who still
hadn't learned their places. There had been a time or two
when Honey felt like she was being tested by little things
she'd pick up through the grapevine. They'd been
attempting to bait her into a response, but when you are a

beautiful woman on the arm of a powerful man, there really isn't much more that needed to be said.

"You guys ready?" Brutus asked once the photographers had gotten enough shots of Shai and Honey.

"In a second," Shai craned his neck to scan the crowd. He spotted someone, who Honey couldn't see, and waved them over. A few seconds later, Star came busting through the crowd with Paula doing her best to try and keep up. "We gotta do it again."

"Shai, you can't be serious?" Honey asked with an attitude.

"I promised her she could do her walk and you know I'm a man of my word." Shai took Star by the hand and led her back toward the house. With little other choice, Honey reluctantly followed.

After entering the party - for the second time - and letting Star do her Princess wave, Honey was ready to embrace her moment. Star had gone off with Paula again, while Shai and Honey made a brief circuit of the yard to greet their guests. Honey had received more kisses on the cheeks and people trying to rub her stomach for luck than she could count. She received everyone graciously, but knew half of the people wishing her well were full of shit, and her hormones were making it hard for her to hold her tongue. She was actually glad when Shai branched off to handle his business and instructed Brutus to take her to their table.

Brutus took Honey gently by the hand and navigated the crowd. She watched his muscular back through the suit jacket as he guided her towards the table. He moved like a black shadow, occasionally plucking people out of the way who stumbled into their path or got too close to Honey. Women's eyes seemed to follow Brutus as he moved and Honey couldn't say that she blamed them. Brutus was as handsome as he was deadly.

"How you holding up?" Brutus asked over his shoulder as if he could feel Honey staring at him.

"I'm cool for now. I just didn't expect there to be this many people," Honey told him.

"I don't know why not. You and Shai's special day has been the talk of the street for the last two months."

Hoodlum II: The Good Son

"Funny, you spend so much time around the house making sure we're good, I didn't know you still kept your ear to the streets like that," Honey joked.

"Just because I'm not technically in the streets anymore doesn't mean I'm not aware of what's going on in them. It's my job to keep you guys safe from enemies foreign and domestic," he said seriously.

Their table was situated on a slightly raised platform that would give them a view of the entire yard and everyone in it. Honey had decided to forgo the traditional baby shower chair and instead would be seated in a brass throne, with Shai occupying one similar. Shai had been against it, saying that the thrones were overkill, but she argued him down until he finally relented. For Honey, the shower was as much about celebrating their pending new addition to the family, as it was flaunting her position. Humility could find her another time; that day she was out to stunt.

Brutus helped her up the few stairs and into the throne. He took a minute to relay some last-minute instructions to the two members of his team who had been assigned to guard that section, before preparing to take his leave. "I gotta go make the rounds, but I ain't going far. If you need anything at all, just let me know."

"I'll be sure to do that," Honey said, not meaning it quite like it sounded.

Brutus gave Honey an awkward smile before excusing himself and disappearing into the ground.

"You and that fucking mouth, Melissa." Honey cursed herself for the slip. Since Shai was gone a lot, she often found herself in the company of Brutus. He had become more like a friend than a bodyguard, so sometimes she got a little more comfortable around him than what some would have deemed appropriate, but it hadn't always been like that.

Initially Honey had been leery of the smooth chocolate brother with the mysterious past. He was a new face, and in the lifestyle they led, having new faces around could be dangerous. Shai never talked to her much about Brutus' past, but from what she had been able to piece together from ear-hustling and asking some of the soldiers, Brutus and Shai went back as far as high school. He, Shai and Swann were like the three amigos, until Swann and Brutus had a falling out, but he and Shai remained cool. Rumor had it that Brutus had even saved Shai's life once when a man tried to shoot Shai over his daughter. After graduation, Shai went off to college but Brutus had entered the military. Supposedly he was a part of some sort of black-ops team that had participated in some truly gruesome shit. Honey spent a lot of time around Brutus, and after having gotten to know him, she found it hard to believe some of the stories were true…but if he didn't have a monster hiding somewhere inside him, there was no way Shai would have trusted him with his life, let alone the lives of his family.

"You better keep them goo-goo eyes to yourself." Giselle startled Honey when she appeared in the seat next to her. She was the mother of Swann's daughter, and Honey's friend. She was a pretty Spanish girl who was teetering on the chunky side, but still had a nice shape.

"Girl, what you talking about?" Honey tried to play it off.

Giselle gave her a look.

Honey sucked her teeth. "Damn, I'm engaged not dead!"

"Yeah, but you will be if Shai had reason to believe you getting too close to the help," Giselle warned. "Though the nigga is fine as all hell." A sly smile crossed her face.

Honey chuckled. "And you talk about me. If I were you, I'd take my own advice. Shai can push a button and make it happen, but Swann is the button."

"Chile please," Giselle waved her off. "Swann is too busy chasing pussy to worry about what I'm doing."

"Get out of here. I thought Swann cleaned his act up?"

"He has, meaning he's putting a little more shade on his bullshit," Giselle said honestly. "He got a second phone he doesn't think I know about, and now he takes his whores to New Jersey instead of fucking them in hotels in the city."

"Damn girl, you on it! How the fuck do you know all that?" Honey asked, impressed by her friend's detective skills.

Giselle shrugged. "Because men are sloppy. Find a receipt here, a dirty glare from a bitch you never met there, and eventually shit starts to add up."

Hoodlum II: The Good Son

"That's crazy." Honey shook her head in disbelief. "So, if Swann is out there playing, why do you stay?"

Giselle laughed. "Because I got time in. You must be bugging if you think I'm gonna spend eight years of my life polishing that ignorant ass nigga and teaching him how to boss up to let my feelings open the lane up for some random bitch to reap the benefits of my work. They can have his dick so long as I got papers on his heart and his bank account. The only thing Swann loves nearly as much as our daughter Mara is fresh pussy. I don't like it, but it's something I've come to accept. It's just a part of who he is."

"Damn Giselle, you better than me. The last time I caught Shai on some bullshit, I left him," Honey said, recalling the time she had caught Shai messing around with a young stripper from Miami named Reign. It hadn't been the first time she had caught him cheating, but it was the last straw for her. "I cut that nigga smooth off. You should've heard him pulling up in front of my sister's crib at 3A.M. singing "Ain't Too Proud To Beg" at the top of his lungs," she laughed. "He knew that I was really leaving him that time."

71

"And you'd have been a damn fool," Giselle countered. "Sweetie, our men are two young, fine and powerful niggas who operate on the wrong side of the law. Thirsty bitches come with the territory. Let them take the headaches, abortions and gun charges, while we rest and dress in the finest shit. I ain't stressing myself over something I can't change. As far as I'm concerned, my baby daddy can knock down all the pawns he needs to feed that ego, so long as everybody is clear on who the queen is." She sat back and crossed her legs for emphasis.

As it generally went after their chats, Giselle had given Honey some food for thought. They were roughly the same age, but for as long as she had known Giselle, she had always had a wisdom about her that women only acquired with time and experience. When Honey had first met Giselle, she and Shai hadn't been dating that long, while Giselle had already been with Swann for years and had a baby by him. Honey had been dating hustlers all her life, but none played anywhere near the level Shai was at. It was Giselle and her familiarity with the family who assisted with Honey's transition to the next level.

Hoodlum II: The Good Son

Over the years, Honey had grown closer to Giselle than some of her oldest friends, including Paula.

One of the servers ascended the steps holding a platter full of champagne flutes. She was a cute girl, brown skinned with short hair and an ass that threatened to burst from the black slacks she was wearing. Across her wrist was a tattoo of a rosary. Giselle glared at her, before snatching two flutes from the platter, downing one while keeping her eyes locked on the server. The server ignored Giselle's look and turned the platter to Honey.

"What are you, retarded? Don't you see she's pregnant?" Giselle snapped.

The server covered her mouth in embarrassment. "Oh! I'm sorry. I didn't realize."

"Don't be sorry, be careful. Now scat," Giselle shooed her away.

"Giselle, why did you have to be so rude to that girl? She's just doing her job!" Honey scolded her.

"One of her jobs. When she ain't serving drinks, she shakes her ass at that strip club Swann loves to spend our money in. Found a video of her in my dumb ass baby daddy's phone. I almost didn't recognize her fully clothed, but that tattoo on her wrist gave it away."

"Cut it out, Giselle. Rosaries are popular tattoos. I'm sure she ain't the only one with it," Honey reasoned.

"Yeah, that tattoo is common, but that ass is undeniable," Giselle said in a matter-of-fact tone, before going back to her sipping.

Honey sat laughing at her friend's theatrics, while looking out over her guests. She spotted her man, shaking hands and handling business like a boss was supposed to. He stopped to embrace an older man who Honey had seen on television once. He was some kind of politician, though she was unsure of what office he held. It made her heart swell with pride to see her man.

Finally growing into his new status. He had come a long way since she had first started dating him, and would go even further if she had anything to say about it.

Her proud moment was short-lived as a pretty young girl came into the picture. Next to Honey, she wasn't much to look at, but she seemed to be holding Shai's attention.

Hoodlum II: The Good Son

"Yo Giselle," Honey tapped her leg to get her attention. "Who is that bitch? The one with the tiny black skirt on."

Giselle's eyes narrowed as she saw what Honey saw. The girl and Shai were smiling a little too hard at each other for her taste. "I don't know, but I'll go find out if you want." She stood, but Honey stopped her.

"Nah, just chill for a minute. I wanna see how this plays out before I start handing out split wigs."

CHAPTER 7

Now that Honey was out of his hair, it freed Shai up to handle more pressing business. He had a lot to take care of that day, and was already running behind schedule.

Shai moved through the yard, shaking hands and whispering into the ears of his guests. He had put together quite the function, and people were climbing over each other to show their appreciation, especially for the free food and drink. The event served two purposes; to celebrate the pending birth of his and Honey's child and to address family business. With as hot as the streets were, meeting with some of his affiliates out in the open was becoming increasingly riskier. Since his ascension to the throne, he was under constant surveillance. He could barely take a piss without a cop standing over his shoulder offering to hold his dick. He had to be careful how he moved and who he was seen associating with. There was a guy in the organization who had gotten years on a conspiracy charge just for hanging out with the wrong muthafucka and Shai would be damned if he was going out like that. Tommy had warned him about the

Hoodlum II: The Good Son

weight that came with the crown, but it still couldn't prepare his little brother for how heavy it was. He had a whole new respect for his father for being able to live like that for all those years and still hold onto his sanity.

His newfound notoriety was one of the reasons he decided to handle his business at the house that day under the cover of the baby shower. All of his normal haunts, as well as those of his associates, were susceptible to being bugged or watched, but not his home. Shai had invested tons of money into personal security and all the latest anti-surveillance gear, including cell phone jamming towers that he could turn on and off at his pleasure. He even had the property swept for bugs twice per week. The police or anyone else couldn't get within one hundred yards without Shai knowing about it. He spared no expense fortifying his home, which is why it was one of the only places he felt safe discussing business.

"Behold the prince of the ghetto!" Chance King approached wearing a broad smile with his arms spread.

Bringing up the rear were his wife and two of his children.

"Good to see you, Chance, and thanks for coming." Shai hugged the older man.

"Stop that. You know me and the family wouldn't miss this. We were just in the car saying how happy we were for you guys! Ain't that right, Ghost?" The eldest King boy grumbled something inaudible.

"Sup, Ghost?" Shai addressed him.

"Ain't shit. Just chilling. Congratulations, by the way," Ghost said dryly.

"Thanks." Shai matched his tone.

"And you remember my wife, Maureen, don't you?" Chance draped his arm around her and nudged her forward.

"Now that can't be Mrs. King? Surely it's one of your daughters and you're playing a trick on me." Shai took her hand in his and kissed the back of it. "How are you, Mrs. King?"

"I'm fine and after all this time I think it's okay for you to call me, Maureen." She blushed.

"Watch that shit, youngster." Chance half-joked.

"You gonna kiss my hand too, Shai?" a voice spoke up. She was a walnut-colored young woman with rich brown eyes, wearing a short black dress that hugged her athletic frame.

Shai had to do a double take to make sure his eyes weren't playing tricks on him. "Lolli?" The last time he had seen Lolli, King had been at Hope's sweet sixteen party. Back then she had been a scrawny girl with braces, who was beating the dog shit out of a boy who tried to touch her developing boobs.

"Careful, Shai. I'd hate to have your future baby mama get in her feelings over the way you're staring at my daughter," Maureen warned.

Shai composed himself. "I'm sorry, I didn't mean any disrespect. It's just that I hardly recognized little Lolli."

"I ain't so little anymore, huh?" Lolli's tone was flirtatious.

"You ain't got nothing to worry about, mama. You know Lolli don't like boys no more," Ghost remarked.

"Shai ain't no boy," Lolli shot back slyly. She was doing it just to get under Ghost's skin.

"The both of y'all cut that shit and act like you got some home training!" Chance cut in. "As a matter of fact, go busy yourself at the bar or something. I need to talk to Shai."

"Maybe I should stick around, pop," Ghost suggested.

"Nah, I got it, Ghost," Chance assured him. "Go on with ya mom and sister."

Ghost continued to linger, until his mother rested a reassuring hand on his. "Come on, baby. Let your daddy tend to his business."

Ghost gave Shai a last look before allowing his mother to lead him away.

"That kid of yours has got some serious trust issues," Shai said after the others had gone.

"In this line of work, can you blame him?" Chance asked seriously. "Ghost can be a little stiff, but the boy is a damn good son. I can always depend on him in a pinch. I wish I could say the same about that other boy of mine."

"Shadow giving you grief?" Shai asked after the youngest of the King children.

"Grief is a nice way to put it. It's more like a heart condition," Chance sighed.

"He in the streets?" Shai asked in surprise. He knew that Chance felt the same way about Shadow as Poppa had about him and kept him away from the family business.

"Hell nah, man. I'd never let Shadow anywhere near this mess. Besides that, he ain't got the stomach for what we do. He's a little on the tender side if you ask me. I don't mind that so much, though. Him being spooked of the life will keep his ass out of prison. It's his lack of motivation that gets on my damn nerves. I got him a summer internship at one of my realty offices and he would either show up late, high or not at all. I had to fire him. Can you believe that? I had to fire my own kid!" He shook his head in disappointment. "I don't know how I produced a kid that lazy. Seems like all he wants to do is smoke weed and chase pussy."

"I know a thing or two about that," Shai said, recalling how he was in high school. "It's a phase, Chance. He'll grow out of it."

"I sure hope so. But forget all that. This is your special day and I'm heaping all my problems on you. How does it feel knowing you're gonna be a daddy soon? I know you're happy!"

"Yeah, but to be honest I'm more nervous than anything. I don't know nothing about being a dad," Shai admitted.

"Neither did I my first time around, but by the third one I pretty much got the hang of it," Chance joked.

"Third? Sheesh, I just wanna make it through the first one without fucking up before I start looking that far down the road."

"You're gonna be a great dad, Shai, just like your old man. Poppa Clark had a good heart, and he was always very fair. I'm sure those same qualities have rubbed off on you." He patted Shai on the back good-naturedly. "That also brings me to a little piece of business I need to rap with you about."

Shai should have known it was coming; it was Chance's style. Unlike some of the other Clark associates, Chance had made more money with words than he did bullets. He had a way with getting you comfortable enough to drop your guard before making his play. Chancellor King was the only gangster Shai knew that had been elected into a city office position twice. In addition to running his crime family in Five-Points, he also sat on the City Council. Rumor had it that he had his eyes set on one day running for mayor, and for as slick as he was, Shai didn't doubt that he at least had a boxer's chance of winning.

"I already know, the expansion," Shai cut to the chase.

"Right," Chance confirmed. "Look, I don't mean to be bringing this shit up on the day of your baby shower, but's it's kind of a time-sensitive matter on my end. I got some irons in the fire that this move is depending on."

"The consummate hustler," Shai smirked. "Chance, I wanna help you out on this but this is a decision that can't be made overnight. There are other things that factor in before I can say yay or nay on this."

"You mean like Wongs?" Chance raised an eyebrow.

Shai was thrown off by the statement, but tried his best not to let his face betray it. "I just need to make sure it all makes sense."

Chance laughed. "Shai, I'm a politician. It's my job to spot bullshit before the bull even knows it has to take a dump. I know you got a thing going on with the Wongs, but I can assure you that my interest in that territory won't affect your money or theirs. This move I'm trying to make is totally legit. I got my eye on some property down that way and wanna jump on them while they're still letting them go for below market value. No street shit." He all but confirmed what Swann had told Shai earlier.

"Maybe not now, but who's to say it'll stay that way when Ghost is in charge?" Shai asked, letting Chance know that he wasn't the only one who had done their research.

Chance's brow knotted. "Shai, can I speak freely?"

Shai shrugged. "I wouldn't respect anything less."

"This is bullshit," Chance said flatly. "We both know that the only reason you're stonewalling me over this is because you don't wanna hurt Billy Wong's feelings and potentially hurt your heroin profits. You been getting money with the Wongs for the last couple of years, but the Clarks and Kings been making money together for nearly two decades. I don't wanna sound out of line or petty, but don't that count for nothing?"

Chance had a point. The Kings had always been good friends to the Clarks, and on occasion even allies when beef popped off. Poppa Clark had a great deal of respect

Hoodlum II: The Good Son

for Chance for his loyalty and the old man knew it, which is why he had attempted to use it as his trump card. It was a classic Chancellor King move that Shai saw coming even before he opened his mouth.

Shai nodded as if he was weighing the old man's request. "You've spoken your piece, and now I'll speak mine. All these things you say are true; my father respected you and the friendship between our two families. He was always big on friends, but this isn't a matter of friendship you've brought to me. This is about profit. As you so graciously pointed out, I get money with the Wongs. If I shrink the space they have to move in, it shrinks what they've been kicking back to my family for the good deed. That being said; I couldn't begin to even consider such a move unless I had a guarantee that it wouldn't affect my bottom line."

"You trying to muscle me?" Chance's eyes flashed anger.

"Chance, as someone who knows my pedigree, you should know better than that. I got too much respect for you and your history in this city to ever come at you sideways. All I'm saying is that one hand washes the other and two wash the face."

"I get it," Chance said reluctantly. "So how much you talking, or do you want points off the deal I'm gonna make?"

"Neither," Shai said, much to Chance's surprise. "I wasn't gaming when I said I respected our family's friendships. I know with retirement pending you're just trying to set yourself a nest-egg and my hand don't belong in that."

"So, what you want?" Chance asked suspiciously. Shai smiled, and extended his hand. "Only a friend if I ever find myself in need."

Chance looked at Shai's hand as if it was a poisonous snake. "Okay," he reluctantly shook it.

"Glad we understand each other. I'll be in touch," Shai said over his shoulder as he walked off to mingle with the rest of his guests.

CHAPTER 8

"About time you pried yourself loose. I thought he was gonna spend the rest of the night yapping your ear off," Angelo said when Shai approached. As usual, he was dressed in a gray suit and white shirt. His hair was cropped close on the side with the top growing out only slightly longer. It had once been rich and black, but you could now see the first signs of silver popping up.

"You know Chance likes to talk." Shai gave Angelo dap.

"More like negotiate. What did he want this time?" Angelo asked.

"How do you know he wanted anything?" "Because a man doesn't spend twenty minutes whispering about the weather."

Shai laughed. Angelo had always been very perceptive, which is why he spent so many years as the eyes in back of Poppa Clark's head. "Pressing me about that expansion again."

Angelo shook his head. "That Chance King and his dreams of glass towers in the sky. Fool owns damn near every piece of property south of Houston and is still looking to snatch up more land? Greedy muthafucka."

"That ain't greed, Angie. That's foresight. Real estate is big business, and I'm kinda tight we didn't really dig our claws into it," Shai said.

"What you talking about? I know for a fact that Poppa owned some buildings uptown and three houses in the Bronx that I can think of off top of my head. Not to mention the spots I didn't know about," Angelo pointed out.

Shai shook his head sadly. "Damn near all that shit was in the wind. I had to liquidate most of the properties held by Clark Lansky realty to get up the money to spring Tommy from the can."

"Damn, I had no idea. What about the lots in Queens that he was planning to build the casino on?" Angelo asked hopefully.

"You mean the three empty acres of concrete foundation that we can't do shit with?" Shai corrected him. "When my father was killed, most of the people who were in with him on the casino found other shit to do with their money. Even with Sol still at the table with us they feel like it's too big of a risk for someone who doesn't know shit about that side of the business."

"That's fucked up, with a capital F. Couldn't we still move forward on our own with it?" Angelo asked.

"I'd thought about it, but to be honest we don't have the connections or the capital to pull it off," Shai admitted.

"Listen Shai, I got about five hundred thousand tucked for a rainy day. It's yours if you need it," Angelo said sincerely.

Shai smiled at his friend's display of loyalty. "I appreciate it, man, but no thanks. We ain't hardly hurting for no paper, we just ain't got it to make a move that big without feeling the pinch on the backend. Besides, even if we did finish building the hotel and casino, without the gaming licenses and nod from the zoning board that my father's so-called friends were supposed to take care of, we'd never be able to open for business."

Angelo shook his head. "What the fuck happened to loyalty?"

"It died with my father," Shai sighed.

About then, Swann ambled up. Trailing him, scowling at everything moving, was one of his young wolves. Tech was his name if Shai recalled correctly. "I see you crawled out of that hole and finally came out to get some of this love."

"This ain't love, baby boy, it's one big ass hustler's convention. Half these niggas got a business proposal in one hand and a knife in the other," Shai laughed.

"I'm glad you're in a good mood, because I wanted to have a few words with you about my little man, right here," Swann ushered Tech forward. "You remember, Tech, right?"

Shai studied the young man for a few seconds. "Yeah, yeah... I remember you. The last time we seen each other, you and your man pulled some Wes Craven shit and dropped a body part off to me in the middle of having lunch."

"My fault about that. My homie Animal can be kinda literal in his tasks sometimes. It won't happen again," Tech said apologetically.

Hoodlum II: The Good Son

"Let's hope not. We like to move quiet around these parts, but you and your Dog Pound can be a little loud for my tastes. Unnecessary bodies bring unwanted heat."

"I feel you, Shai, but rest assured we ain't never put a nigga down unless he had it coming or got too attached to his goods," Tech laughed. Shai didn't.

"Well, if you plan on working for me then you need to tone it down. Nobody dies unless I say so," Shai told him.

Tech's cheek twitched, but his expression never changed. "With all due respect, Shai, I didn't hook into Swann because I wanted a job. I'm looking to prove my worth." The declaration caught everyone by surprise, especially Swann.

"Ah, Shai, I don't think he meant…" Swann began, but Shai cut him off.

"Nah, let him speak," Shai insisted.

Tech could feel the tension between them. It wasn't what he had intended, but it lingered nonetheless. Shai was a man who could have him and everyone he had ever come in contact with wiped off the map with one phone call. He had to choose his next few words wisely. "What I mean to say is; we would be honored if you could find a seat for us at your table. Your bloodline is official and your family is like hood royalty, but at the same time you already got enough hands in your dinner plate. The Dog Pound has always operated independent and I didn't realize that rocking with y'all was gonna change that. For as much as we would appreciate you feeding us, we'd rather you showed us how to fish."

Shai looked at Swann, who appeared embarrassed, before turning his attention back to the young man. "And what makes you think I'd even consider teaching you anything?"

"Because you're familiar with the Pound's body of work," Tech said honestly. "No slight to any of your people, but when the shit hits the fan, you want a nigga like me standing in between you and whatever the other side is planning."

Shai stood analyzing Tech for what seemed like an eternity. In his eyes he could see that the young man believed everything he was saying. There was a conviction to Tech's words that reminded him of how Swann carried himself at that age, which was the only reason Shai didn't dismiss him like he would have any other soldier trying to get close to him. "You got a set of balls in you like I haven't seen in a long time. If Swann is smart, he'll keep you close."

Tech wanted to smile, but instead he just nodded. "Thanks, Shai. That means a lot coming from you."

"Thank me now, but you might hate me later," Shai said prophetically, before patting Tech on the shoulder letting him know their conversation was at an end.

"Tech, go grab us a few shots. I'll catch up with you in a few," Swann said, picking up on Shai's signal.

Tech was rough around the edges, but smart enough to know when he was being dismissed. "That's what it is then," he gave Swann dap. "Congratulations on the baby, Shai. Hope we get to talk again real soon." He walked off.

"That little nigga is a headache," Angelo said once Tech was out of earshot.

"Yeah, but he's also incredibly vicious, which ain't a bad trait to have during these troubled times," Swann said.

"God forbid," Shai chuckled.

Angelo's cell phone rang in his pocket. He fished it out and looked at the screen before frowning. "I need to take this." He excused himself and answered his cell.

"Tech is a knucklehead," Shai continued, "but tolerable. It's his little crime partner that creeps me the fuck out. That boy has got some very deep issues - issues that I don't want anywhere near me or my family."

"No worries, Shai. Tech got all them little niggas in line," Swann assured him.

"For their sakes I hope so. I won't have another Amine poisoning this family," Shai said. Amine had been one of the youngsters on the come-up when Shai had first gotten kicked out of school and first started dabbling in the family business. He'd been one of the first examples Shai had to make when he came into power. His big mouth and disloyal nature had cost the Clarks a great deal, and as a result Shai had adopted a policy of whacking weeds as soon as he noticed them sprouting.

Angelo was heading back in their direction. He had a worried expression on his face.

"Everything good?" Swann asked before Shai could.

"Nah, man." Angelo extended the cell phone to

Hoodlum II: The Good Son

Shai. "It's Sol," he answered the question in his eyes.

"Yeah?" Shai spoke into the receiver. Within a few words his expression matched Angelo's. "Wait, not on the phone. I'll be there to handle it personally. Give me an hour," he ended the call.

"What's good?" Swann asked once Shai had gotten off the phone.

"I gotta out by the airport and handle something real quick. Angelo, go find Big Doc. I need y'all with me. Swann, you keep the party going and tell Honey I'll be back shortly," he tossed the phone back to Angelo.

"Shai, if it's drama, I'm going with you. Don't leave me here to play host," Swann said.

"Ain't no drama, my nigga. Just another headache to deal with," Shai told him and walked off.

Swann watched his friend walking away, shaking his head. "A boss' work is never done."

CHAPTER 9

"So, tell me why we gotta do this again?" Bruno asked from his perch on the cushy armchair. He was a brutishly built man with a chiseled jaw and large block head. He squirmed in his seat trying to flex the shoulders in his suit jacket into giving him some extra room. He hated suits, primarily because he had to pay extra money to get them tailored to fit his large frame. Bruno was far more comfortable in sweatsuits and sneakers, but Louie had insisted that they all get dressed up for the function.

"Because Frankie sent us. Mr. G needs a favor done," Louie replied. He was seated across from them in a chair similar to the one Bruno sat on, absently picking the dirt from beneath his fingernails. For the last thirty minutes, they had been sitting in the receiving room waiting for an audience with their host.

"Then how come Frankie didn't come instead of sending us?" Bruno asked.

Louie stopped his picking and turned his gaze to Bruno. "What are you, trying to be cute or something?"

Hoodlum II: The Good Son

Bruno looked over at the weasel-faced man. Louie was known to fly into murderous fits over little things so Bruno was careful not to provoke him. "I didn't mean nothing by it, Louie. It's just that for an occasion like this one, I'd think Frankie would've wanted to be here, or maybe even Mr. G personally. We're just button-men."

"Speak for yourself," Mel interjected. He was a handsome man with evenly tanned skin, and dark hair that he wore high and slicked back. "You humps still got a little ways to climb up the ladder, but I'm a lock to get made the next time they open the books."

Louie laughed. "You've been saying that for the last five years and you're still right down here with the rest of us, doing Frankie's dirty work."

"Hey, Louie," Mel flipped him the bird. "Right here, huh?"

"Listen, fellas," Louie began, "I'm sure we all got better shit we could be doing other than kissing this shine's ass, and those of you who want to leave are free to do so, but I'm not gonna be the one to go and tell Frankie that we don't wanna do this for him." The men exchanged looks, but no one made an attempt to leave. "Just like I thought. We don't have a choice so we might as well as make the best of it. Let's speak our piece, drink up some of that high end booze they're serving on the lawn and get the fuck outta here."

"From the looks of this place, I'll bet everything is top shelf." Mel picked up a vase and examined it. "Say, how much do you think we could get if we were to bring a couple of the guys out here to knock this place over?"

"How about you and your next of kin wiped off the map?" Louie took the vase from him and returned it to the shelf. "I keep telling you mopes that these ain't no average darkies we're dealing with, but yous don't seem to be listening." Unlike Bruno and Mel, he was familiar with the family who owned the property and had seen what they were capable of.

Bruno shook his head. "Man, these are definitely different times we're living in when a man like Mr. G goes out of his way to pay respect to some spear-chuckers from Harlem."

"That's one thing we can agree on, Bruno," Mel agreed. "I mean, I understand keeping relationships good with the coloreds and all, but Mr. G has practically given him a seat at the table. Between us, I ain't the only one who is looking at this whole situation funny. Cosa Nostra breaking equal bread with the blacks?" He shook his head sadly. "Fat Mike Tessio is probably rolling over in his grave."

"A grave our young friend put him in," Louie reminded them. "See, you boys were still knocking over liquor stores when Fat Mike got the big idea in his head to go against the Clarks. To that fat son-of-a¬bitch's credit, he nearly pulled it off when he had Poppa Clark and his oldest boy Tommy hit. With them out of the way, the lane would've been wide open for Fat Mike to do as he pleased in Harlem, but he never factored in the baby brother. When he took the reins, shit got real on both sides of the color-line. Mr. G didn't just hand Shai Clark his respect, the kid earned it."

Before the conversation could go any further, the door to the adjoining room opened. Louie stood at attention, followed by Bruno and Mel. From the other room stepped a bookish looking man, wearing wire rimmed glasses and a pale green suit and white shirt. Louie couldn't recall his name, but he had seen him around the Clarks before and knew he was a part of their inner circle.

"Apologies for the wait, gentlemen," the man in the pale green suit greeted them. "I'm Jackson Duffy, but everyone calls me Jackie. I work for the Clarks."

"A black guy with an Irish name," Bruno snickered, which got him a sharp look from Louie.

"Louie Gaza," he introduced himself with a handshake. "And don't worry about the wait. We see you guys got a lot going on today."

"Yeah, we're having a family gathering so we'll try and get you guys in and out of here as soon as possible," Jackie said with a smirk, indicating that he hadn't missed the crude joke. "If you boys will follow me, Mr. Clark is waiting." Jackie turned on his heel and lead back the way he had just come.

From the legendary stories Louie had heard about the legendary Trinidadian crime family that had went head to head with the American Mafia, he had expected their meeting to be in a conference room around a big table, or at the very least some plush-looking office straight out of The Godfather, but he was thrown off by what he saw when he crossed the threshold. It was a small, yet cozy space. Lining the walls were the tallest bookshelves Louie had ever seen outside of a library, each shelf brimming over with books. Dominating the other side of the room was a large picture window that invited in the noonday sun. When Louie spotted the man sitting in the corner, reading a copy of Soul On Ice, he had to blink twice to make sure he wasn't seeing a ghost.

He had put on some weight, and now wore his hair in neat, shoulder-length dreadlocks that made him a dead ringer for his deceased father, but their physical appearances were where their similarities ended. Poppa Clark had been a reasonable and fair man, but Tommy was a thug and a savage. He had earned the moniker Tommy Gunz on the streets for his preference to settle disputes with bullets rather than words. Tommy was a tyrant and next in line to inherit his father's throne, but a bullet to the back changed his fate.

"You're the last person I expected to see at this meeting." Louie said.

"I imagine not. You eat a dozen or so bullets and everybody writes you off for dead. I'm still very much alive, just won't be running any marathons anytime soon." Tommy patted the armrest of his motorized wheel chair.

"I didn't mean it like that, Tommy Gunz. It's just that Frankie said I'd be sitting down with the head of the family, Shai Clark," Louie explained.

"Well, my baby brother is unavailable at the moment so you'll be having an audience with me today," Tommy told him.

Louie and his men exchanged unsure glances. "Is there a problem?" Tommy asked.

Louie is hesitant. "Listen, T. I don't want you to take this the wrong way, but... "

"I don't want you to take this the wrong way is usually what a muthafucka says right before they insult you," Tommy cut him off. "Now I've noticed that since I got passed over for the big chair and slapped in this little one, people been acting like they forgot how Tommy Gunz gives it up, but make no mistake that I am still the bark and the bite of this thing of ours. My brother wears the title as head of this family, but let's not forget who brought the fear of the Clark name to the table. You can put whatever you got on the table with me, or get the fuck out. Don't make me no difference."

"Okay, Tommy. No need to get your panties in a bunch," Louie said in an easy tone. "Like I was saying earlier, Frankie the Fish sent to speak with Shai about a sensitive matter, but since your brother isn't here, maybe you can help."

Tommy shrugged. "Frankie the Fish ain't never been no friend of mine or my family, so what the fuck would make him think we'd even consider it?"

"Let me be a little clearer. Frankie sent me, but the favor isn't for him. It's for Gee-Gee," Louie told him.

Hearing the old mobsters name got Tommy's attention. Genaro Giovanni, or "Gee-Gee" as he was called by those closest to him, was the former underboss and current boss of the Cissaro family. Back when Poppa Clark had been grooming Tommy to succeed him, they had been involved in backdoor heroin deals with a Cissaro capo named Fat Mike. When Tommy tried to cut ties with Mike and started buying their heroin from the Chinese, the fat man had orchestrated the shooting which left Poppa dead and Tommy in a wheelchair. During his recovery, Shai had assumed control of the Clark family and his first order of business was the extermination of Fat Mike and anyone loyal to him. Shai and the Clark soldiers laid waste to Mike's men, but left the fat man to be handled by his own people. He exposed Mike's double dealing to Gee-Gee, and in turn the underboss had him whacked. This took care of the Fat Mike problem, but it also frayed their relationship with the Italians. With a novice, Shai, now at the head of the family, and the veil of protection from the Italians lifted, it was open season on everything Poppa Clark had built. The year or so that followed was a bloody time for the Clarks. Enemies came from far and wide to try and claim their piece of the empire. Shai did as best he could, but the

Clarks had taken on heavy casualties and lost a lot of money during the war. For a time it looked bleak for Shai, but he refused to fold. Gee-Gee was impressed by his resilience and this is what caused him to approach Shai with a proposition that would put an end to the fighting and solidify his claim to the Poppa's empire. No one could say for certain what went on in that room during their meeting, but when it was all said and done,

Hoodlum II: The Good Son

Gee-Gee found himself at the head of the Cissaro table and Shai had usurped Tommy for their father's throne.

"Okay, I'm listening," Tommy said.

"Got a rabid dog that needs to be put to sleep. We'd need someone from your organization to handle it," Louie told him.

"The Cissaros have got plenty of killers on their payroll. Why do you need us to do it?" Tommy asked.

"It's somewhat of a sensitive nature. He's a made guy; a member of the Meloni family," Louie confessed.

This brought a smile to Tommy's face. The Melonis were an outfit out of New Jersey. They were a small family, but gaining quite the reputation for their brutality. Word on the streets was that over the last few months, they had been encroaching on Cissaro operations. "Guineas whacking their own now? And you call us savages," he snorted.

"Look, we didn't come here to be judged by some fucking..." Mel began, but the gun that appeared on Tommy's lap cut him off.

"You finish that sentence and this quiet chat we've been having is going to get real noisy," Tommy warned.

"Everybody just calm down." Louie stepped between them. "Listen, Tommy, if it were up to me I'd kill this piece of shit myself, but if it blows back it could start a war between the Cissaros and the Melonis and we can't afford that right now. It'd be bad not only for our business, but for the Clarks too."

"That's a white boy problem. We ain't got a dog in that fight. Maybe we'll just sit back and let the Melonis thin your numbers out some more," Tommy said sarcastically.

Louie laughed. "You're a funny guy, T. But let me ask you this; what do you think will happen if the Melonis manage to sink their hooks into New York and start calling shots? Unlike us, they ain't no friends of the negro community. No offense."

Tommy weighed it. "Okay, let's say that we do decide to help you out with your little problem. What's in it for the Clarks?"

"Our undying gratitude."

Hoodlum II: The Good Son

"Fuck outta here," Tommy waved him off. "Us doing this favor for you could have a fallout of epic proportions. You're gonna have to do better than that."

"Well, what do you want?" Louie asked, not sure he really wanted an answer.

"You can start with letting me in on that new gun deal you're putting together behind Gee-Gee's back."

The statement caught Louie by surprise and his face said as much.

"What you surprised that I know your little secret? C'mon man, just because my legs have stopped working doesn't mean my ears have. Don't nothing move in this city without me knowing about it."

"Tommy, it's a small thing. Just me doing a little business on the side to keep up with my alimony payments," Louie tried to downplay it.

Tommy leaned in and gave Louie a look. "That's funny, because I happen to know for a fact that you ain't married."

"I come here to make a good faith deal and you're gonna extort me?" Louie chuckled. "Okay, you got me. I know a Russian guy who's got some connects down south that I've been making a little money from, but it's a small thing. We don't have the means to get them up here in a large enough volume to take on any partners."

Tommy's wheels began to spin. "What if I could solve that problem and provide you with a way to get the guns up here in bulk? Maybe three to four dozen at a time?"

Louie did the math in his head. That was double what he was currently moving. Getting his help moving that many guns at one time, he could he could afford to cut Tommy in and still make a ton good chunk of change. "Then I'd say, maybe there's room for another hand in the pot after all."

"Figured you'd see things my way," Tommy smirked. "Of course I'll have to charge you a little something extra for transportation costs.

"I come here to negotiate a good faith deal and you're trying to grease me?"

Tommy laughed. "I hardly think soliciting murder qualifies as a good faith deal, but whatever. Those are my terms. Now we can either keep dancing around and wasting either other's time or seal the deal so we can both go on about our days." He extended his hand.

Hoodlum II: The Good Son

Louie looked back at his entourage. Both Bruno and Mel looked like they were against it, but Louie didn't figure he had a choice. If he didn't go along with it, what was to stop Tommy doubling back and exposing his backdoor deal? He had witnessed what happened to the last person who had tried to put one over on their organization and wanted no parts of it. "Fucking ballbreaker," he grumbled and shook Tommy's hand.

"Thought you'd see things my way," Tommy smirked triumphantly. "Now you're excused. I'll have my boy Duffy come see you tomorrow so we can work out the details of our new business arrangement."

"Fuck you, Tommy. You just make sure that whoever you sent to clip this prick does it painfully and slowly. Oh, and pay special attention to his face. Mr. Gee would like it very much if this prick's family couldn't have an open casket funeral." Louie stood to leave.

"Say Louie, if you don't mind me asking: what did this guy do that has Mr. Gee so in his feelings about it?" Tommy asked curiously.

Louie shrugged. "He's got a thing for little girls."
"Say no more. He's fucking dead." Tommy vowed.

"Anything else I need to know about this guy?" "Yeah, don't take him lightly. Nicky might be a
   baby-raping piece of shit, but make no mistake - this guy is a stone killer. Whoever you send after him, make sure they're up to the task."

   Tommy waited until Louie and his bunch had gone before letting a sinister grin spread across his face. Sitting with Louie and his boys was the last thing he had expected to be doing that afternoon. Shai was the mouthpiece of the family those days. Him being unexpectedly absent and allowing Tommy to highjack the meeting was either dumb luck or fate finally throwing him a bone.

   Tommy had a long and turbulent history with the Cissaros, since before the events leading to his father's murder and his current physical status. Though Fat Mike might not have been the shooter, he set the wheels in motion, and Tommy held all of the Cissaros accountable by association. During his long months of recovery, all he could think about was revenge against those who had changed his destiny and that of his family. When the subject of the truce between the two sides had first been presented, Tommy was the most animate in his opposition of it. His little brother was more of a politician than the warlord Tommy had been in his day, so he understood him wanting to end the bloodshed and get back to the money, but that didn't mean it sat well with him. Had it been up to Tommy, he'd have kept killing until the last of their enemies were dead, but he was no longer calling the shots - his baby brother was. Publically he would support his brother in whatever decisions he made concerning the family, but in secret, Tommy plotted and waited for an opportunity to strike back at his enemies, and Louie might have provided him with just that.

"Did you get all that?" Tommy spoke to the seemingly empty room.

"Yes," a voice spoke back. A figure peeled itself from the shadows near the window and stood next to Tommy. He was a tall man with a shaved head, dressed in a dusty priest's robes. A black leather patch covered his left eye, lying just over a scar that went from his forehead to his cheek. To most, he was known as the Clark family executioner, but to Tommy he was simply called Priest.

"These fucking dagos kill me. The only time they even halfway show the proper respect is when they need a damn favor!" Tommy spat.

"It's been like that since the beginning. The only reason Poppa even tolerated them was because they were able to open doors that were previously closed to us," Priest said.

"Well Poppa ain't here, and we been took them doors off the hinges. If it were up to me, I'd sever ties and kill the whole stinking lot of them."

"Well, it isn't up to you anymore," Priest said. He didn't mean any offense; just making a point.

"Don't be funny, Priest. You've always been better at killing than you were at making jokes," Tommy said.

"Personally, I think the whole thing stinks to high hell. The Cissaros have got at least a half dozen qualified killers on payroll who could undertake the task?" Priest shook his head. "I don't like it, Tommy."

"Truthfully, I don't either, but I can't pass up an opportunity to put that prick Gee-Gee in our debt and dipping into Louie's pockets at the same time. Shai breaks bread with the Italians, I'm fonder of bleeding them."

"Poppa used to always say that all money ain't good money, Tommy," Priest warned.

"Well we see where my father's philosophies got him, don't we?" Tommy asked. This quieted Priest. He wheeled himself over to the desk and reached for the drink resting on it. Tommy had just lifted it when the glass slipped and shattered on the floor. "Muthafucka!" he began flexing his fingers as if they had gone to sleep.

Priest knelt and began cleaning up the glass. "Your hands giving you trouble again?"

"A little numbness from time to time, but nothing I can't deal with." Tommy shook both his hands to wake them up. "It's a small price to pay to be able to wipe my own ass again. I've never been one to believe in miracles, but our mutual friend got me re-thinking my stance on that."

After Tommy had received the news of his paralysis, he'd slipped into a deep depression. To make matters worse, the shit treatment he'd received while in the prison infirmary only made things worse, as he had contracted two infections that caused further nerve damage. By the time he was released and able to receive proper care, he was in such poor health that things didn't look good for him. Shai spared no expense, taking his brother to the best specialists around the country, but none of them were hopeful. When conventional medicine failed them, an unconventional remedy presented itself.

One of Priest's acolytes, The Black Lotus, had come to them during their times of troubles and told them of a man who was said to be able to do what the doctors could not. He fashioned himself a faith healer, but upon their first meeting looked to be anything but that. Dressed in leather and motorcycle boots, with a black duster that looked like something out of a Terminator movie, Shai and everyone else had been suspicious, but they had exhausted all their options and Tommy was desperate so he consented. By the third week of what the healer referred to as conditioning, there was still no improvement in Tommy. By week four, Tommy was ready to write the faith healer off as a charlatan and arrange to have him killed, but something quite unexpected happened...his finger twitched. In under a year Tommy had regained the use of his arms and hands. He still couldn't walk, but the man he had come to know only as The Cross, made him hopeful.

"About this gun business," Priest interrupted his thoughts. "I'm not sure how Shai is going to take this. You know he has a strict policy about the Clarks not getting involved with guns. It's too risky."

"And selling heroin isn't?" Tommy shot back. "If Shai was so worried about what was going on with the Italians, he'd have been here to take this meeting instead of running off to do God knows what with Angelo and Big Doc. He ain't gonna have shit to say about this little deal I made because we ain't gonna tell him... at least not yet. This deal is about me, not the family. I'm used to earning my way, not depending on the mercies of my little brother."

A disapproving look crossed Priest's face.

"You got a problem with that, Priest?"

"My job is to pass judgment on our enemies, not members of this family. I am here to serve the Clarks," Priest told him.

"And you'd do well to remember it."

"Do I even want to know how you found out about Louie's gun connect?" Priest asked.

"A little jumpoff I'm knocking down is connected to the guy Louie is getting the guns from," Tommy said, much to Priest's surprise. "Don't look so shocked. I can't feel shit below the waist but I still get the occasional erection. These days sex is more of a psychological thing for me than for pleasure."

"I guess The Cross' treatments worked a little better than we expected," Priest said in awe.

"You don't know the half," Tommy flexed his hand. "Now about this shit bird Mr. G wants clipped."

"I'll take care of it. The Black Lotus is in town - I'll set her to the task," Priest offered.

"Nah, we'll save her for something more befitting of someone of her talents. We'll let one of the soldiers take care of it." Tommy thought on it for a few ticks. "As a matter of fact, those little niggas from the Dog Pound are always looking for a come up. We'll put one of them on it."

"Tech? Maybe Brasco?"

Hoodlum II: The Good Son

"Tech has got his head shoved too far up Swann's ass for me to trust him to keep this quiet, and I don't like that fat fuck Brasco. We'll give it to the other one - the little fucker with the grills and bushy hair."

"No!" Priest blurted out to Tommy's surprise. "What I mean is, he's barely a child. If this Nicky that we've been asked to murder is Nicky The Gent, then he's a real piece of work. I'm not sure Animal is ready," he tried to clean it up.

"Have you forgotten that this child, as you call him, presented my brother with a human head to prove himself?" Tommy reminded him. "I'd say he's more than qualified."

Before Priest could try and argue further, Duffy walked in. He seemed startled when he noticed Priest in the room. "I'm sorry, T. Didn't know you had company." He apologized, quietly wondering how Priest had managed to slip passed him.

"It's fine, Priest was just leaving." Tommy said, dismissing the assassin.

Priest gave a curt nod before slipping from the room.

"That guy give me the creeps," Duffy said once Priest had gone.

"He should. Priest has been putting niggas in the ground since before either of us were born. I can give the history of the Brotherhood another time, but for now I need you to do something for me."

"Anything, T," Duffy said excitedly. He couldn't wait to get out of that suit and back into the streets.

"I need you to make a run into Harlem to get something for me." Tommy grabbed a slip of paper and a pen from the satchel hanging from the arm of his wheel chair and scribbled an address down on it.

"Sure, T. Anything. What do you need me to get?" Duffy asked, stuffing the slip of paper into his pocket.

"Not a what, but a who. Tell the Animal that the Clarks have need of his services."

The mention of his name made the hairs on Duffy's arms stand. He had never met The Animal, but the stories he'd heard painted him as a homicidal imp that got his jollies off the misery of others. Duffy wasn't entirely sure if the stories had been exaggerated or if the devil really did walk the earth, but he wasn't too happy about being the one sent to find out.

"You got a problem with what I'm asking you?" Tommy noticed Duffy's hesitation.

"No, no problem at all." Duffy checked himself.

"Glad to hear it. And as far as me receiving any more appointments, ain't my problem or concern. I ain't Shai's secretary. They can wait for him to come back or go the fuck home." Tommy wheeled himself over near the widow and gazed out at the lawn.

"I figured you'd say that and I told him as much, but this guy says he's your family," Duffy explained.

Tommy cocked his head. "Family? Ain't much of that left besides me, Shai and Hope. Whoever the fuck it is, tell them I said, 'Beat it,'" he capped, loud enough for whoever was waiting outside to hear. Tommy dismissed Duffy and picked up his book to go back to his reading.

"Damn, that's how Nappy Black do his family these days?" Tommy heard a familiar voice from the hallway, and it froze him. There were only two people who referred to him as Nappy Black: his brother Shai and the man who had given him the nickname in the first

119

place. He dropped the book and wheeled himself towards the door so fast that he nicked one of his fingers in the spokes.

Standing there, still trying to convince Duffy to let him pass, was a face Tommy hadn't seen in years; a face not all that different from his own. He was tall and dark-skinned, dressed in jeans, combat boots and a tattered fatigue jacket. He had shaved off his dreads and now wore his hair in a low afro that had begun to gray around the temples. He had aged quite a bit, but his lips still wore the mischievous grin he would always flash at Tommy as a kid, right before convincing him to do something that would likely get him into trouble.

Seeing that Tommy was watching, Duffy doubled his efforts to get the man to leave. He was about to lay hands on him when Tommy motioned for him to stand down. Duffy didn't like it, or the looks of the man, but it wasn't his place to argue with Tommy.

"Pardon yourself, lil' nigga." The man popped the collar of his jacket and bumped Duffy as he passed him.

"The devil must be slipping if he let you sneak out of hell," Tommy glared up at the man.

Hoodlum II: The Good Son

The man placed his hand over his heart and flashed Tommy a mock-wounded look. "Now what kind of greeting is that for your favorite cousin?"

PART II
"FAMILY TIES"

CHAPTER 10

"I think you coming in person is a bad idea," Big Doc said for the fifth time as he pulled the car into one of the empty parking spaces.

"I don't like it either, Angie, but Sol wouldn't have asked me to come unless it were absolutely necessary, especially in the middle of my baby shower. Let's go in, see what the fuck is going on and get out." Shai climbed from the backseat.

Angelo led the way through the crowded parking lot with Big Doc bringing up the rear and keeping Shai wedged between them. Both men's eyes constantly swept back and forth for danger. It was the middle of the day and the Newark airport Ramada was busy with guests coming and going so the chances of someone trying something were slim, but you could never be too careful.

When they stepped through the automatic glass doors, they were greeted by a tall white man, with a head full of wavy black hair. His black suit was perfectly tailored and the white shirt beneath was freshly starched. He wore no tie, and left the top few buttons undone so you could see the gold Star of David hanging from his neck. Big Doc stepped forward to intercept the man, but Shai waved him off.

"What's good, Jacob?" Shai extended his hand. Jacob was Sol Lansky's nephew. He and Shai had met years ago when he was still in high school and Jacob was home visiting for the holidays. He was a graduate of Harvard Law, and had spent the last ten years in Israel working for the government. He was ex-Mossad and from what Shai had heard, very good at what he did.

"Nothing," Jacob said flatly. Worry lines were etched across his face.

"Is your uncle..." Shai began, but was cut off when Jacob raised a finger to his lips for silence.

"Not here. Too many prying ears." Jacob looked around suspiciously. "Follow me, please." He led them to the elevators. The entire ride up to the fourth floor, Angelo and Big Doc exchanged suspicious glances. If Jacob noticed, he showed no signs of it as he kept his face neutral. When they got off, they headed to a room at the end of the hall. Jacob removed a key-card from his jacket pocket, but paused. "I trust anything you see beyond this point will remain between us."

Shai nodded in agreement. "Jacob, what's going on?"

"I can show you better than I can tell you." Jacob slipped the key into the slot and released the lock. He pushed the door open and stood to the side for Shai to enter. Jacob was family, but Shai was no fool, so he let Angelo enter first.

"Holy shit!" they heard Angelo say from inside the room.

Big Doc went in next with Shai following close behind. When Shai beheld the scene in the room, all he could say is, "What the fuck have you done?"

*

Sol Lansky sat in a chair in the corner, steel gray eyes staring straight ahead and a cigarette burning between his withered fingers. Normally Sol was the epitome of composure, but he looked nervous, which was a bad sign. He spared a glance at Shai, before going back to his staring.

The hotel room was a mess; empty bottles of whiskey and beer littered around and clothes strewn across the chair and spilling onto the floor. On the nightstand, a used condom sat atop of mound of cigarette butts in an overflowing ashtray. It looked more like a drug house than the cozy hotel the adds billed it to be, but it wasn't the filth that held Shai's attention. It was the girl stretched out across one of the twin beds. She was a thin blonde with plastic breasts and icy blue eyes that stared out into space. From the dried blood caked around her nose and mouth, Shai could tell she had been dead for a while. Sitting on the other bed, sobbing and wrapped only in one of the thin hotel sheets, was the man Poppa Clark had once called one of his closest friends. Back then he had been running for assistant District Attorney for Manhattan, but his sights were set on higher offices. When things were moving slow for him in New York, he pulled up stakes and joined the political race in New Jersey. For the last year, Bill O'Connor had occupied the office of Deputy Mayor of Newark.

"What the fuck did you do?" Shai snapped at the

quivering man.

"Shai, this wasn't my fault!" Bill said with a quivering voice.

"So you're trying to tell me this bitch offed herself?" Shai snapped.

"This is bad... all bad." Big Doc shook his head in disbelief. "You shouldn't be here, Shai."

"My thoughts exactly," Angelo agreed. "Let's get the fuck outta here!" He grabbed Shai by the arm and started pushing him towards the door.

"Wait! Don't leave. I need your help!" Bill jumped off the bed and rushed towards Shai to keep him from leaving. He was stopped when Big Doc dropped him with a punch to the gut.

"Take it easy!" Sol moved between them.

"Fuck do you mean take it easy?" Shai turned angry eyes to Shai. "You've got me standing in a hotel room three feet away from a dead body! What the fuck were you thinking calling me here?"

Sol moved closer to Shai and lowered his voice to a whisper. "I was thinking how we could turn this tragedy into an opportunity. Shai, you ever known me to do anything without a seeing the bigger picture?"

"No," Shai huffed.

"Then hear him out," Sol urged.

Shai didn't like it, but he reluctantly agreed. "Okay, what's the story?" he asked Bill.

"I'm still not sure what happened," Bill began, trying to stop his voice from shaking. "She's one of my regular girls. We get together once or twice per week, do a little blow and fuck. There was nothing different about this day."

"Except I'm guessing your little trysts don't usually end with her dying," Shai said sarcastically. "Cut to the chase, so I can go."

"I usually get the coke from my guy in the city," Bill continued, "but I was coming in from Philadelphia last night, so I had my driver go into Newark to score in the hood. I know it was stupid, but she was geeking, and this broad turned into a real freak when she was nice and tuned up. We got at it for a while and I go to take a shower. When I come out, she's on the bed having some type of seizure and foaming at the mouth. I tried to give her CPR, but there was nothing I could do."

"So why not call the cops instead of Sol?" Shai asked.

"A married deputy mayor found in hotel with drugs and a dead prostitute wouldn't play out well in the morning paper," Billy answered sadly.

"That still doesn't answer my question; what the hell am I doing here?" Shai folded his arms. He knew where it was going, but needed to hear it.

"Well, in this terrible pinch, Bill decided that it was best to reach out to his friends to help him," Sol answered for him. "What good are friends if you can't turn to them in times of need?"

Shai laughed. "Friends? Is that what we are now? You know, my dad once called you his friend. I can remember all those years ago, sitting in his office and hearing him say to me, 'Shai, my friend Bill is going to be instrumental in helping me build my dream casino.' When he was killed, you turned your back on us and my father's dream." He reminded him.

"It wasn't like that, Shai!" Bill's voice was pleading. "When Poppa was no longer sitting at the head of the table, the others felt like it was too big of a risk. Tony and those guys didn't want anything to do with it."

"But Poppa looked at them as his friends. It was an honor reserved for you," Shai sneered. "I'm sorry, Bill. I can't help you. Maybe because of your new standing as Deputy Mayor, the judge will show you lenience." Shai started for the door.

"Please!" Bill threw himself at Shai's feet. "I can't go to prison. If you help me, I'll give you anything you want! Anything!"

Shai looked down at the man groveling at his feet and frowned. Growing up, he had always looked up to Bill O'Connor as a man of great power and respect. What he was reduced to that day disgusted him. "How the mighty have fallen," he mumbled. "Get up Bill, you're embarrassing yourself."

"I'm sorry, Shai." Bill pulled himself back onto the bed, wiping his runny nose with the back of his hand.

"I didn't mean to involve you in any of this shit, truly I didn't."

"It's okay, Bill," Shai softened his tone. "It's like Sol said: what good are your friends if you can't turn to them in times of need? We are friends, aren't we?"

Bill nodded.

"Good," Shai smiled wickedly. "Who else knows about this?"

"My driver," Bill told him.

"And what about the person you got the drugs from? Do you think your driver could point him out?" "I don't know. I guess so."

Shai thought for a few minutes. "Okay, Bill. No need to worry. This is what's going to happen next. You're going to tell Angelo how to get in contact with your driver, then you're going to go into the bathroom, clean yourself up and go home."

"What are you going to do?" Bill asked nervously.

"Better if I spare you the details. Like I said, go home, have a nice dinner with your wife and get some rest. By the time you wake up in the morning, this will all have been a bad dream."

Bill dropped to his knees and kissed Shai's hand. "Bless your heart, Shai. I owe you a huge favor for this."

"You owe me more than a favor, but we can discuss it at a later time. Now go get cleaned up. I need to speak to my people in private."

Bill nodded sheepishly and went off into the bathroom.

"Well played, Shai," Sol smiled proudly.

"You set this whole thing up, didn't you?" Shai accused.

"Not at all. I simply laid a puzzle in front of you and let you solve it," Sol said innocently.

"Whatever, you cagey old fuck!" Shai joked, tossing one of Bill's discarded socks at him. "Big Doc, after I leave I need you to stay behind. Call in a cleanup crew to take care of the mess. Then see the person on duty at the front desk and persuade them to turn a blind eye while we take care of business."

"Sure. We'll get rid of her too," Big Doc said.

"Nah, no civilians. Either bribe her or threaten her; I don't care which. Just get it done. And make sure they wipe the surveillance tapes between the time Bill came in with the whore and the time I leave."

"Wait, you're really going to help this scum bag?" Angelo asked in disbelief. "After that snake shit he did to Poppa, I say let that fucker burn!"

"What he did to Poppa is exactly the reason that Shai isn't going to leave him twisting in the wind," Sol spoke up. "Poppa Clark showed us all the advantages of having political allies, but even at the height of his reign, his reach had never extended as far as having a deputy mayor in his pocket."

A light of recognition went off in Angelo's eyes. "So you're going to make him a business partner?"

"After what he did to my father, that piece of shit ain't fit to sit at our table, but I got a nice spot on reserve for him at my feet," Shai said with a sinister smile. "Gentlemen, I feel the winds of change starting to blow."

CHAPTER 11

Tech stood off to the side, smoking a cigarette and watching Shai as he moved through the crowd of guests. From the way people bent over backward to kiss his ass, you'd have thought that he was the President. Hard to believe that just a few years prior, he had been just another spoiled athlete who didn't know shit about the streets.

He found himself stuck somewhere adoration and repulsion at the new Don of New York. Tech came from a world where you had to earn your stripes, but Shai had inherited his. Tech tried not to feel resentful towards Shai, but he couldn't help it. Tech had been in the streets for most of his life, laying homies and enemies to rest, and yet he was still trying to claw his way up from the bottom of the barrel while Shai pranced around giving orders to dudes he felt were way more qualified to sit in the big chair. He was by no means a hater, but his young mind still had a hard time processing it. He'd once expressed his feelings to his big homie Castro, and she'd told him he was suffering from growing pains. He had no clue what the fuck it meant, and the only thing she offered in the way of an explanation was that he'd understand it when he was older.

"You must be more important than I gave you credit for, if Shai allowed you into his personal space." Jewels eased up on him. The boy walked so light that Tech hadn't even heard him approach. "What y'all talk about?"

"Nothing much, just some hood shit," Tech downplayed it.

Jewels gave him a disbelieving look. "Yeah, right. I been running with this crew strong for six months and still ain't never had a one on one conversation with Shai. Only reason he checking for you is because you under Swann," he teased him.

"Fuck outta here. I don't need an endorsement from another nigga to prove my worth. The Dog Pound stands on their own," Tech said proudly.

"Whatever nigga," Jewels dismissed the statement. The two of them stood around making small talk, sipping and people-watching. Near the path that led to the house he spotted two members of Brutus' security team escorting a trio of white guys back down the driveway towards their car. "Yo, who them cats right there?" he nodded at the men. One of them looked familiar, but he couldn't put a name with the face.

Jewels glanced in the direction Tech was looking in and frowned. "I don't know. I ain't never seen them before, but Shai has got all kinda important white people running around here. They're probably some politicians or some shit."

Tech looked at how they were dressed; off the rack suits, and low-end shoes. "Nah, those ain't no politicians," he said suspiciously.

"Whoever they are, they're leaving the big house and whatever goes on in there ain't none of our business... at least not yet. But fuck them dudes, what's good with shorty who keeps looking over here at you?" Jewels nodded across the yard.

There were three girls sitting at a table with an old woman wearing a large hat. The smallest and youngest looking of the girls was staring in their direction, but when she saw that Tech noticed, she turned away.

"Man, I ain't stunting that little girl," Tech lied. He had actually noticed her when she walked in.

"Little girl?" Jewels gave him a funny look. "Man, no matter their ages, ain't none of the chicks who run with Ms. Ruby can be considered a little girl."

"Ms. Who?" Tech wasn't familiar with the name.

Jewels shook his head. "You really don't get out much, do you? Ms. Ruby is a gangster with a cunt. All the girls she takes care of are in the life and involved in everything from selling pussy to catching bodies. At least that's what I heard."

"So you trying to tell me that girl is some kind of prostitute or something?" Tech asked in disgust.

"Nah, man. I didn't say all that. I don't think she's pretty enough to be one of Ruby's whores, but if she's sitting at that table, she's something. We should go over there. You can take the runt, and I'll get at the white girl."

"I'm good," Tech said, trying to keep his heart from thudding in his chest as he watched the white girl lean in and whisper something to the other one and they both looked in his direction. He wasn't sure what to make of it and that unnerved him. Tech was handy with a pistol, but a total novice when it came to the opposite sex.

"Let me find out you scared," Jewels taunted him, picking up on Tech's apprehension.

"I ain't scared of shit!" Tech declared.

"Then let's go over there and press them broads," Jewels challenged. Seeing that Tech still refused to move, he took the initiative. "Matter of fact, you can stay your scary ass here and I'll put the ball in play for you," he said as he started over towards the girls.

"Stop playing, Jewels!" Tech called, but Jewels was already on his way.

*

"'Come to the baby shower,' she said. 'It'll be fun,' she said," Belle mumbled while picking over her garden salad.

"You hush that complaining, Lulabelle, before I send your ass home," Ms. Ruby checked her. "There are at least a half dozen girls who would've killed to be here, but I brought y'all. It's a high honor to be invited into the home of the Clarks. It means we're important."

"If we're so important, how come Shai had time to say hello to everyone except us?" Belle capped.

Ms. Ruby shot Belle a look that silenced her. Belle's delivery was crude, but it didn't make her wrong in her observation. They were there for almost an hour before Shai finally made an appearance. Ms. Ruby watched him taking his time, working through the yard greeting all his guests. He looked like he was finally going to make his way around to them, when one of his men handed him a cell phone. Less than five minutes after Shai had taken the call, he had vanished and she hadn't seen him since. Shai had always been a gentleman, and she doubted if him rushing off before speaking to her and her girls had been a slight, but there was obviously something big going...big enough to make him take off from his own baby shower. The lingering question was what?

Once she was sure Ms. Ruby wasn't going to bite her head off, she went back to brooding over her salad and people watching. She hadn't meant to sound ungrateful. In fact, Belle was extremely thankful to have been selected as one of the lucky few girls who would accompany her to the baby shower. As the newest member of the house, and the roughest around the edges, it hadn't been an easy transition for Belle. She often found herself failing to fit in with the other girls and wondering if Ms. Ruby hated her.

Plucking a grape tomato, Belle busied herself looking everywhere but at Ms. Ruby and the other girls. Her eyes fell to the other side of the yard and she spotted a young man who looked just as out of place as he did. He was taking short drags of a Newport, and watching everyone who passed too close to him as if they were going to pull a knife out and stab him. He was a wolf trying to mingle amongst sheep, and she could smell it coming off him over the scent of fresh grass.

"I see you," Natalia whispered into Belle's ear, startling her.

"What you talking about, girl?" Belle asked as if she had no clue what Natalia was talking about.

"Bird watching," Natalia said slyly. "Which one you got your eye on; the thug ass nigga with the box braids, or the cute one rocking all the fake jewelry? Let me guess... the thug, right? Yeah, Tech-9 seems more your speed."

"You know him?" Belle asked, not meaning to sound as interested as she did.

"Not personally, but I heard a few stories," Natalia dangled. "They say he's the ring alpha in a pack of young wolves who call themselves the Dog Pound."

Belle was familiar with their crew through reputation. Let the streets tell it, the Pound was composed of a bunch of hardened killers, spewed from the bowels of hell to do the Devil's work. Looking at the skinny piece of chocolate standing about a yard or so away from her, she had a hard time matching his appearance to the stories of their exploits.

"He ain't all that," Belle rolled her eyes. She watched as the cute one with the cheap jewelry exchanged words with Tech. Whatever he was selling, it didn't look like Tech was buying it. After some debate, the one with the cheap jewelry started making his way in their direction.

*

Tech's heart filled with dread, as he watched Jewels amble over to the table where Ms. Ruby and her girls were sitting. He'd been trying his best to fly under the radar so as not to embarrass himself or Swann, but Jewels' clown ass was about to blow it and have him on Front Street over some high school shit. He'd considered running Jewels down and knocking him out before he could pull the trigger on the debacle, but causing a scene at Shai's baby shower would have only made a bad situation worse. By that point, he had no choice but to ride it out and hope that the damage wasn't irreparable.

Jewels in all his confident swagger peppered the ladies at the table with some slick words, with intentions on greasing the wheels of furthering his own gains. He thought he had opened the lane up until he tried to slide into the empty chair between the white girl and the brown skinned one, and Ms. Ruby placed her cane across the seat and prevented him from sitting. She capped something to Jewels that brought a dumbstruck expression to his face, before casting him back in the direction he had come.

"Why you play so fucking much?" Tech asked once Jewels had made it back.

"I was trying to cut to the chase for you, baby boy," Jewels told him. "But dig, I got a message for you." "From shorty?" Tech asked hopefully.

"Nah, from the old lady," Jewels said to Tech's surprise.

*

Belle sat up a little straighter when she saw Jewels coming in their direction, trying to keep her game face on, but she was really nervous. It was obvious from his and Tech's body language that he was coming as an envoy, but she hoped that it wasn't on his behalf, because she had no interests in him.

"What's popping ladies?" Jewels greeted the women at the table.

"Not a damn thing if you can't come with a better opening line than that," Natalia shut him down.

"Damn, no need to be so cold, snowflake. I come in good faith," Jewels said, thinking he was being cool, and not taking into account how insulting the statement was. He tried to sit down, but the old woman placed her cane across the chair.

"And there went the snowball's chance in hell you had," Ms. Ruby cut in. "Is that how they teach you young men to approach ladies these days? If so, it makes me glad I ain't got no sons," she laughed. "State your business and be gone, baby."

Jewels found himself embarrassed, so he decided to shift some of the blame to his friend. "Pardon me, Ms. Ruby. I didn't mean no disrespect, it's just that my homeboy wanted to talk to shorty," he nodded at Belle, "but he's a little shy."

Ms. Ruby looked over at Tech, before turning her attention back to Jewels. "Is that a fact? Well you tell your little friend that any girl in the company of Ms.

Ruby is a lady, and not a hoodrat. If he got a mind to court Belle, then he needs to come over here and do so in his own words."

"Jeez, why did you have to embarrass me like that?" Belle whined once Jewels had gone.

"I ain't doing nothing but teaching you a lesson about how women of respect are supposed to conduct themselves," Ms. Ruby informed her. "Now had you let that boy send his friend to fetch you, you'd be at his call from here until whenever. Now if he comes to you, then you've established two things: how serious he is about his intentions and the fact that you are not to be summoned like some damn dog. Anything you do in life must always be on your terms. Remember that, Lulabelle."

Ms. Ruby had just dropped some real game on her, but Belle's young mind couldn't pluck out the gem in the statement. She was more focused on being told what to do. She watched Jewels say something to Tech and and sat in anticipation, waiting for him to start laughing and blow her off. To her surprise, that wasn't what happened at all. Her heart fluttered in her chest as he began walking in their direction.

"Uh, how are you ladies doing today?" Tech asked awkwardly.

"Well and yourself, young man?" Ms. Ruby replied, looking him directly in his eyes. She noticed that Tech couldn't return her gaze. He was either nervous or trying to hide something he didn't want her to see. She reasoned it was a bit of both.

There was an awkward silence hanging in the air. "So, do you work for Shai too?" Brain asked. It was a forward question, but that's how she was.

"Um, no. I'm a friend of Swann," Tech told her. "You got a name, friend of Swann?" Ms. Ruby asked.

"Yes, they call me Tech," he said as he extended his hand.

Ms. Ruby took his hand and instead of shaking it she examined it, turning it over to study his palm. "Dirty fingernails, and calluses," she said as she released his hand and frowned. "Shai must be getting laced if he's allowing corner boys this close to where he lays his head."

145

"Ms. Ruby!" Belle said in embarrassment.

"No, it's cool," Tech assured Belle before turning his attention back to Ruby. "I ain't no corner boy, ma'am. Ain't been one in a while."

"But you're still in the streets, yes?" she shot back.

"For the moment, but I'm hoping to turn my luck around sooner than later," Tech told her with a wink.

Ms. Ruby studied him for a few beats. "I like you, Tech. You're a bit on the raggedy side, but you're honest. That's a rare quality, especially in a den of thieves," she said as she motioned to the guests around them.

"Thanks... I think."

"So," Ms. Ruby picked up her water glass and took a light sip of the whiskey she had poured into it from her flask, "what's your business with my Belle?"

"My business?" Tech didn't understand the question. This drew a laugh from Brain and Natalia, but a quick look from the old woman hushed them.

"I mean, what do you want? What are your intentions?" Ms. Ruby clarified.

Tech shuffled his feet uncomfortably. "I dunno... just a little conversation I guess."

"You sure that's all you want?" Natalia asked slyly, and the girls giggled again.

"You know what? I think that's my cue to bounce," Tech said, trying to hold his anger. He knew when he was being mocked, and decided to cut out before he did or said something stupid.

"I swear, sometimes I think y'all go out of your way to embarrass mc!" Belle fumed, as she watched Tech walk away.

"Hush, child. We wasn't doing nothing but having a bit of fun with the young man. He should have thicker skin," Ms. Ruby said as she took another healthy sip of her drink.

"Yeah, for a tough guy, he sure is sensitive," Brain added.

"So what you gonna do, New Fish; sit there looking sad or let that fine little piece of meat walk away?" Natalia taunted her. "If you don't want him, I'll give him a whirl."

"You keep those whorish hands to yourself!" Belle said as she tossed a napkin at her.

"What did I tell you about table manners?" Ms. Ruby glared at all the girls. She let her eyes linger on Belle, who was watching Tech with a sad expression on her face. "Natalia is right. If you want him then go get him, but just be mindful that you really want what you're chasing, hear me?"

"Yes, ma'am." Belle got up and went after Tech.

"Wow, I've never seen Belle act like that over a guy before," Brain said as she pushed her glasses up on her nose.

"I was wondering when she would start noticing the opposite sex. Frankly I was beginning to wonder about her," Ms. Ruby joked.

"You are deplorable," Belle said as she rolled her eyes.

"No, baby. I'm just an old woman who remembers the thrill of the chase and the pain of the fall. You girls make sure you keep your good eyes on Belle and that boy," Ms. Ruby told them, before looking around for the waiter to bring her another drink.

Natalia was absently picking at the chicken on her plate when her eyes happened to drift to the front of the house. A tall man was wheeling Tommy out of the house, escorted by two members of the security team. She removed her compact mirror from her purse and applied a quick coat of lipstick. Blotting her lips with the napkin, she got up and excused herself from the table.

"And where are you going?" Ms. Ruby asked.

"To the bathroom. I'll be back in a bit," Natalia lied. Before Ms. Ruby could press her further, she skirted off.

*

Tech was cursing under his breath and wishing that he had something to hit. He didn't know why he had let Jewels gas him into approaching that girl, and had ended up getting embarrassed for it. He had been having a decent time up until then, but after that he was ready to go.

A pair of rapid footsteps behind him caused Tech to spin. To his surprise it was Belle, jogging in his direction. "Fuck do you want? To crack some more jokes on me?" he snapped before she had even reached him.

"Damn, why you gotta say it like that?" Belle asked.

"I don't know, maybe because your homegirls just spent the last few minutes clowning me," Tech replied.

"I'm sorry about that. Ms. Ruby has had a little too much to drink and Natalia is just rude," Belle said. "You gonna slow those long ass legs down so we can talk, or are we gonna keep having this conversation at thirty miles per hour?"

Tech stopped. "What?"

Belle looked him up and down. "Look, I know you're tight about the ribbing they gave you, but ain't no need to get all stank like I'm bothering you. You're the one who sent your friend over asking if you can talk to me."

"I didn't send him," Tech said.

"You didn't?" Her eyes flashed hurt.

"No. I mean yes. I mean... shit, I don't know!" Tech threw his arms up in surrender. "Look shorty, I ain't really good at this kinda thing."

"Neither am I. So how about we stop making it a thing and just talk and see where we end up?" Belle suggested. "Look, let's start over. I'm Belle," she said as she extended her hand.

Tech's demeanor eased. "Tech," he said as he took her

HOODLUM II: THE GOOD SON

hand. And just like that, the fuse was lit.

CHAPTER 12

It had been slightly over two hours since Shai had slid off from the baby shower to respond to Sol's summons. There was no doubt in his mind that Honey was going to be beyond pissed, and rightfully so. He hadn't expected to be gone that long, but then again, he hadn't expected to walk into a murder scene either.

Sol chose to ride back in the SUV with Shai and Big Doc, with Jacob trailing them in his car. Sol hadn't said much during the ride back, but Shai could see his brain working behind his eyes. The irony of the man who had turned his back on the Clark family at one of their lowest points finding himself in a bind that only the Clarks could fix hadn't been lost on Shai. It was either the universe doing Shai a solid by allowing him to repay the slight done onto his father, or Sol was a far better manipulator than Shai had given him credit for. He suspected it was a bit of both. Sol could find a way to turn a profit from anything, including the tragic death of a young whore. He was the kind of dude who secretly took out life insurance policies on his soldiers, so he made money whether they lived or died. It was his ruthlessness when it came to making a dollar that ensured he'd always be an asset to his business partners, and why he had been able to outlive most of his contemporaries in the underworld. The better Shai got to know Sol over the years, the more he understood why his father had kept him so close.

"So, you just gonna keep staring at me or speak whatever is on your mind?" Sol said as he turned to Shai.

Shai thought about bullshitting him, but Sol had known him since he was a kid and would see right through the veil, so he was honest with him. "You took a hell of a gamble back there, calling me to help that piece of shit O'Connor."

"Did I?" Sol asked with a raised eyebrow.

"Damn, right. For all you know, I could've told that piece of shit to go to hell. After what he did, I wouldn't have been wrong."

"No, you wouldn't have and yet you didn't," Sol pointed out. "Crushing him right off would be convenient, but an empty victory. Exploiting the situation and making Bill your bitch not only furthers your own gains, but it'll also feed that ever-growing ego of yours."

"So I've got an ego now?" Shai asked.

"You've always had an ego, Shai, it's just gotten bigger over the last few years. No shame in that, though. Every man in a position of power has been a bit of an egomaniac, including your father. The difference between the two of you is that Poppa was better at hiding it. That's a skill you haven't mastered yet, but in time you will. My question to you now is, what do you plan on doing with this blessing that has fallen into your lap?"

"First? Clean up the mess this fucking idiot has made. He's no good to me in prison, at least not now."

"Well your cleanup crew should've made it to the hotel by now, so that won't be a problem much longer," Sol said.

"I mean the entire mess," Shai corrected him.

Sol didn't have to ask what he meant to know what he was getting at, and the thought made him shiver. "Do you think that's necessary?"

Shai shrugged. "Maybe, maybe not. Why take unnecessary chances?" And with that, he turned his attention to the window letting Sol know it was no longer up for discussion.

When they arrived at the house, security waved the two cars through the gates without stopping them. The crowd seemed to have thinned out, but there were still a good amount of people wandering the yard. Shai spotted Honey off to the side talking to Brutus. He watched as his head of security touched his wife's arm and say something, causing her to blush. It was an innocent enough gesture, but something about it sounded an alarm in Shai's head. When they spotted the SUV, they put a respectable amount of distance between them. Brutus went off to attend to his duties while Honey came to meet the SUV. Shai was barely out of the ride before she started in.

"Where the hell were you?" Honey barked.
"Sorry, babe. I had to take care of something. I'll tell you about it later." Shai said coolly.

"Nigga, you leave in the middle of my baby shower... our baby shower, and I'll tell you about it later is the best you can come up with?" Honey shot back. She was talking so loud that people were starting to look.

Shai shot her a look that told her to leave it alone, but Honey was on a roll.

"You can't silence me with a look like I'm one of your flunkies, oh great king of the hill. I need an explanation!" Honey insisted.

"I'm afraid that it was my fault," Sol cut in. "My car broke down and Shai had to come out and get me," he lied.

Honey looked from Sol, to his car in the driveway. "You know what? Both of y'all are full of shit!" She stormed off.

"I swear sometimes that broad acts like she's my mother," Shai grumbled.

Big Doc patted him on the back good-naturedly. "Still time to run before she forces your ass down the aisle."

"Fuck you," Shai said as he swatted Big Doc away playfully. Just then, one of the black-clad security guards walked up. He was a young light-skinned dude, with nervous brown eyes and a slight overbite. His name was Tre, if Shai recalled correctly. He served as Brutus' second in command.

"Sorry to bother you, Mr. Clark..." Tre began, but Shai cut him off.

"Shai is fine," he corrected him.

"Right. Shai. Sorry to intrude, but your brother Tommy asked me to bring you to him as soon as you got back," Tre said.

Shai sighed. "Tell him to give me a few minutes. I don't feel like climbing all those damn stairs up to the library right now."

"Tommy's actually not upstairs. He's by the pool house."

This surprised Shai because Tommy rarely left the library, let alone the house. "If he's feeling up to being out and about, why is he back there instead of up here on the main lawn with everyone else?"

"You want me to tell him you're busy?" Tre offered.

Shai looked across the lawn at Honey, who was chatting with Giselle and shooting him dirty looks.

Lingering not too far from them was Brutus, looking like the cat that had swallowed the canary. When he noticed Shai watching, he flashed a guilty smile. "Nah, I need to step away for a minute anyhow before I do something I might regret."

*

Shai had to walk nearly a half block to get to what they referred to as the pool area, but it was unlike any pool you'd see in any of the other suburban homes in the area. In an ode to their old house, Shai had recreated the emerald lagoon that his father had always been so proud of. There were palm trees, artificial grass and even rock slates that you could lay out and sun bathe on when the weather was nice. Lining the bottom of the pool were green tinted lights that when turned on, gave the effect of swimming in an emerald pool. It was truly a marvel to behold.

Tommy was sitting in his wheelchair, beneath the shade of one of the trees. To Shai's surprise, he wasn't alone. Perched on his lap was a young white girl. Her red-painted nails traced a line along his ear as she whispered softly into it. Swann was also with him, along with a few of the soldiers. In the center sat someone who had his back to Shai, so he couldn't see his face. He was jawing with the men and laughing as if they were all old friends.

"Who's that guy?" Sol asked, voicing what they were all wondering.

"I have no clue," Shai said as he walked up ahead with Sol and Big Doc trailing him. As Shai drew closer, he could hear the stranger in the middle of a story that seemed to be holding everyone's attention.

"So, I'm in this guy's bedroom," the man was saying. "The wife is tied up on the bed, while I'm giving the husband the beating of his life trying to get him to tell me where the shit is. I had been working this guy for about a half hour and he's still pretending he has no clue as to what I'm talking about. By now I'm figuring that this tough son-of-a-bitch is willing to die with his secret, so I aim to oblige him. So I go in my bag of tricks and pull Bertha out," he said as he stacked his fists as if he was tightening his grip on a baseball bat, "and I'm getting ready to send this tight-lipped piece of shit to the Great Beyond, when the wife throws herself at my feet and starts trying to scream something through the duct tape. I'm silently thanking God, thinking this bitch has come to her senses and is about to tell me where her old man's stash is so I can get the fuck outta there, but of course my life can't ever be that easy."

"So what happened?" one of the soldiers asked in anticipation.

"What happened was, I snatch the tape off her mouth and she informs me that I've wasted the last half hour of my life kicking the shit out of the wrong guy. As it turns out, the husband had a twin and she was having an affair with his twin brother, so he really didn't know what I was talking about," the stranger told them.

"Damn, that would've had me tight. You did all that for nothing?" Swann asked.

"I wouldn't say it was for nothing. I never got the stash, but I did get the snatch. I figured any bitch with a pussy good enough to turn brother against brother had to have a biblical vagina, and running up in a saint has always been on my bucket list!"

Everyone erupted with laughter, as if it was the funniest joke they'd ever heard. Shai looked into the eyes of the soldiers - his soldiers - and saw adoration of a total stranger. It unnerved him, and he made a mental note of every face in the comedian's audience. Having had enough of the show, Shai cleared his throat to announce his presence.

Swann was the first to notice him, and quickly stood at attention. The soldiers made to follow suit, but Shai motioned for them to remain seated. "Don't get up on my account, gentlemen. I thought the party was being held on the main lawn, but it looks like the real party is back here. My invitation must've gotten lost in the mail."

"We're just back here shooting the shit, little bro," Tommy told him.

"Obviously," Shai said as he looked around at the cups of liquor and discarded weed clips in the ashtray on the floor. "So, how was your spontaneous journey?" Tommy asked sarcastically.

"Apparently not as much fun as your little get-together," Shai shot back. "Nobody told me we were having guests that weren't on the list," he said as his eyes fell on the stranger.

As if feeling Shai's gaze on his back, the stranger stood and turned to face him for the first time. "Well look who's all grown up," he said, as he looked Shai up and down.

Shai found himself momentarily stunned when he took in the stranger's features; that angular face, brown skin. It was almost like looking in a mirror. "Do we know each other?" he said as he finally found his voice.

The stranger laughed. "Damn, I know I put on a few pounds since the last time we saw each other, but I haven't changed that much, have I?"

Shai looked to Tommy for an explanation, but all he got from his brother was an amused smirk. "Listen, homie," he began in an irritated tone, "I ain't never been big on guessing games. Identify yourself or get the fuck off my property."

"Harley Livingston," Big Doc spoke up from behind Shai. From the tone of his voice, he clearly wasn't happy to see the visitor.

"What's up, Doc? Been a long time."

"Not long enough," Big Doc spat.

Harley smiled. "I see you still got that sour ass disposition. I don't blame you though, Doc, I blame your upbringing."

Big Doc took a threatening step forward, but Sol blocked his path. "A time and a place for everything, my friend," he said as he patted Big Doc's broad chest.

Big Doc cast one last lethal glare before backing down. "Shai, if you need me I'll be at the bar getting a drink... or three." He turned and stormed off.

Shai looked from Big Doc's departing back to the man called Harley. "Is there something I missed?"

When Tommy decided that his brother had toiled in confusion long enough, he filled in the blanks. "Shai, this here is our cousin Harley. You probably remember him as Hammer."

At the mention of his nickname, the pieces finally fell into place for Shai. He hadn't seen Hammer since he was a kid, but stories of his exploits had been told in his house for years. Harley had gotten the name Hammer because he had a fondness of bashing men's skulls in with a sledgehammer. He and Poppa were first cousins, having come to America from Trinidad together in the early eighties. The two of them had made their names doing freelance hits for the mob all through South Florida. When things got too hot, Poppa came to New York and got into the heroin business, but Hammer stayed in Florida. In the first few years he would come up and visit frequently, but after a while he began to visit less and less, until the visits stopped altogether and Hammer fell off the grid. Most had assumed him dead, but the fact that he was standing there said that he wasn't.

"How you been, little cousin?" Hammer asked as he embraced Shai, snapping him out of his thoughts.

"Good," Shai said awkwardly. He still wasn't sure what to make of his cousin's sudden appearance after so many years.

"Man," Hammer said as he held Shai at arm's length and gave him the once-over, "I haven't seen you since you were about eight-years-old. You ain't a kid no more. You the man now!" he exclaimed as he slapped Shai on the back.

"Something like that," Shai said, straightening his suit. "Say, can you guys give us a minute? Me and Tommy got a little catching up to do with our estranged cousin," he told Swann.

"No problem. It was an honor to meet you, Hammer." Swann shook the older man's hand enthusiastically.

"Likewise, kid. Maybe I'll see you around," Hammer told him.

"I sure hope so," Swann said. "Let's go, fellas!" He gathered the soldiers and led them towards the exit. He noticed that the white girl hadn't moved from Tommy's lap. "Sweetie, are you hard of hearing?"

Natalia looked to Tommy for approval.

"It's okay, snowflake," Tommy said as he patted her on the ass playfully. "I'll hit you up later on tonight, but in the meantime, I need you to look into that situation we discussed. You're my eyes and ears on this, ya dig?"

"You got it, Tommy Gunz." Natalia kissed him on the cheek. She sashayed passed the men, giving Swann a challenging look.

"Bitch, get yo white ass on," Swann quipped as he gave her a shove.

"I ain't gonna be too many bitches," Natalia hissed.

"You'll be kicked the fuck out in a minute if you don't get a move on," Swann warned. "Tommy throwing your young ass a little play and you acting like you the queen of Sheba or some shit." The two of them continued to exchange words on their way back to the main lawn.

"You need me to stick around, Shai?" Sol asked

"I got it," Shai said without turning around.

Sol nodded, and gave Hammer one last distrustful look before going to catch up with Swann and the others.

"I see my cousin Thomas done real well for himself,

and set you boys up pretty nice," Hammer said as he looked over the property. "This is a far cry from the condo we shared in Liberty City."

"This is my house. We sold Daddy's mansion a few years back," Shai told him.

"Right, I forgot you're in the big chair now. No offense, but I always thought it would've been Tommy to succeed my cousin when he passed.

"Sometimes things happen that are beyond our control," Tommy said.

"Man, I was sure sorry to hear what happened to Poppa. Please accept my condolences," Hammer said sincerely.

"So sorry that you missed his funeral?" Shai shot back.

Hammer shrugged. "It's like your big brother said, 'Sometimes things happen that are beyond our control.' For as much as I would've liked to make it back here to see my cousin off, the good folks of Combinado del Este had other plans."

Unfamiliar with the name, Shai looked to Tommy.

"It's a prison in Cuba," Tommy explained.

"Got into a little spat with one of the locals in a bar down there over a piece of trim that didn't belong to either of us. He ended up dead and I ended up getting fifteen years in that shithole, but I was able to liberate myself in a little over seven. They planned on leaving me in there to rot, but there ain't been a cage built yet that can hold the Hammer."

"So you're a fugitive?" Shai asked.

"All depends on how you look at it. I like to think of myself as a man who prefers to find his own way, rather than have my steps dictated by others."

"And what brings you this way?" Shai was suspicious and didn't bother to hide it.

"I got a little business to handle in New York. That and the fact that I never got to come and pay my respects after Thomas died, so I figured I could kill two birds with one stone. From what I gathered since I been here, it seems I've come right on time. Tommy told me about that little piece of trouble y'all been having with people trying to poach on my cousin's legacy."

"Is that right?" Shai shot Tommy a dirty look. "And what else you and my brother been back here gossiping about?"

"C'mon, Shai. Don't take it like that. Tommy was just bringing me up to speed on what I missed while I was rotting away in a Third World prison. I know I'm a little on the old side now, but I'm still a soldier at heart and in times of war, you'll need all the soldiers you can get."

"For one we ain't at war, and for two, we've got more than enough soldiers. Though I do thank you for the offer," Shai said in a less-than-sincere tone.

"Okay, I get it. You're just as suspicious of new people as your old man was," Hammer said. "Well, let me lay my cards on the table so that we all understand each other. I didn't come here today looking for no handouts, so let's get that straight off the muscle. I ain't doing so good financially these days, but I ain't never been no beggar. I'm definitely trying to eat, but I ain't looking for you to feed me. I'm old school and believing in earning my way, and all I'm asking for is a chance to prove it."

Shai measured Hammer's words. They seemed sincere enough, but it wouldn't have been the first time someone who called themselves family came wearing a grin, but holding a knife behind his back. "Look," he began in an easy tone, "I'm dealing with a lot today, so maybe we got off on the wrong foot."

"I can dig it, Shai. You probably got a million niggas coming at you on the daily with their hands out. I remember how it was when I was running things down in Miami. Being a boss comes with a lot of stress. I'm sure I didn't help matters much by just popping up like this, especially when y'all are having a private get-together. Let me get out of your way and we'll talk another time if you want. I'm glad I got a chance to see you though," Hammer said as he gave Shai a hug, then Tommy.

"You sure you don't wanna chill? You're more family than half the muthafuckas out there eating and drinking up our shit," Tommy offered.

Hammer looked to Shai, who didn't seem to be feeling the idea. "Nah man, I'm gonna cut out. I got some shit I need to take care of on the streets anyway. I'll get with you later." He turned to leave.

"Yo Hammer, where are you staying in case I need to reach you so we can finish our talk?" Shai called after him.

"I'll be around," Hammer said over his shoulder on his way out.

Tommy waited until Hammer was out of sight before ripping into Shai. "What the fuck is wrong with you, Slim? That man is not only a street legend, but he's family and you treated him like some bird nigga looking for an opportunity to suck your dick!"

Shai spun on him, eyes blazing. "First of all, lower your fucking voice. If I wanted this to be a public conversation, I wouldn't have told Swann and them to leave. Tommy, you out here praising this dude like you ready to give him the keys to the palace and you only known him a few minutes!"

"Shai, you bugging. We knew Hammer all our lives, you were just too young to really remember him," Tommy waved him off.

"Exactly, I was too young to remember him and Poppa never went out of his way to make sure I did either, so that tells me something about our friend the Hammer. Think about it, T. We knew all the war stories, but whenever we'd try to ask about Poppa's relationship with Hammer outside of hustling, he never gave us a straight answer. For as much as our father loved to praise fallen legends, how come he never heaped no great amount of praise on Hammer?"

"Slim, I hear what you're saying, but try and see it my way. Hammer isn't some random dude; he was Poppa's old running buddy. Dudes from that era that are still around and able-bodied enough to put in work are like unicorns, bro. Think about the advantages to having someone like the Hammer with us?"

"Or the damage he could do," Shai countered. "Black, you know how much I depend on your counsel. You've been my guardian angel since before I inherited the throne. You love me, and I know you'd never intentionally steer me wrong, but this isn't about me. Every decision I make has to be with the good of the family in mind. We don't know that the guy who walked in here today is the same man Poppa trusted to have his back two decades ago. Time changes all things, especially the hearts of men."

Tommy let out a sigh, knowing his brother had a valid point. "You're right, Slim. I'm sorry if it sounded like I was trying to undermine you with all this, it's just that there's a part of me that's still trying to wrap itself around the fact that Poppa isn't here. Hammer represents a part of our father's history and could help us get to know Poppa in ways we never could growing up. I guess that's why I wanted to keep him close."

Shai laid a reassuring hand on Tommy's shoulder.
"Black, you ain't the only one tugging a heavy heart
behind them. I think we all miss Poppa, and that's all the
more reason we do all we can to preserve his legacy.
The best way to accomplish this is leading with our heads
and not our hearts."

"So you think we should cut Hammer loose?" Tommy
asked.

"Not necessarily. For now we'll just keep him at a safe
distance until we're sure what his agenda is," Shai told
him.

"And who says he's got an agenda?"

Shai smirked. "If there's one thing that you taught me
growing up, it's that there's always an agenda."

"And here I thought you weren't listening," Tommy
said as he playfully punched Shai in the leg.

Their moment was broken up when Brutus came
jogging out to the lagoon. He was usually the picture of
calm, but there was a worried expression on his face. Shai's
first thoughts were that something happened with Honey
or the baby, and it filled his heart with dread. "What is it?"
he asked nervously.

"I'm sorry to bother you, Shai. We've got a problem at the front gate," Brutus told him.

"Don't I pay you niggas to handle that kind of shit?" Shai snapped. He hadn't meant to come across like that, but it was rare that he got to bond with his brother and Brutus was intruding on that.

"You know I wouldn't have come back here fucking with you unless I didn't have any other choice," Brutus told him. Then he hesitated. "Well, spit it out nigga!" Tommy ordered. "It's your sister."

*

Brutus led the way down the driveway, with Shai bringing up the rear, pushing Tommy. He was moving so fast that Tommy feared he would flip the chair over. Before they had even made it to the gate, they could hear the shouting. Some of the guests had wandered from the baby shower to partake the spectacle that was unfolding at the front gate.

They heard the shouting long before they made it to the foot of the driveway. When they rounded the bend, the first thing he noticed was a young man leaning against a motorcycle. He watched with an amused look on his face as Swann, along with two members of the security staff, tried to calm a young woman. She was tall and curvaceous, dressed in black leather pants, the matching motorcycle jacket and high-heeled boots. Her long back hair was mussed, and plastered to her face. Dangling from her hand was a pink and black striped helmet that she waved threateningly while addressing security. Swann had his hands raised submissively, trying his best to get the girl to calm down, but she was too far gone to hear anything he was saying. He made the mistake of touching her arm, and was rewarded by her bringing the helmet around and nearly missing his skull. Reflexively, Swann's fist balled, and had it not been for Shai, he couldn't say for sure what he would have done, family or not.

"What the fuck?" Shai's voice boomed.

"My fault, Shai. I tried to get her to chill, but as you can see she ain't really hearing me," Swann explained.

Shai patted his shoulder. "It ain't your fault, my nigga. I saw it all. Disperse this crowd, I got it from here," he instructed as he continued towards the girl. Her legs were shaky and her eyes were bloodshot. "Hope?"

"There's my big brother!" the youngest Clark child said,

way louder than she needed to. "I told you niggas that I was connected!" Her drunken eyes passed over the security staff mockingly.

"Hope, what the fuck are you doing here? You're supposed to be away at school," Shai asked, trying to make heads or tails of what he was seeing. Hope was the baby girl of their family and the straight arrow of the three children. She had managed to keep her nose clean through all of their ups and downs, and seemed the most likely to avoid their family curse. After high school, she had gone off to attend Howard University, and she rarely came home unless it was a holiday or special occasion. She put distance between herself and the family, and Shai couldn't blame her, considering how they lived. She was grown now and Shai had no illusions as to her being an angel, but he didn't know the drunk ass broad standing before him.

"I needed a little break so I figured I'd come see my family, but your little toy-cops trying to act like I can't get into my own house," she slurred. "You got all these leaches in here sucking on the blood of my family, and your little toy-cops trying to tell me that me and mine ain't welcome!"

Shai looked to Brutus for an explanation.

"They showed up drunk, and tried to ride the bike up the driveway. I asked homie to park it and walk up, so as to avoid a potential accident and that's when baby sis wigged out," Brutus explained.

"Fuck is you to call me baby sis, like we got history?" Hope said drunkenly, waggling her finger in Brutus' face. "Nigga, you ain't really family. You just another nigga eating off our plate, waiting for a chance to try and snatch the whole meal. Just because I don't come around as much don't mean I'm blind to what's going on. You think I don't see the way you look at my brother when his back is turned? The way you look at his woman? You just like the rest of these muthafuckas, waiting to lay claim to something that don't belong to you."

Brutus' face darkened. "Shai, if you don't need me anymore, I'm going to go and make the rounds."

"Yeah, handle your business. And I'm sorry about all this," Shai said apologetically.

Brutus nodded and continued on his way. "You better watch that nigga, Shai," Hope fake-whispered. "He got larceny in his heart."

"And you got alcohol in your blood. How the fuck you

gonna show up at Honey's baby shower drunk like this?" Shai snapped.

"Chill out, Slim. I ain't drunk. I'm just a little tipsy," Hope declared, before throwing up in the driveway. "Damn, maybe I'm a little more faded than I thought," she laughed, before pitching forward into Shai's arms.

"Jesus on a damn cross," Shai sighed, looking down at his drunken sister. "Yo, y'all get her up to the house," he directed the two members of his security team who had been standing by watching. When they took his sister off his hands, he turned his attention to the smirking young man on the motorcycle. "Who the fuck are you?"

"Oh!" The young man straightened his posture and extended his hand. "My name is Snake. Me and Hope been dating the last few months."

Shai looked at his hand, but didn't shake it. "You bring her here in that condition?"

"On my kids, she was already on one when I picked her up," Snake lied. He and Hope had been getting thrashed together, but her tolerance for liquor happened to be lower than his.

"Fucking idiot," Shai mumbled, before heading back

towards the house.

"Mr. Clark," Snake turned to Tommy. "I know this might be a bad time, but in case I never get this opportunity again, let me just say how much respect I have for you and your family. You were like a God to me growing up. I was as excited as a kid on Christmas when Hope said I'd finally get to meet you today." Tommy glanced up at him. "What did you say your name was again?"

"Snake," he repeated.

"Well, Snake, how about you get on your fucking crotch-rocket and wheel your ass outta here before I have my boys stick you somewhere cold and dark," Tommy said coldly.

"But I was just trying to pay my respect, you know? Give you your props," Snake explained, not understanding what he could have said to offend him.

"And so you have. Now get the fuck from around here!" Tommy spat, before turning in his chair and wheeling himself back up the driveway.

"Could this day get any worse?" Shai was grumbling when Tommy finally caught up to him.

"Give it time. It's still early," Tommy laughed and kept

wheeling up the path. Had he bothered to turn around, he'd have noticed the murderous look Snake was giving him.

CHAPTER 13

Duffy breathed a sigh of relief when he walked into his one-bedroom apartment, which was located on the Upper East Side and boasted a view of the FDR drive. It was small, but nice. He kicked his shoes off and massaged his sore feet. He was glad when Tommy cut him loose for the night. It wasn't that he didn't enjoy the luxuries of the Clarks' fancy parties, but only in small doses. Galas weren't really his thing; he was a street nigga and always more comfortable in his element.

He had quite a bit to do, but first he had to get mentally and physically prepared. He twisted up a blunt of sticky from his stash, and fired it up while changing into something more fitting of the task at hand: black jeans, a hoodie and Timberlands. Strapping his glock to his hip, Duffy hit the door and went out into the concrete jungle.

Duffy pushed his E-Class Mercedes through Harlem at slightly above a cruise. The engine was so quiet that if the car hadn't been moving, he wouldn't have even known it was running. It was a hell of an upgrade over the Toyota Celica he had been pushing a year prior, and a leap from his days riding the trains and buses to get where he needed to go. Tommy Clark had not only upgraded his means of transportation, but his life.

He had first met the eldest Clark male on Riker's Island. Duffy had been there fighting a gun possession charge. He had gotten into a shootout with a rival crew and took two bullets before they arrested him. His wounds were what landed him in the infirmary where Tommy was being kept. At first, he had no clue who Tommy was, but from the respect he was shown by staff and inmates alike, Duffy knew he was someone important on the streets. Back then, Tommy was still getting used to dealing with his condition, so he wasn't the friendliest cat. He kept to himself and rarely talked unless it was to bark on one of the guards or the doctors. The other inmates waited on him hand and foot, with hopes of Tommy putting them on, but Duffy kept his distance. For as much as he wanted to cut into Tommy like the rest of them, he knew following the trend would get him nowhere. For nights on end, he toiled over ways to put himself on Tommy's radar, but there was nothing you could offer to a man who had everything. He needed to find a way for Tommy to notice him, and he found it with a book.

Duffy was street smart, but had never been academically sound. He couldn't read very well, so sometimes he had to read aloud to himself to make sure the words were right. It drove the other inmates crazy, but none of them had the nuts to come over and shut him up. One day he had been reading a copy of a book called *Gangsta* that he had gotten from the prison library. He had just dog-eared his page and closed his book for the night, when Tommy spoke to him for the first time.

"Keep going," Tommy said from his bed.

At first Duffy wasn't sure who he was talking to, but when he looked over, Tommy was staring at him. "The book, keep going. I wanna know if the nigga is gonna make it out of New York."

Duffy wasn't sure what else to do, so he opened the book back up and kept reading. It was almost day-

Hoodlum II: The Good Son

break before they got to Lou-Loc's tragic end, and for a while after he was done, Duffy and Tommy discussed the book. This became their thing, and every night, Duffy would read while Tommy got lost in the stories. This is how their friendship developed. Duffy had once asked Tommy why he made him read to him every night instead of listening to some of the audio books that the library carried, and Tommy simply replied, "Because the narrator's voices don't take me back to where I come from."

Eventually, Duffy was sent back into general population to continue fighting his charge. A few months later, Tommy was going home to his family. He promised Duffy that he would reach out and try to do what he could for him once he was back on the streets, but that's what most prisoners say when they're going home and their friends were still left sitting. Duffy hadn't put much stock into the promise, until he had a random legal visit from a man he had never seen before who introduced himself as his new counsel. It took nearly a year of court dates and vanishing witnesses, but the charges against Duffy were eventually reduced and he was released with time served and ten years felony probation. Duffy didn't like the idea of spending the next decade at the end of a leash, but it beat serving time. On the day he walked out of the courtroom, Tommy was there to greet him. He had been a man of his word, and from that day forward, Duffy had been on the Clark payroll, but his loyalties were with Tommy.

When Duffy arrived at the address Tommy had given him, he had to look at it twice to make sure he hadn't read it wrong. It was an old building in Harlem that looked like it hadn't been lived in for some time. Most of the windows were boarded up, but he could see the faint glow of a light in one of them. Somebody was home.

Cautiously, he got out of the car and approached the building. There was a thin piece of plywood that served as the entrance, if you could even call it that. Upon closer inspection, he saw words spray painted just above the door: "Welcome to hell." It was a bad

omen, but Duffy would rather take his chances with whatever was lurking within the dark building than disappoint Tommy Clark. Against his better judgment, he stepped inside.

Hoodlum II: The Good Son

The first thing Duffy noticed when he crossed the threshold was the cold. It had nothing to do with the temperature outside; more like an unsettling chill in his bones. He ventured deeper into the building, crunching glass and debris under his Timberlands. He noticed that the floor was littered with more junk food and candy wrappers than anything. At the end of the hall, a staircase loomed. The dim light at the top of it flickered on and off as if daring Duffy to continue. He did.

Duffy crept up the rickety stairs. Seemingly coming from all around him, he heard the faint sounds of what thought were children giggling. He stopped to listen closer, but there was nothing. With his gun now in hand, dangling at his side, Duffy continued up to the next floor. When he reached the landing, he felt the chill again. This time it was different, as if someone had moved passed him. Duffy turned but didn't see anything except two rats in the corner, fighting over a discarded cupcake.

"You know where you at, blood?" a voice came from behind

Duffy spun and found himself pointing his gun at empty space. "Who the fuck is that?"

"We asking the questions," someone to his left said.

"You know who you're fucking with?" Duffy said as he swept his gun back and forth, trying to find a target.

"You must be hard of hearing." A beer can skirted down the hall and bounced off Duffy's feet, causing him to discharge his gun. The sound of the shoot echoed off the walls, making Duffy's ears ring.

"Muthafucka!" Duffy clutched his ear. At the end of the hall, he could see a youthful looking boy. He couldn't hear him, but from the way he was doubled over and pointing, Duffy could tell he was laughing at him. "You little shit! I'm gonna kick your ass!" He charged down the hall in the direction of the boy and got within arm's reach of him, before a foot came out of one of the abandoned apartments and tripped him. Duffy spilled onto his hands and knees, scraping one of his palms. Before he could right himself, something smashed into the back of his head and everything went black.

*

Duffy awoke with a splitting headache. He was no

Hoodlum II: The Good Son

longer in the hallway; instead he had been moved to one of the apartments. He was parked on a rotting wooden chair with a shaky leg, and his hands zip-tied behind his back. He wasn't sure how much time had passed, but running late to carry out Tommy's errand was the least of his concerns.

There were two burning trash cans positioned a few feet away from him, which explained the light he had seen from outside. Loitering around them were several children. Most of them were dusty and looked like they missed a few meals, but they all wore the same look in their eyes; one of hunger. It was something straight out of *Lord of the Flies*. Just beyond the children, he spotted the young boy who had been taunting him in the hallway. His body was half turned as he whispered to someone sitting on a tattered couch. Duffy couldn't see his face through the veil of shadow, but he could make out a pair of dirty red Converse planted on the ground. They must have felt him watching them because their conversation abruptly stopped, and the young one stepped forward.

In the light, Duffy could get a better look at him. He was young, and dark skinned; maybe about thirteen-years-old, with the eyes of a man twice his age. He moved through the children and planted himself directly in front of Duffy. "You should've heeded the sign outside, blood."

"This is Hell and everything that passes through Hell that ain't of Hell is food," the next boy spoke up. He was slightly older and stockier.

"You're making a mistake, kid," Duffy struggled against his bonds. "I'm with Tommy Clark!"

"Broken Gods have no voice in The Below," a voice called from the couch. "All that pass through those gates are either dogs from out of this pound or food. Since I don't see no fangs in your mouth, you must be food."

"Food! Food! Food!" the children all chanted in unison.

"Ashanti," the voice continued, "feed this trespasser to the pups and let the rats have what's left of him." He stood and began walking deeper into the shadows.

"You got that, big homie," the little one who he called "Ashanti" said as he drew a butterfly knife from his dirty jeans and flipped it back and forth expertly. "Nothing personal, fam," he said as he moved in for the kill.

"No!" Duffy screamed and began thrashing wildly.

Hoodlum II: The Good Son

There was no way he was going to meet his end in a vacant building at the hands of a juvenile delinquent. He threw his weight to one side and managed to tip the rickety chair over. His plan had been to try and break the rotted chair and try to get free, but his shoulder took the brunt of it and the chair held.

"Stop fighting and I'll try and make sure you go quick," Ashanti said as he knelt beside him and pressed the knife against his throat.

"Animal!" Duffy blurted out. The room went quiet, and the one who had been sitting on the couch stopped short. The children parted like the Red Sea as another youth made his way through them. From the angle Duffy had landed, he couldn't turn to see his face, but he had a clear view of the red Converse blazing a trail across the floor in his direction.

"If you've come looking for the Bastard Son of Harlem, you're either a fool or an enemy. Answer truthfully or die ugly," he told Duffy. It wasn't a threat; more like a fact.

Duffy knew he had to choose his next few words wisely, for they may have been his last. "Look man, all I know is that Tommy Clark sent me to find someone called The Animal." After a few seconds, he and the chair were pulled upright. For the first time, he could see the face of the one he assumed to be the leader of the bunch. He was dark-skinned with almost feminine lips, and a mess of wild black curls crowning his head.

The wild-haired young man studied Duffy for what felt like an eternity under his lifeless eyes. When he finally opened his mouth to speak, Duffy could make out the gold grills in his mouth that spelled out his name. "Then look no further."

PART III
"MURDER BY THE POUND"

Hoodlum II: The Good Son

CHAPTER 14

When Hope woke up the following morning, she was a mess. She had spent half the night throwing up, and the other half trying to keep her head from spinning. Not only did every single muscle in her body ache, but even the hairs on her arms and legs were sore. If she never saw another drink in her life, it would be too soon.

After laying in the bed and looking at the ceiling for about a half hour, Hope was finally able to move. She dragged herself into the bathroom, where she threw up twice more before finally feeling a little better. She didn't trust her shaky legs enough to get in the shower just yet, so she settled for washing her face and brushing her teeth. She attempted to put her hair in a ponytail, but decided against it when fire shot through her scalp. It had truly been one of the longest nights of her life.

When she came downstairs and entered the kitchen, all eyes turned to her. Shai, Honey, Tommy and Star were already seated and having breakfast. She could have only imagined how she looked, hair everywhere, still dressed in her motorcycle pants beneath her bathrobe.

"Auntie Hope!" Star jumped up from the table. She rushed across the kitchen and leapt into Hope's arms, probably never knowing how close Hope had come to dropping her on the floor. "I didn't know you were here! How come I didn't see you at the party?"

"Auntie was tired when she got in and went straight to bed," Honey answered for her. "Come back and finish your breakfast." Reluctantly, the little girl did as she was told.

"Good morning all," Hope greeted her family, as she pulled out a chair at the table. She grabbed a plate and began piling bacon from the platter onto it, but the minute she bit into the greasy pork, she felt her stomach lurch.

"For some of us, at least," Tommy teased her.

"Glad you didn't die in your sleep from alcohol poisoning. At one point, we weren't so sure which way the coin was going to flip," Shai said coldly.

"Shai!" Honey was embarrassed by his cruel remark.

"Shai my ass," he shot back. "This chick shows up pissy drunk to our baby shower, embarrasses us in front of our guests and I'm supposed to sit here and smile like it didn't happen?"

Hoodlum II: The Good Son

Honey could see that Shai wasn't going to let it go. "Star, baby," she turned to her daughter, "why don't you take your breakfast into the living room so you can watch TV while you finish?"

Star looked from her mother to Shai, who was glaring daggers at Hope. "If they're letting me eat in the living room, that means somebody is about to get it!" She took her plate and hustled off through the double doors.

"Shai, I'm sorry that happened," Hope said apologetically.

"Not as sorry as I am," he said. "That was some straight bullshit you pulled, and I expect better of you, baby sis. At this stage of the game, I shouldn't have to still be telling you how important appearances are when it comes to this family. You're not a little girl anymore."

"Then why don't you stop treating me like one?" Hope shot back. "Yeah, I know I fucked up by coming in here sloshed like that, but I'm a college kid and that's what we do; drink in excess. You act like you ain't never came in here blasted after a night of hanging with Swann and them while you were on break."

"Those cases were few and far between. Besides, it's a

different kind of situation."

Hope shot him a look. "How do you figure that?"

"For one, I'm a guy. For two, I've always been the rebel. That kind of shit was expected of me from time to time. You? You're the good girl, Daddy's princess. How do you think that makes you look?"

"Like a young woman who is finally learning to live a little!" Hope shot back. "Shai, between you, Daddy and Tommy, I've always been kept on a short leash. I never missed a day of school, never slutted myself out with boys, and kept my distance from family business. And we ALL know that is no easy feat," she said as she looked back and forth between Shai and Tommy. "I do everything right and the one time I decide to blow off a little steam, you gonna sit here and try and judge me?"

Shai rubbed his temples in frustration. "Hope, nobody is trying to judge you. It's just that you got everything laid out for you to be somebody great in this world, and I just don't want to see you get sidetracked."

"You mean like you did?" Hope asked in an accusatory tone.

"Why don't the both of you tuck your fangs and quit

Hoodlum II: The Good Son

this damn arguing," Tommy cut in. "What's done is done, and unless one of you geniuses have secretly invented a time machine, I don't see much we can do to change it. Hope fucked up, and she knows it, Slim. Ain't no sense in beating a dead horse."

"There you go defending her again, Tommy," Shai fumed.

"I ain't defending nobody, Shai. I'm just trying to enjoy my damn omelets in peace!" Tommy cut a piece of egg away with his fork and scarfed it down. "You're right in everything you're saying, but I think in focusing on her being drunk, you're missing the most important question," He turned to Hope. "What the hell are you doing in New York in the middle of a school year?"

"I just needed a break," Hope told him. "I'm acing all my classes and finals aren't for another three weeks. I needed some personal time, so I took it."

"So, I'm sure if I did some investigating your story will hold up?" Tommy challenged.

Hope shrugged as if it was nothing, but her eyes looked nervous. "Do what you gotta do, big brother."

"Indeed, I will," Tommy assured her. "For your sake, I

195

hope you're keeping it real, because if I find out you're lying, this tongue lashing Shai put on you ain't gonna be shit compared to how I'm gonna react and that's on Daddy."

Hope seemed to shrink in her seat. She was nineteen, technically grown, and not living at home anymore, but Tommy could still make her regress to the little girl who would threaten boys with the prospect of her crazy older brother beating them up. Wheelchair bound or not, Hope wanted no parts of Tommy's

wrath. Everyone under that roof feared Tommy to some degree, whether they chose to admit it or not.

The doorbell rang, and to Hope's relief, took some of the heat off her. The Clarks were dysfunctional, but only amongst each other. She was relatively certain they wouldn't clown in front of an outsider. A few seconds later, her temporary reprieve expired when Brutus' man Tre escorted Swann into the kitchen.

"Damn, nigga. Why you all on my back like I don't know where I'm going already? You see me every day," Swann was barking on Tre when he walked in.

"Brutus said everyone except the people who live her

need to be escorted..." Tre was explaining, but Swann cut him off.

"Everyone except me, lil' nigga!" Swann snapped. "Let's get something straight once and for all; I been guarding the Clarks' backs since you were in grade school. Stay in your lane, or you might find yourself in a head-on collision," he said as he jabbed his finger in Tre's chest.

Tre's jaw tightened as his eyes went from the finger to Swann's eyes. He knew the man was dangerous with a gun, but with the hands Tre reasoned he could take him. He weighed his options, then looked to Shai. His eyes said, "What would happen if Tre tried it?" so he took a step back. "You got it, big man," he said as he raised his hands submissively.

"Muthafuckin' right I do." Swann popped the collar of his shirt and sneered triumphantly at Tre.

"Mr. Clark, I'll be out front if you need me," Tre said.

"Thanks Tre," Shai dismissed him. He waited until the young man was gone before addressing Swann. "Why are you always fucking with that kid?"

"Because I don't like him," Swann said honestly.

"Him or his boss. Something ain't right with them, I just can't put my finger on it." His eyes drifted to Honey when he said it. "But fuck them clowns. Looks like I arrived right on time for breakfast!" he exclaimed as he parked himself in the chair next to Hope and grabbed a piece of bacon off her plate.

"You're disgusting. You didn't even wash your hands when you came in here," Hope quipped as she pushed the plate away from her. She doubted she'd be able to finish her food anyhow, but Swann sticking his hand in her plate made her want it even less.

"Shut yo' drunk ass up. You probably need an aspirin more than you need this bacon anyway," Swann teased her.

"I've had two lectures already this morning and I don't need another one." Hope sucked her teeth.

"You're lucky a lecture is all I'm giving you after the shit you pulled. You almost cracked my skull with that helmet," Swann reminded her.

Hope was so twisted she could only remember bits and pieces of the day before. "I'm sorry," she said in an embarrassed tone.

Hoodlum II: The Good Son

"We good, lil' sis. Just don't pull it again or me and you gonna have to box," Swann warned. "So, who was that joker you rolled up with? What's his name again? Fake or some shit like that, right?"

"Snake," she corrected him, "and he's a friend from school."

"That douche-bag is a student?" Shai asked in surprise.

"Yes, what did you think he was?"

"A fucking dick rider," Tommy cut in. "You should've heard that nigga! 'Mr. Clark, you're my idol!'" he mocked Hope's friend. "He was trying to get too friendly too fast and I don't trust cats like that."

"Please," Hope waved him off. "Snake is harmless."

"Yeah, aight," Tommy said disbelievingly. "Still don't change the fact that I don't know him or like him, so you might wanna keep that in mind the next time you try and bring an outsider in this house."

"Yes, sir." Hope said sarcastically. "Well, my head is spinning so I think I'm gonna go back to bed," she said as she excused herself from the table.

"That Hope has sure grown into a piece of work,

hasn't she?" Swann said as he watched her walk away.

"Indeed she has, but she's still our baby sister," Tommy said in an icy tone.

Swann caught the accusatory undertone. "C'mon, Tommy. You know I didn't mean it like that."

"I know you didn't, Swann. I'm just saying, feel me?"

Swann nodded.

"So, what brings you here at this hour? Your ass usually doesn't get out of bed before noon," Honey quizzed him.

"You know the early bird catches the worm, sis. I actually have something I need to talk to Shai about," Swann said seriously.

Honey caught on right away. "Well, let me give you boys the room1" She got up from the table and walked around and kissed Shai on the cheek. "If you need me, I'll be upstairs."

Swann remained silent until Honey was gone. "Dig it, Shai. I spoke to Angelo and he..."

Shai raised his finger to silence Swann. "Never in the house. You know better than that. Let's go out on the deck and talk," he said as he got up and walked out of the kitchen doors that led to the wooden deck that overlooked the backyard. Swann followed, pushing Tommy.

"Shai, your ass is paranoid as shit," Swann said when they were outside. "All this money you spend on counter-surveillance and you're still worried about the FEDS bugging your crib?"

"It ain't the bugs with wires I'm worried about. It's the ones with bills to pay or troubles to shake," Shai said as he cast a glance through the glass doors at the maid who was clearing the table. "Now what's Angelo talking about?"

"The boys came through and cleaned up that mess at the hotel. Everything went off without a hitch," Swann told him.

"And the desk clerk?"

"Big Doc let her live, as you ordered. He gave her ten grand and assured her that we knew where her mom and kid rested their heads, but I think it was a bad idea not to kill her too," Tech said.

"For what, trying to make an honest buck?" Shai questioned. "No harm is to come to that woman."

Tech looked at Tommy, who shook his head in

disappointment. "Whatever, man. As far as the driver, we got a line on him. Angelo has a few of the boys sitting on his house. I told them just to watch for now and not do anything until we see how you want to play it."

Shai looked to his older brother, who he had filled in on the situation with the deputy mayor the night before. "What do you think, big bro?"

Tommy mulled it over for a few ticks. "It's possible that he keeps his mouth shut as to not get himself crossed up in this shit, but I say why take chances. If it were me, I'd make sure anything that happens going forward can't be traced back to this family. The kid who sold Bill the drugs needs to go too."

"That's a lot of collateral damage," Swann said.

"You get a bump up in rank and you squeamish about blood now? That ain't the Swann I raised." Tommy glared at him.

"Nigga, you know I'm still about my business, rank or not," Swann assured him.

"Then why are you here looking for my brother's blessings to do something that you already know needs to be done?" Tommy questioned. "As an underboss, it's

Hoodlum II: The Good Son

your job to anticipate what Shai needs before he knows he needs them. I ain't getting on you, just schooling you, little bro. Feel me?"

"No doubt, and you're right," Swann agreed. "It's just that with something as sensitive as this, I just thought all orders should come down from the top."

Tommy shrugged. "Tell yourself whatever you need to help you sleep at night. I'm gonna leave you girls to it. I've got some reading to catch up on," he said, and wheeled himself back into the house.

"Your brother can be a real dickhead sometimes," Swann said when he was sure Tommy was out of earshot.

"If I recall correctly, you were the one defending him yesterday," Shai reminded him. "Tommy is a sour-puss, but he isn't wrong. We need to wipe this slate totally clean."

"I'll make sure it gets handled," Swann assured him. "So, what's on your agenda for today?"

Shai shrugged. "Probably sit around here and relax. I think there's an afternoon game on today."

Swann shook his head. "Man, it seems like all you do lately is sit around the house. When is the last time you hit the streets?"

"I thought the idea was to keep me insulated from the bullshit?"

"I don't mean like that, Shai. I mean when is the last time the king has left the castle to mingle with his subjects? I know you miss it; the sights, the sounds, the bitches throwing themselves at you."

Shai smiled. "I can't front, I do sometimes, but it's too risky."

"What is reward without risks? I know you love sitting in this big ass house, watching T.V., baking cookies with Honey, or whatever the fuck you do these days but sometimes it's good for morale to let the soldiers see your face."

"So, what do you suggest?"

Now it was Swann's turn to smile. "I thought you'd never ask."

CHAPTER 15

Two hours later, Shai was pushing across the George Washington Bridge, reunited with an old friend; his gold Lexus GS300. He hadn't driven it in years, and almost felt funny behind the wheel. Shai had at least a half dozen cars in addition to the throwback, which was nearly twenty years old by that point, but that car had always been special to him. It reminded him of happier times.

"Yo, do you remember this?" Swann pointed to a small burn hole in the passenger seat where he was sitting.

"How could I not?" Shai laughed. It had been three days since Poppa Clark presented Shai with the car. He and Swann were coming back from a night of partying, and Swann had gotten so drunk that he fell sleep with the blunt in his hand and burned the seat. "Poppa threw me a good beating for your bullshit."

"And grounded you for a week," Swann added.

"The bullshit about it was that it wasn't even my fault because I was dead sober. I was always getting in trouble for your bullshit."

"Nigga, don't act like I haven't taken my fair share of lumps for you," Swann shot back. "I corroborated plenty of your lies, which is probably why Honey hates me now. I'm surprised she even let you come out with me today."

"My woman don't let me do shit. I'm a grown ass man. But she wasn't exactly happy about it," Shai snickered. "She beefed a little, but she'll get over it. I left her some shopping money before we broke out."

"The quickest way to a woman's heart is through her pocketbook," Swann joked. "But seriously though, when you first met shorty, did you ever think you'd be damn near married to her and be expecting a kid?"

"Hell no," Shai said honestly. "Honey was a wild girl, not really my speed, but the heart wants what the heart wants."

"Indeed, it does," Swann agreed. "I was skeptical at first, but I gotta admit that she has stood tall with you

through some very trying times. She's earned my respect."

"Why do you think I wife'd her up?"

"Speaking of which; did you two kids set a wedding

date yet?"

Shai cut his eyes at him. "Where did that come from?"

"Giselle," Swann told him. "After we got home from the baby shower, she started talking that marriage

shit again, so I know her and Honey been conspiring.

The only time she ever gets to rocking the boat is after talking to yo chick," he said as he pointed at him for emphasis.

"Yeah, she did come at me on some set a date shit yesterday," Shai confessed. "Lately she really been on this marriage trip. Haven't I already given her the life and the loyalty?"

"Yeah, but it's the title that's the real prize. Any bitch can be a baby mama, wifey or even a fiancé, but it takes a certain class of woman for you to stand up and put it on God!"

"Thanks for putting even more pressure on me," Shai said in a worrisome voice.

"My fault, Slim," Swann patted him on the back. "Look, if you ain't ready to marry Honey, then come out and tell her as much."

"It ain't like that. Honey been in my corner for years. It's only right that I make it official, but I wanna do it when I feel like the time is right, not because it's what she's pushing for. That's like you and Giselle been together probably three times as long as we have, but y'all ain't tied the knot yet. You gonna do it in your own time, right?"

Swann got quiet.

"You do plan on marrying Giselle, don't you?" Shai asked.

Swann looked at his best friend seriously. "Shai, I'm about to give you some real talk. I love Giselle. I let her into my heart and that's a privilege another bitch will never have, but I ain't looking to give nobody but Mara my last name right now. We getting big money out here, Shai, and things are going great, but I ain't nowhere near where I need to be to get comfortable enough to ease up on this money. I pray that one day I get to stop and smell the roses with my lady and my kid like you and Honey, but right now I'm out here chasing this power and everything that comes with it. To be honest with you, I'll probably end up a beautiful young corpse before a

Hoodlum II: The Good Son

devoted husband."

Swann just laid some heavy shit on Shai. The two of them had been down for so long that Shai had always looked at them as equals, but in truth, they weren't. Swann had money and power, but he wasn't a boss, because he still answered to Shai. This gave him food for thought and his next order of business would be figuring out a way to give Swann more independence, maybe even allowing him to start his own family.

"So, what's the deal with Tommy and that white bitch?" Swann changed the subject.

"Beats the hell out of me. She looks familiar, but I don't know for sure if I ever seen her before. She's one of Ms. Ruby's girls," Shai told him.

"Then she's either selling pussy or was casing your joint. You know Ruby and all them little hood boogers she takes in are scandalous as hell," Swann half joked. "Not on no funny shit, but I didn't think Tommy still had much use for women, considering his condition. You think he can still get it up?"

Shai gave him a look.

"Hey, I'm just asking."

"Well ask him yourself the next time you see him," Shai challenged.

"No thanks. Whether he's got legs or not, Tommy is still a dangerous muthafucka and not to be played with."

The two of them continued to chop it up about this and that, as they coasted through Harlem. It had been quite some time since Shai had revisited his old stomping grounds. He came into Manhattan frequently, but it was always on business and with an entourage. It had been ages since he and Swann had mobbed out two-deep, bending corners and taking in sights. It was a nice day, so Harlem was busy with activity. It seemed like every block they turned on, they knew somebody. Shai felt like the president as people waved and shouted to them in greeting. Shai pushed the car down 7th, across 125th and past White Castle. Harlem had undergone some changes, but he was glad to see one of his old haunts still standing. There had been plenty of nights when he had Swann had staggered into the burger joint, drunk and hungry after the club. The burgers tasted like sweet life, but he would always pay for it when he spent half the next morning bound to the toilet while the meal ran straight through him. Those were the days. It was cool being the boss of an organization, but sometimes he longed for the days when he was able to just hang out and shoot the shit.

They looped through a few more blocks before Shai navigated them to their destination. It was a non¬descript little spot on 113th and Lexington Avenue, where you could grab a take-out plate that was sure to have you coming back. It was called Daddy's House, and was fast becoming one of the key spots to pull up to in Harlem if you were hungry. The menu wasn't much to look at, mostly soul food and burgers, but their fried chicken was the stuff of legend. Shai pulled up in front of a fire hydrant and clicked his blinkers on.

"Fuck is you, hungry?" Swann asked, noticing where they were.

"Nah, but it's like you said - sometimes it's good for morale to let the soldiers see my face," Shai told him and hopped out of the car.

Big Doc sat with a group of hard-looking men at one of the tables outside the establishment. They were entrenched in a conversation about God only knew what, but from the way he held their attention, it must have been serious. When Big Doc spotted Shai, his eyes lit up. "Now this is something you don't see every day," he said as he stood and embraced Shai. "Fuck you doing down here in the slums?"

"Just strolling down memory lane," Shai told him. "What up with you though, B.D.? Thought today was your day with your kid?"

"It is. He's inside fucking with one of those video games," Big Doc said.

"You know those games cause brain damage?" Swann added.

"No more than all that dro you smoke is rotting yours."

"Dro was yesterday, haze is the thing of tomorrow. You better step into the new millennium, OG," Swann capped.

"Haze, dro, kush...I can't keep up with all these different kinds of weeds you youngsters keep popping up with. Back in my day, we kept it simple and called it all chiba," Big Doc said with a chuckle.

The door to Daddy's House opened and a group of school-aged kids filed out. In the lead was Baby Doc. He

Hoodlum II: The Good Son

was the spitting image of his father, dark with cubed features, but he had a petite build like his mother. He was swigging an orange Tropical Fantasy soda, and shoving chips into his mouth. Bringing up the rear were Tech and Jewels. Tech wore a sour scowl, while Baby Doc and some of the other kids teased him about something.

"Well, if it ain't the get along gang," Swann joked as he rubbed Baby Doc's head playfully. "What you little hooligans up to?"

"Just got finished taking your boy's money!" Baby Doc said proudly, thumbing at Tech. "Kicked his ass three games straight in NBA JAM!"

"Watch your damn mouth! And what did I tell you about drinking these damn things?" Big Doc snatched the Tropical Fantasy from his son's hand. "These things will make you sterile."

"Quit believing in oldwives tales, B.D," Shai spoke up. When the kids noticed Shai for the first time, they all rushed him, shouting his name and hitting him up for dollars like they always did. Shai pulled out his bankroll and began handing out bills in between warning them about the ills of the streets and telling them to stay in school. After handing out about one hundred dollars in singles, the kids dispersed to go for another round of video games.

"Shai, niggas like you make it two easy on them kids. Where's the lesson in giving away money instead of making them earn it?" Swann questioned.

"The lesson is that a good king makes sure no man, woman or child goes without," Shai capped.

"That's deep," Tech said, reminding them he and Jewels were even standing there. He wasn't sure what kind of response he had been expecting from Shai, but the silent glare wasn't it. "Thanks again for inviting me to your baby shower," he said, more to break the uneasy tension than anything else.

"I told you I was gonna have you moving in different circles," Swann said to rescue Tech from his embarrassment. "I tell my peoples all the time that you're a young man with potential."

"That remains to be seen. Swann, let me holla at you for a minute," Shai said in a displeased tone.

Tech watched as Swann and Shai stepped off to the side so they could speak out of earshot. Shai's body

Hoodlum II: The Good Son

language wasn't hostile, but it was rigid. The conversation only lasted for a few seconds, but it was long enough for them to come to an understanding.

"Yo, I'm gonna go in here and get something to eat. I'll get with y'all in a few." Shai gave Big Doc dap, then Swann. Tech held his hand out too, but Shai just looked at it and continued walking inside.

"Yo, what's up with your man?" Tech asked Swann. The day before, Shai had laid a compliment on him, and now he was acting like Tech had cooties.

"Give me a second," Swann said, tapping Tech's arm and walking him down the block.

"I'm starting to get the feeling that your boy ain't feeling me," Tech said.

"It ain't like that, T. Shai's the boss, so all eyes are always on him. He's gotta be real careful how he moves. I've seen a nigga catch a dime for talking to the wrong muthafucka. That's why all the soldiers talk to him through me," Swann explained. "Give Shai some time and he'll warm up to you just like I did. But onto more pressing business. Where's your little man? I had kinda hoped to talk to both of y'all about some work."

"Who, Animal? I ain't seen that little nigga in a few days," Tech said.

"Everything okay between y'all?"

"Yeah, man. You know I can't keep track of that strange lil' nigga. He comes and goes at his leisure," Tech lied. In truth, he wasn't sure what was going on with Animal lately. Ever since the hit they pulled for the Clarks where Animal inadvertently blinded the victim's elderly mother, something changed in Tech's protégé. He had become more withdrawn and was more distant. Tech had even gone by his apartment that morning to surprise him with an order of his favorite meal (broiled eel from the Japanese market,) and to give him the play-by-play from the baby shower, but Animal was already gone. Where, only God knew, but if Tech had to guess, he was probably skulking around in that abandoned building with the band of misfits he'd adopted. He spent more time with those dirty ass kids than he did the Dog Pound. Tech had seen Animal in funks before and normally he would snap out of them within a few days if given enough space, but this was different. The more he stayed away, the deeper he sank. Tech wouldn't admit it to the others, but he was really starting to worry.

"Well we ain't really got time to wait on him to find his way back home. Need this done ASAP and it's at least a two-man job. You got somebody else to ride out with you?"

Tech looked over his shoulder at Jewels, who was watching them intently. "Yeah, I can maybe scare somebody up. What you need, blood?"

"Someone to disappear."

CHAPTER 16

After grabbing his food, Shai came back outside and rejoined his troops. He had his sleeves rolled up, enjoying the greasy fried chicken and watching the ladies go by. "Damn, sometimes I forget how much I miss this shit."

"Then you need to get out here with us more often instead of being in the crib with your head stuck up Honey's ass," Swann said.

Shai sighed. "Man, there you go again. You starting to sound like a real hater."

"Or a jealous girlfriend," Big Doc added. "Shai, don't listen to this nigga. Ain't nothing wrong with monogamy."

"Ain't too much right about it either," Swann shot back. "Variety is the spice of life. Sampling other pussy makes me more appreciative of the one I got at home."

Big Doc gave him a look. "You sound dumb as shit. The object of the game is to win the prize at the end. You don't win and keep playing. That's madness."

"Nah, that's pimp shit," Swann capped. "Look, you can let Shai talk that devoted boyfriend shit to you, but I

Hoodlum II: The Good Son

know him better than that. That hound dog I used to turn these streets with is hiding in there somewhere. All it's gonna take to bring him out is catching the scent of the right bitch."

"I think you're wrong, Swann. Shai has gotten busted enough times to have finally figured out that it's safer for him to keep his dick in his pants."

"Then put something on it," Swann challenged. "I got a stack that says the hound dog I used to run these streets with is still hiding somewhere in there and all it'll take is the scent of the right bitch to pull it out of him."

"You're on!" Big Doc said confidently. The two shook hands to seal the bet.

All Shai could do was shake his head in amusement while his friends wagered on the strength of his infidelity. His attention was drawn to the curb as a candy-red Hummer pulled in front of Daddy's House and double parked. It was sitting on large rims with windows tinted so heavily that it was impossible to see who was inside. Music boomed so loudly from the speakers that it set off the alarm it was double-parked next to. Both Big Doc and Swann stood at the same time, forming a barrier between

Shai and whoever was in the vehicle.

The kids came out of Daddy's House and lined up on the curb, pointing and trying to peer through the tints to see who was in the nice car. The driver's side door popped open, and out lumbered a mountain of a man. He was high yellow with a clean-cut head and shoulders almost as wide as the vehicle. One of the little kids wandered too close, but a scowl from the man sent him scurrying away. He was known in underworld circles as Red Devil, or Devil for short.

Devil opened the back door first and out stepped two attractive young girls, one light-skinned and the other dark. They were both fine and dressed in tight clothes that showed off their curvaceous figures. Swann and Doc eyed the girls openly, whispering about what they would do to them if given the chance, but it was the third girl, the one who was riding shotgun, that caught Shai's eye.

She was a leggy doll with skin like the color of almond milk, and rich black hair she wore in long boxed braids that swayed every time she moved her head. Dressed in tight jeans, doorknocker earrings and construction Timberlands, she was the embodiment of a

Hoodlum II: The Good Son

B-girl. When the little kids caught sight of her, they all squealed and rushed her, begging for autographs and pictures. She smiled graciously and accommodated the children. Devil let the autograph signing go on for a few minutes before dispersing the children and heading towards the table where Shai sat, with the ladies trailing him.

"Who that?" Shai asked Big Doc and Swann.

"Man, where have you been; living under a rock? That's Lady Monet. She's one of Big Dawg's newest artists," Swann explained.

Shai had never heard the name Lady Monet, but he was familiar with Big Dawg. It was a record label started by a gangster-turned-rapper who went by the name of Don B. To Shai's knowledge, they specialized in gangster rap, but Lady Monet looked more like a movie star than a gangster.

"Young Swann, what it do?" Devil ambled to the table where they were sitting and greeted him. He and Swann knew each other from the streets, as they were affiliated with the same gang.

"Ain't shit, blood." Swann gave Devil dap. "What

221

brings you this way?"

"When I heard you niggas stopped selling bricks to sell chicken, I had to come and see for myself if the rumors were true," Devil joked.

"Don't go believing everything you hear," Shai said, wiping his hands with a napkin. "So, who are your friends?" He was speaking about the girls, but his eyes were locked on Lady Monet. Though she was wearing sunglasses, he could feel her watching him too.

"This is Lisa, Genie and Lady Monet, also known as Man-Eaters. They're Big Dawg's newest act," Devil made the introduction.

"A pleasure," Shai greeted them with a nod.

"So says you," Monet capped, clicking her gum.

"Show some respect when you're speaking to this man!" Devil warned. "Shai ain't no regular nigga, he's the new king of Harlem."

"Cut that out, Devil. I ain't the king of nothing but my house," Shai said modestly.

"Funny, he looks like a regular nigga with chicken grease on his face to me," Monet capped.

Shai grabbed the napkin and wiped his face. "I see this

Hoodlum II: The Good Son

one has got jokes."

"Jokes, and a set of pipes that are out of this world. That little mulatto is gonna make us richer than we already are!" Devil boasted.

"And what the fuck are we, chopped liver?" the dark-skinned one capped with an attitude. This was Genie.

"Tuck your claws, ma. You know we do this shit in three-part-harmony," Monet said reassuringly.

"Y'all bitches can argue about who is gonna sing the lead later. Can we get some food now? I'm starving!" Lisa said dramatically.

"Here." Devil pulled out his bankroll and started counting out bills. "Y'all go in and get whatever you want." He handed the ladies some money and the three of them disappeared inside. "Man, all them bitches do is eat and smoke weed," he joked. "Say, I just came through to grab some food for the girls, Shai, but being that you're here, Don B. has something he'd like to lay on the able for you."

"If y'all will excuse me, I left something inside," Shai excused himself from the table and went back inside Daddy's House.

"What's good with your man? My breath stink or something?" Devil was confused by Shai's abrupt departure.

"Devil, you been around long enough to know nobody talks street business with Shai directly," Swann explained.

"Aw, man. I know what it is, so you know I'd never come at you like that," Devil said sincerely. "I came to talk some legit business. You know we just opened a new club downtown, right?"

"I'd heard something about it," Swann told him.

"Well, we're doing something for the anniversary of True's passing," Devil said as he crossed himself. "We wanna do it real big to honor his memory; booze, bitches, the whole nine yards. Bad Blood is going to headline, but Man-Eaters are the opening act. All the biggest players are coming out and ain't none bigger than the Clark family. It'll look real good to have y'all in the building. Bottles on us, of course."

"Shit, me and a few of the homies will slide through and show out. I don't know about Shai, though. You know he don't do clubs like that," Swann said honestly.

Hoodlum II: The Good Son

"Yeah, I'd heard he was kinda skittish these days,"
Devil laughed mockingly. "Well, maybe the good king
will change his mind when he hears what Don B. would
like to offer him. Let me give you the short version," he
said as he pulled out a chair and sat down.

*

Shai stood in the window of Daddy's House, watching
Devil talking to his men. Big Doc's face was unmoved,
but Swann seemed very interested in whatever Devil had
to say. That meant that whatever it was would likely be
laid at Shai's feet before the day was out.

That's how it worked. Everybody wanted something
from him and Devil was no different.

Whatever the OG was pitching to Swann to take back
to Shai, he had already made his mind up that he would
shoot it down. It didn't have anything to do with Devil;
he was a solid dude and true street nigga, but Shai knew
that anything he brought to his table would be on behalf
of his boss, Don B. Shai and Don B. knew each other, but
they weren't friends to speak of nor would they be. Don

225

B. was arrogant, but he knew how to make a dollar, which Shai respected, but that was about where the buck stopped. There was no doubt that Shai could stand to benefit from doing business with a man like Don B., but he wouldn't. Don B. was a man without honor and that was a deal breaker for Shai.

Once he grew tired of watching them, he turned his attention to a more pleasant scene. Genie and Lisa floated over to where the old-school arcades were set up, engaged in a game of Ms. Pac-Man. Lady Monet was standing at the counter waiting for her food, and trying her best to ignore the constant advances of wayward young men. They were on her like flies on shit, and he couldn't say that he blamed them. She wasn't quite as pretty as Genie, or had as much body as Lisa, but Monet had presence. It was like when she entered a room, she sucked the life out of it. It was easy to see why Don B. pushed her as the front woman for the group.

Shai watched in amusement as Lady Monet fended off advances with sharp words and an occasional hand slap. For the most part she was holding her own, but there was one dude who looked to be getting a little too aggressive.

Hoodlum II: The Good Son

He was a short, thick cat, who Shai had seen around a
few times, but didn't know him by name. He was
invading her space, and letting his hands roam uninvited.
Shai turned to her protector, Devil, who was still
occupied with Swann and unaware of the situation
brewing. Shai was halfway across the room before he
even realized that his feet were moving.

"Nigga, is you hard of hearing? I said fuck off!"
Monet was saying when Shai approached.

"Bitch, I was good enough to trick on you when
you were sliding up and down that pole at Shooters
and now you wanna act brand new because you got a
little record deal?" the kid pressed her.

"Just because you tipped me a few times don't mean
you own me. And even if I was for sale, the price would
be way too high for your slum ass. Now be gone!" Monet
barked and turned her back to him.

"You rotten whore!" He spun her back around and
raised his hand to slap her, but Shai caught him about the
wrist before the blow could fall. He spun, ready to turn
his anger on Shai, but froze when he saw who it was.

"I know you been here enough times to know what

happens to niggas who try to show out up in here," Shai said in an icy tone.

"My fault, Shai. Just having a little misunderstanding with my lady. I'll take her outside and finish this conversation." The kid took Monet by the arm and tried to pull her out, but Shai stepped in front of him.

"Nah, I think you'll leave... alone, and count yourself thankful that you're making your exit on your feet and not in a bag," Shai told him.

"Damn, it's like that?" the kid asked in disbelief. Shai didn't answer, just continued to glare. "You got it." He began backing towards the exit. "And bitch I'll see you again real soon," he told Monet.

"You good?" Shai asked once the threat had passed.

"Yeah, and thanks, but I had it under control," Monet told him.

"I'm sure you did, but I wasn't willing to gamble that pretty face of yours on it," Shai smiled.

"Your order comes to $62.50," the girl working the register said as she sat the bags of food that Monet and her crew ordered on the counter. Monet was reaching into her purse to pay, but Shai stopped her.

Hoodlum II: The Good Son

"Nah, her money is no good here," Shai told the cashier. She gave him a knowing glance and went back to take another order.

"Damn, first you save me from that stalker ass nigga and now you're going to pay for my food? You're either a real gentleman or somebody who thinks they got a shot at getting some pussy," Monet said sarcastically.

"I'm neither, shorty. Your food is on the house because I own the joint, and I ain't got no immediate interests in your pussy."

"Not yet, you don't, but give yourself some time." She ran her index finger down his shirt, letting it stop briefly at the pocket of his shirt before pulling her hand away. It was a subtle gesture, but the message behind it resonated.

"You cocky as hell, ain't you?"

"But of course. Every good performer should be." "So, is that what this is? A performance?" he asked.

"I don't know, is it?" Monet invaded his space. She wasn't close enough to touch him, just enough so that he could feel her body heat.

The scent of Monet's braids invaded Shai's nose, and tapped on the walls of his self-control. "You're treading on dangerous ground, ma."

"Why? What you gonna do, stab me with that notorious pole of yours?" Monet began pacing a tight circle around Shai. "I know all about you, Slim," she playfully addressed him by his nickname. Shai didn't bother to hide his surprise. "When you and your crew first walked up, you acted like you didn't know who I was."

"I never said I didn't know who you were. Devil just assumed that," she corrected him. "I was born and raised in Harlem. You'd have to be living under rock to not know who Shai Clark is. Besides, this isn't the first time our paths have crossed." She stopped her circling and stood in front of him.

"I think I'd know if we met before."

Monet removed her sunglasses and bore into Shai with her hazel eyes. "You mean to say this face isn't familiar to you?"

Before their game of words could go any further, Devil appeared behind them. "What's this?" he asked, giving both of them accusing looks.

"Ain't nothing," Shai said with a guilty look on his

Hoodlum II: The Good Son

face.

"Looks like something to me," Devil insisted. "Well if you must know; Shai was in here doing your job. Where the fuck was you when that creep ass nigga was in here trying to take my goodies?" Monet changed the subject.

"What? Somebody tried you? Where the nigga at?" Devil looked around angrily.

"I told you, Shai already took care of it," she repeated.

"Well now that Shai has saved your honor and you got your food, let's get going. Don B. is expecting us at the studio." Devil grabbed her arm and began half-dragging her towards the door.

"Why don't you take it easy?" Shai suggested.

Devil stopped and gave Shai a menacing look. "No disrespect, Shai, but this lady is property of Big Dawg, and none of your business," he said, and continued shoving her out.

Shai followed them outside, watching as Devil shook Monet and barked on her on the way to the car. Shai wanted to intervene and have his men swoop in and rescue Monet, but to do so would have potentially sparked a beef with Big Dawg. Don B. and his minions weren't in the streets anymore, but they still had heavy ties. They were no match for the Clarks, but it would have put Shai in the awkward position to have to explain to his solders that they were about to shed blood over a woman that Shai didn't even know. So instead, he was forced to sit by and watch as Devil whisked Monet and the girls away.

Shai folded his arms in quiet reflection of the things that just played out. It was then that he noticed something in his shirt's breast pocket. Curiously he dug into his pocket, only to find the Monet had slipped one of her business cards into his pocket when she touched him inside Daddy's House. She was slicker than a pig in shit, he'd give her that. Shai smiled as he slid the card back into his pocket. When he turned back around to rejoin his crew, he saw Big Doc placing a rolled-out knot of bills into Swann's outstretched hand.

CHAPTER 17

The Mall at Short Hills in Milburn, New Jersey was crowded as usual. People hustled about, window-shopping and darting in and out of the high-end stores it was famous for. It was one of the premiere shopping areas in the tri-state, and one of Honey's favorite places to unwind. Because she was pregnant she couldn't smoke weed, so she turned to retail therapy to relieve some of her stress.

The last forty-eight hours had been rough on her. Though she was looking forward to her baby shower for months, she was relieved when it was over. She knew there would be a lot of people in attendance, but wasn't prepared for the small parade running through her backyard. Sitting out in that hot ass sun playing hostess was taxing. It would have probably gone smoother had Shai not run off and left her to handle it on her own. He seemed to be doing that a lot lately; leaving her to handle things by herself. It was one of the downsides of Shai's new position.

Most of Honey's friends envied her for having landed

Shai. He was young, handsome and caked up. She would listen to them go on and on about how great it would be to have what they had, but that's because they were on the outside looking in. They didn't know about the lonely nights sitting by the phone, hoping that she didn't get the call that her man was locked up or dead. For the most part, Shai kept himself insulated from the street aspect of the business, delegating responsibilities through Swann, but he still had one foot in the life he promised to put behind him. There was a time when all he could talk about was legitimizing the family, and though it was still the goal, the sense of urgency wasn't there anymore. When she'd asked him about it, all he would say was, "As soon as we get to where we need to be." It sounded and smelled like bullshit to her. Shai kept Honey on a need-to-know basis as far as his business went, but she knew what they brought in from their legitimate holdings allowed them to live beyond comfortably, so she couldn't understand his reluctance to let go of the streets. Was it the money that kept him bound to the old ways, or the God-like power that came with being the boss?

"Girl, are you even listening to me?" Paula snapped

Hoodlum II: The Good Son

Honey out of her daze.

"Huh?" She turned to her friend as if she was just noticing her.

"I said I wanna run up in Bebe. They're having a sale," Paula repeated.

"Sure," Honey said in a disinterested tone. "Where is your head at today?" Paula asked, noticing the troubled look on her face.

"I'm sorry girl, I just got a lot on my mind."

"Apparently so. We've been in this bitch for two hours and you've only hit one store," Paula said, nodding at the single plastic shopping bag in her hand. "The Honey I know could burn a mall down twice in that amount of time."

"Must be this pregnancy weight slowing me down," Honey half joked.

Paula looked into her friend's eyes. "You're definitely carrying around some extra weight, but it don't have nothing to do with being pregnant. You stressing that bullshit Shai pulled yesterday? Girl, I don't blame you. Had my man run out on me in the middle of our baby shower, I'd be pissed too."

"He didn't run out on me. He was called away on business," Honey corrected her.

"The way he dashed out of there, it must've been pretty damn important. What was that all about anyhow?" Paula asked.

"Nothing," Honey brushed her off. Paula was her bestie, and she confided a great deal in her, but never family business. She and Honey had history, but Paula was still technically an outsider in their world. "Damn, I'm hungry," she said as her stomach grumbled.

"Didn't you just eat when we first got here?" Paula reminded her.

"You keep forgetting that I'm eating for two. Let's run over to Legal Seafood. I could go for some shrimps," Honey suggested.

Paula sucked her teeth. "You know there's gonna be a wait. By the time you get done stuffing your face, all the good sale shit will have been picked over. Why

don't we send Brutus to grab you some cookies or something to hold you over?" she suggested.

Honey looked over her shoulder at the bodyguard who

Hoodlum II: The Good Son

was shadowing them through the mall. "No, I don't wanna bother him sending him on no errands."

"Shai pays him to make sure you're good at all times, and getting some food into your greedy ass will do just that. Brutus, can you come here for a second?" Paula called to him before Honey could stop her.

"You ladies okay?" Brutus approached. He had shed his normal black suit and was wearing a button-up shirt and cotton slacks over leather shoes.

"Honey is hungry. Be a dear and make a Starbucks run for us, please?" Paula batted her eyes.

Brutus looked hesitant.

"Brutus, we're in a crowded ass mall. I don't think you have to worry about anybody trying to kill us in the ten minutes it'll take you to get us some snacks," Paula said.

Brutus looked at Honey, who nodded that it was okay. "Aight, but wait right here for me until I get back. Don't move!" he insisted before walking off.

"Damn, that nigga be sounding more like your man than your bodyguard. What's really good with that?" Paula asked suspiciously.

"Ain't nothing up with it. Why are you always trying to make something out of nothing?" Honey downplayed it.

"Bitch, how long have we known each other? I know when you're trying to hide something, which is what you're doing now."

"You tripping, Paula."

"No, I'm reading the signs," Paula shot back. "All I know is that ever since that night, things have been different between the two of you."

"What night?" Honey faked ignorance.

"Bitch, don't play with me. You know just what night I'm talking about."

Indeed, Honey did. It was about a year ago. She and Shai had gotten into a big argument over her finding out about some skank broad he had been creeping with. She knew Shai dabbled in hoe-soup from time to time, but for the most part, his bitches always knew their places. This one was different, though. She was going around town telling anyone who would listen about her plans to unseat Honey from the throne, and it had gotten back to her through the grapevine. When she confronted Shai about

Hoodlum II: The Good Son

it, of course he tried lying, but the Honey knew too much
to be making it up. They had said some hurtful things to
each other, which lead to Honey storming out. She had let
Paula convince her to go out to the club to blow off some
steam that night, and they both ended up getting so drunk
that neither of them were in any condition to drive home.
There was no way she was going to ask Shai to come get
them, so they ended up calling Brutus.

He must have been out partying himself because
instead of his usual black suit, he was wearing a cream
turtleneck and matching Gucci shoes. Paula could
remember how Honey kept drunkenly commenting on
whatever cologne he had on. Paula got dropped off first
at her apartment in the Bronx, then Brutus left to take
Honey home. It was roughly an hour drive from Paula's
place back to the estate, but two hours later, Shai was on
Paula's phone asking her if Honey was there. Of course,
Paula pressed Honey about the lapse in time, but to that
day she had never given her a straight answer.

"Brutus and I are just friends. Nothing more," Honey
said, but Paula still didn't believe her. Not wanting to talk
about it anymore, Honey busied herself looking at a pair

of shoes in the window of Prada. "Now those are hot."

"Those would look good on you," Paula said, joining Honey in admiring the high-end stilettos.

"Yeah they would, but ain't no way I can get these swollen feet into them, and by the time I drop my load and this weight, they'll be out of season. I'll bet you'd crush the building with them, though."

"You know my pockets ain't set up to do much more than look," Paula said honestly.

"What good is having money if you can't blow it on your bestie? Now come on!" Honey grabbed Paula by the hand and pulled her inside the store.

Honey and Paula spent the next twenty minutes trying on different shoes. She grabbed the stilettos for Paula and found some cute flats for herself. She was at the register, fishing around in her purse for the wallet holding her credit cards when she felt someone standing behind them. She turned, expecting to see Brutus, but found herself looking at the stranger she saw at the baby shower.

"Sorry, didn't mean to startle you," he said easily. "You're Shai's lady. Honey, right?"

Hoodlum II: The Good Son

"Depends on who's asking?" Honey reached deeper into her purse and fingered the baby 9mm at the bottom of it.

"My fault. Where are my manners? We didn't get a chance to meet formally, but I'm Shai and Tommy's cousin, Hammer," he introduced himself.

That explained why his face was familiar to her. The Clark men had very strong genes. "Nice to meet you, Hammer. Now how can I help you?"

"I was actually wondering if you were here with Shai? I need to holla at him about something. I called the house, but he wasn't in," Hammer told her.

"So you stalked his lady to the mall?" Honey asked suspiciously.

"Nah, this was purely coincidence," Hammer chuckled. "I was in here grabbing something for a friend of mine when I spotted you," he explained, raising the Prada bag in his hand. "Look, I didn't mean no disrespect, I just need to get with my little cousin. It's kind of important. Do you have a cell phone number or something?"

"I don't know you well enough to give out that kind of

information." Honey gave him a distrustful look. Something about Hammer creeped her out. She didn't know him, but she was sure she didn't like him. "I'll let Shai know you're looking for him," she said, and collected her bags and attempted to leave. Hammer blocked her path.

"A real ride or die, huh? Listen sweetie, I'm not the enemy. Just an estranged relative looking to reconnect with his blood."

"There's gonna be some blood if you don't get the fuck out of our way," Paula said as she stepped between them. She was small, but feisty.

Hammer glared down at Paula. "You must ain't got no man, because if you did, you'd know how to speak when you're in the presence of a real nigga."

"Is there a problem here?" Brutus appeared behind Hammer as if by magic. He was holding the Starbucks in one hand, and a retractable baton in the other.

Hammer looked him up and down comically. "Nah, ain't no problem, pretty boy. I was just leaving."

"Then you need to do so," Brutus said in a threatening tone.

Hoodlum II: The Good Son

"Right." Hammer began backing out of the store. "Shorty, don't forget to give my little cousin my message. He should get with me sooner than later."

"Make no mistake, I'm gonna remember this," Honey promised.

Brutus continued to stand there, glaring at Hammer until he was out of the store. "You okay?" he asked Honey, who looked shaken.

"Yeah, I'm cool. Just get me out of here."

CHAPTER 18

Tech couldn't wait for the sun to go down so he could go about the task of handling the mission Swann handed to him. When his big homie explained the ins and outs of it, Tech was both surprised and honored. Gaining Swann's respect and trust had been the goal since he started taking on jobs for the Clarks.

He wasn't like the rest of the cock-suckers who stood around kissing ass, hoping that Shai would fart sunshine on their heads; Tech was determined to create his own light. Even before forming the Dog Pound with Animal, Tech had been in the streets putting in work. They weren't hurting for money, but they weren't where Tech envisioned them being either. This is where the Clark connection came in. Moving with Shai would put them in a whole different weight class, and open the doors for even bigger scores. The so-called heavyweights being connected would allow him to get close to where little more than suckling pigs waited to be roasted over a spit, and Tech was determined to become the grill master.

This latest task, which Tech figured to be his last

Hoodlum II: The Good Son

obstacle into finally entering the Clark circle of trust,
carried him into the bowels of Newark, New Jersey.
Newark was only about twenty minutes from New York
City, and boasted a vibrant downtown section, but once
you crossed Springfield Avenue, it was like stepping into
a Third World country where the natives were less than
friendly. Tech pushed the stolen taxi through the blocks
of empty lots and houses in various stages of decimation.
All you had to do was read the graffiti on the walls to
know where you were, but the body language of the
young men and women hanging out and about told an
even deeper tale. They were lost souls, fighting to hold
onto what little the corrupt government had left them, and
willing to protect it at all costs. Newark was a city Tech
didn't venture into unless he had to, but even those
occasions it was always was in the company of a local
tour guide and at least half a dozen homies. That night,
though, he was riding two deep.

"You call her yet?" Jewels asked from the passenger
seat.

"Who?" Tech asked, tearing his eyes away from a
woman on the corner who was doing the dope fiend lean.

"You know who, the little bitch from the baby shower. What the fuck was her name again?"

"Belle," Tech informed him, as he hung a right turn on Grove, "and no, I didn't call her."

Jewels gave him a disbelieving look.

"She called me," Tech confessed.

"I knew it!" Jewels laughed. "Man if you had seen the way you and shorty were looking at each other... it was like something out of a movie, dawg. I almost shed a tear!" He wiped under his eye dramatically. "I kinda hope you do get in good with her so I can take a crack at that amazon-looking white bitch."

"Funny you should mention it, because I'm supposed to see her tomorrow. You can be my wing-man and run interference with that old harp, Ruby."

Jewels sucked his teeth. "First of all, nigga, I ain't never the co-pilot; I do the flying. And second of all, I ain't messing with that old broad Ruby. You better have shorty come to the block."

"I tried that, but Ms. Ruby insists that if I wanna see Belle I gotta court her properly...whatever the fuck that means. Homie, we'll go through there, spend about an

246

Hoodlum II: The Good Son

hour or so making the old bird feel respected and then get out of there and into some gangster shit," Tech promised.

"I'll think about it," Jewels said, then busied himself looking out the window. The streets were busy with activity. "Man, you know I heard they got these spots out this way where a bitch will fuck and suck you for thirty bucks!"

"For thirty dollars, she's either an addict or something is wrong with the pussy. No thanks," Tech declined.

"Nah, man. One of my boys told me he hit it up a time or three. Claims these Spanish bitches is some of the finest he's ever seen. I say once we wax these fag, we got get our dicks wet."

Tech shook his head. "Listen, can you get your mind off pussy long enough for us to complete this mission?"

"The two go hand in hand. Once we finish this mission and get in good with Swann, we gonna get all the bitches!" Jewels did a little dance in his seat.

"You can make jokes all you want, but don't sleep just because we're in Jersey. These Newark niggas are a different breed and we're too far from home to call in a lifeline if this shit goes wrong," Tech warned him.

"Nigga, please!" Jewels fished around in the back seat and came up holding a compact machine gun. "This is the only lifeline we'll need," he said as he cocked the slide. "These muthafuckas even peek at us wrong and I suggest you get out of the way because I'm gonna let this thing rock!"

"I'm going to hold you to that statement," Tech said, steering deeper into the hood. When they were about five blocks from their destination, he pulled over behind a BP gas station and killed the engine.

"I thought you filled up before we left New York?" Jewels looked at him quizzically.

"I'm not getting gas, fool. I'm getting our trump card," Tech told him, as he slid out of the car and walked back to the trunk. He gave a causal look around, working his key in the lock. It was more out of habit than fear of being caught. At that hour of the night and in that part of town, the police took their time responding to calls - if they showed up at all. When he was sure that his moment would be an intimate one, he opened the trunk and let his package breathe.

Wayne's nostrils flared as he tried to take in as much

Hoodlum II: The Good Son

oxygen as he could through his nose, because his mouth
was covered in duct tape. His eyes blinked as they tried to
adjust to the overhead streetlight. He'd been riding in the
darkened trunk for the better part of an hour. The whole
time he'd been praying for someone to open the trunk and
give him a glimpse at freedom. His prayers had
seemingly been answered, but the young face staring
down at him ate away at what little hope he'd built.
Wayne had seen the face before, but only once; he was
staggering out of the bar half-drunk and a hooded youth
approached asking for a light, and when Wayne reached
in his pocket to accommodate him, everything went dark.

"Time for you to earn your keep." Tech pulled Wayne
from the trunk and pushed him towards the front of the
taxi. He spun the man around and placed his gun to his
forehead. "I'm gonna pull this tape from your mouth and
you're gonna behave yourself. Do you think you can do
that? Remove your gag and you and me are going to have
a civil conversation. Can we do that?"

Wayne nodded frantically. He didn't know who the
young man was or why he had been abducted, but he was
willing to do whatever it took to see another day. As soon

as Tech removed the tape, he began the tasks of trying to bargain for his life. "Please man. I don't know what this is all about, but I'm just a driver."

"Then drive muthafucka!" Tech shoved him behind the wheel and jumped in the back.

The ten minutes it took him to drive the next few blocks felt like the longest of Wayne's life. His hands trembled nervously as the man in the passenger seat with the gold bracelets looping up his forearm glared at him silently. He couldn't see the machine gun he'd been brandishing when Wayne got in the car, but he knew it was there somewhere, ready to lay him down if need be. His abductor, the one with the braids who snatched him, sat in the back occasionally feeding him directions - not that Wayne needed them. He had taken the drive more than once and knew his way by heart.

"Pull over," Tech ordered on a block between Washington and Broad. On one side of them was a small bodega, where a few young girls in tight jeans were hanging out. On the other, an apartment building. Their position gave them a view of the darkened courtyard where several young men were congregating.

Hoodlum II: The Good Son

"Damn, shorty got an onion!" Jewels said excitedly, rolling down the window to get a better view of the girl he was eyeballing. "Light skinned, what's good?" he called. The girl gave him a smile.

"Are you fucking stupid?" Tech barked from the backseat. "We're here to handle business, not chase pussy!"

"You need to lighten up, man." Jewels said as if it were no big deal.

"Wayne, you see that nigga out there?" Tech ignored Jewels and went back to scanning the courtyard.

Wayne strained his eyes against the darkness. "I can't tell, man. It's dark as shit and my eyes ain't so good."

Tech leaned forward and pressed his gun to the back of Wayne's head. "This help you see a little clearer?"

"The one in the red hoodie," Wayne said, pointing. "He does all his business out of the courtyard."

Tech peered through the window at the man Wayne had identified. He was pacing back and forth, occasionally glancing at his phone as if he were waiting for someone to ring him. Tech had Wayne call and tell the young man that he was in the area and wanted to score some more dope. From his look of anxiousness, Tech reasoned that Wayne was responsible for putting more money in his pocket than that of the dirty politician he drove for.

"Make the call," Tech ordered.

"Look man, I know whatever you're cooking up for this dude ain't good. I did my part and pointed him out. Now how about you let me go my way while you do what you gotta do," Wayne pleaded. He wasn't built to be an accessory to a murder.

"Let me see if I can make this simple for you, Wayne. Somebody is gonna have a conversation with the business end of my gun tonight. Whether it's going to be the dude who sold O'Connor that bad bag of dope or you is your choice."

Knowing that there would be no negotiating with his captor, Wayne pulled out his cell phone. "Hey Jake? It's me..."

Tech drowned out whatever Wayne was saying on the phone and focused on the dealer who had been identified as Jake. His body language would give him a better idea of where he stood than Wayne's words. Reading body

Hoodlum II: The Good Son

language was something he picked up from Animal, and
it paid off. Thinking of his protégé made him wish that
Animal had come along for the ride. Animal and Tech
had been to war together and he always stood tall. The
jury was still out on Jewels. Tech watched Jake walk in
through the back of the building after Wayne ended the
call.

"We all good. He's gonna meet us in the lobby."
Wayne informed Tech.

"Bet, let's do this." Jewels picked up the shotgun and
double-checked to make sure it was loaded.

"Man, we can't roll in there deep. It's bad enough I'm
showing up with a new face, but if I show up with two
new faces he's gonna know something is off," Wayne
explained.

"Fuck that. If you go into that lobby by yourself, I
can't see what's going on. We go together or not at all,"
Jewels said.

Tech weighed it. Everything in his mind told him that
the setup was wrong, but it was his only window of
opportunity. It was either take the gamble or go back and
tell Swann he failed at his task. "I'm going alone. Jewels,

you stay with the car and keep the engine running. I'm going to be coming out fast after I smoke this fool."

"Aight, if you wanna play super hero it's on you, but if you ain't out in five minutes, I'm coming in busting." Jewels chambered a round into the machine gun.

"Stay with the car!" Tech insisted, before sliding out. He was sure he could handle whatever was waiting for him inside the building, but the last thing he needed was to get trapped off in Newark. Once he handled his business, he knew the cats from the neighborhood would be on him like flies on shit. As he followed Wayne towards the building, he cast a glance over his shoulder. The last thing he saw before rounding the corner was Jewels getting out of the car to talk to the girl by the store. For the millionth time he wished he'd brought Animal with him.

*

Following Wayne to the building made Tech feel like he was walking the Green Mile to the electric chair.

Hoodlum II: The Good Son

Wayne seemed shaky, but Tech reasoned he would be too
if he'd been kidnapped and forced to set a man up to die.
There were three or four scruffy-looking cats hanging out
in front of the building, passing around a Black & Mild
and drinking beers out of paper bags. Their eyes roamed
over Tech and Wayne, likely trying to figure out if they
were friend or foe.

"What up, blood?" One of them flashed a gang sign,
noticing the red bandana hanging from Tech's pocket.

"Mack'n," Tech replied in an even tone, and threw up
his set. This seemed to satisfy their curiosities and the
two were allowed to pass without further incident.
Though the lobby window he could see Jake pacing back
and forth. He looked either nervous or anxious; Tech
wasn't quite sure which. When he spotted them, he
slipped on a mask of calm, and hit the button on the other
side to release the lobby door lock with a click. When
Tech stepped inside and the door shut again, he noticed
that he didn't hear it lock. It was then that an eerie feeling
settled in the pit of his gut. Too far to turn back now, he
thought to himself.

"Yo, what the fuck did I tell you about coming

through this joint unannounced?" Jake started right in on Wayne. It was obvious from his tone that he didn't have much respect for the driver.

"Sorry about that. This was kinda spur of the moment. My man needed some work and I figure I'd put the money in your pocket instead of someone else's." Wayne explained.

"Ya man, huh?" Jake looked Tech up and down suspiciously. "How do I know you ain't police?"

Tech matched Jake's glare. "Homie, I came to spend bread, not waste my time answering dumb ass questions. Wayne said you was holding the best bag in town, but if this ain't the case I'll go holla at my man Red in Elizabeth," he said, and started for the door. He didn't really know anyone named Red, but there was always somebody named Red on a blood set.

"Hold on," Jake called after him. "I ain't trying to run you off. It's just that you can never be too careful when dealing with new people, feel me?"

"Nah, I don't feel you, but I ain't here to pass judgment. We gonna do this or not?" Tech asked impatiently.

Hoodlum II: The Good Son

"Yeah, we gonna do this," Jake sneered, opening one of the mailboxes.

Tech wasn't sure why, but he looked to Wayne, who had conveniently edged back. It was then that he spotted something in his eyes - nervous anticipation. Tech reached for his gun, but the cold press of steel behind his ear made him pause.

"Not so fast, blood." Tech recognized the voice as the kid who greeted him outside. He cursed as a hand reached around and relieved him of the pistol in his waist.

"What the fuck is this?" Tech asked Jake, who retrieved a pistol from the mailbox and was now aiming it at him.

"That's what I'm trying to figure out." Jake ripped the front of Tech's shirt and checked him for a wire.

"Wayne, I came in good faith to spend some money and this is how your people gonna do me?" Tech tried to keep up his lie, but knew it was futile.

"Nigga, that's about as weak a lie as my name being Jake. Jake is what we shout when the police on deck, so I knew you were full of shit the minute Wayne called me by that," Not Jake informed him. "The way I figure it, you're either police or a Jack-Boy. Either way you ain't leaving this building... at least not on your feet."

"That's your word?" he asked, locking eyes with Not Jake. He talked the talk, never walked the walk. Not Jake wasn't a killer; at least not yet, and Tech had no intentions on his final resting place being a random lobby in Newark, at the hands of amateurs. He was outnumbered and disarmed, but hardly defenseless. "A soldier's death it is then."

The kid standing with his gun to the back of Tech's head never even saw his elbow coming until it was smashing into his nose, breaking it. His gun went off, sending a bullet bouncing off the mailbox and hitting Wayne in the throat. It wasn't quite how Tech had planned on killing Wayne, but he'd take his victories where he could get them. Seeing the prey now becoming the predator caused Not Jake to hesitate for a fraction of a second, and that was all the time Tech needed to make him regret it. Moving with the grace of a ballerina, he spat a razor from his mouth into his hand and brought it down across Not Jake's stunned face. He howled like a wounded dog, temporarily blinded by the pain that had exploded in his face. His vision cleared just in time to see Tech fleeing through the rear exit.

*

Tech had no idea where he was going, but it didn't matter. He needed to get as far away from the dogs on his heels as quickly as possible. In his pitiful need to appease Swann, he abandoned his normal protocols and walked into a situation blindly. It was a mistake that was threatening to cost him his life.

When he spilled from the exit into the rear courtyard, Tech found that he had gone from the frying pan and into the fire. He was surrounded by an agitated group of young men, obviously put on alert by the sounds of gunfire coming from the lobby. They took one look at the panicked stranger and it didn't take a rocket scientist to know he had been the cause.

"Grab that nigga!" Not Jake came bursting through the door. His hand was across his face where Tech had cut him. From the blood spilling between his fingers, you could tell it was a deep one.

A burly older dude managed to grab a fist full of Tech's hoodie, and yanked him close. He smelled like a mixture of cigarettes and beer. Tech tried to bring the razor into play, but the man knocked it away. Tech struggled to break free of his grip, but the man was as strong as a bear. When he tried to get a better grip on Tech, he slipped out of the hoodie completely and took off.

The Newark thugs hurled profanities and bullets at Tech's back as he zigzagged across the courtyard trying desperately not to get his head blown off. A few yards away, he could see the car parked across the street. Tech hit the black gate separating the courtyard from the street like the Amazing Spiderman and crashed into the grass on the other side. Coming from down the street, he could see the kids who had been in front of the building, all armed and out for his blood. When Tech got across the street to the car, he finally realized why Jewels hadn't already jumped out and laid down cover fire - he wasn't in the car. Tech didn't need to see his enemies closing around him to know that his run was literally over.

Spots danced before his eyes when something heavy

slammed into the back of his head. He went down to one knee, clutching his head. He wasn't bleeding, but was growing a respectable knot. He looked up and saw at least a half dozen angry eyes staring down at him. Leading the mob was Not Jake. In the light, Tech could see the scar he'd gifted him. The gash across his nose was so deep it was a wonder how it was still attached to his face.

"Bitch ass nigga!" Not Jake kicked him in the stomach hard enough to knock the wind out of him. "You dead for what you did to my face."

The next thing Tech knew, he was swallowed by the mob. They rained kicks and punches on every part of his exposed body. He reasoned the only thing that saved him from Not Jake just shooting him and getting it over with was because there were too many of them dog-piling on Tech for him to get a clear shot. The world swam and his ears began ringing from the repeated blows to the head, and he was pretty sure he was about to black out when something warm and wet splashed on the ground just below him. At first he thought it was his own blood, until he looked up and saw Not Jake's body jerk. Not Jake twitched twice more as bullets slammed into his body. Coming out of the shadows, like an avenging black angel, was none other than Jewels!

"Get some! Get some!" Jewels snarled, busting the machine gun. The thugs scattered like roaches, but not before having half their numbers wiped out. When it was done, several dead bodies were scattered on the ground along with a rattled Tech. "I knew this shit was a good investment," he said, kissing the machine gun.

"Where the fuck were you? I said stay with the car!" Tech barked, pulling himself to his feet.

"Relax, nigga. I had to take a leak. I been holding it since we left Harlem," Jewels told him. "Yo, if we hurry, we can catch the ones who ran off!" He eagerly slapped a fresh clip in. "Me and you, baby. Let's take these niggas to war!"

Tech looked from the direction the boys had fled in toward Not Jake's corpse. "Nah, them niggas can breathe...at least for now. We've spent enough time here, and we still got one more stop to make." He slid behind the wheel of the car.

"One more stop? Dude is dead, so what the fuck else

Hoodlum II: The Good Son

could we possibly have to do in New Jersey?"

*

"But mama, why do we to go to Florida? I like it
here." Eight-year-old Alex was sitting on the edge of the
bed, pouting.

"Because I said so!" Jane snapped, tossing a few
things into a small suitcase. When she saw that she scared
her son by yelling at him, she stopped and went to him.
"Look, mama is sorry for being short with you. I'm just a
little stressed. We'll only be in Florida for a couple of
weeks. Don't you wanna see your little cousins?"

"No," Alex said flatly.

"I'll tell you what. If you go and get your underwear
and things together like a good little boy, I'll take you to
McDonald's to get a Happy Meal before we go to the
airport."

"Can I get an ice cream too?" Alex asked hopefully.

"Two ice creams," Jane promised. That was all little
Alex needed to hear to send him scurrying off to do as his
mother instructed. With her son finally out of the way,

Jane was able to go back to what she was doing, which was getting the hell out of dodge. Jane finished packing her suitcase and went into her closet to grab her shoulder bag from its hiding place, behind several boxes of shoes. She peeked inside and did a quick count of the bills. After what she had spent on their plane tickets — and the money she wired through Western Union to her sister in advance to agree to let her stay — she still had seventy-five hundred dollars left. It wasn't exactly a retirement fund, but it would be enough to hold them over until she could find work and get back on her feet.

Jane paused when she saw a pair of headlights shine against her bedroom window. She crept over cautiously and peered out to see a taxi turning into her driveway. "About damn time," she mumbled. "Alex, let's go! Our taxi is here!" she called to her son, making her way down the stairs with her bags. She was moving so fast that she twisted her ankle and almost fell. Jane's nerves were shot and she wouldn't relax until she and her son were safely out of New Jersey.

Jane stopped short of the front door to leave an envelope on the table for her mother to find when she

Hoodlum II: The Good Son

came in from work. Inside it was one thousand dollars and a note letting her know that she and Alex were okay. She felt bad about dashing off that way without at least an explanation, but she figured the less she told her mother, the safer she would be. When she got settled she would tell her everything, but at that moment, her top priority was getting herself and Alex out of town.

"Hurry up, Alex!" Jane yelled again. "Slow ass boy," she grumbled. If he wasn't downstairs by the time she loaded the bags into the taxi, she was going to drag him down. When she opened the door, she found a man standing on the other side, and from the looks of him, he wasn't a taxi driver. Her last thoughts were what would become of her son?

*

Jewels watched Tech as he walked back to the taxi, every so often glancing around to make sure no one was watching. He opened the door and tossed a shoulder bag into the back seat, before getting back behind the wheel.

"What the fuck is that?" Jewels nodded to the bag.

"Tying up a loose end for Swann," Tech told him, before throwing the car in gear and peeling off.

Tech spent the majority of the ride out of Newark in silence, lost in his own thoughts. Every so often he would see Jewels look over at him. He obviously wanted an explanation about their stop at the house and the bag, but Tech honestly didn't have one for him, except that Swann wanted it done.

Tech didn't want to admit it to himself, but he knew he'd fucked up. They had a rule in the Dog Pound - no women and no children. He had broken that rule in his quest to appease Swann. He'd never felt the need to gain the approval of another since he was kind of following Jah around and begging him to let him put in work.

"As long as you stay true to what you believe in, fuck what anyone else says or thinks. Once you stop being your own man, you might as well hang it up," he could hear Jah's voice ringing in his head. His former mentor was probably rolling over in his grave right about then. It was too late to give back the life he'd stolen, but he knew one day the deed would come back on him. Until then, there wasn't much Tech could do but ride it out.

Hoodlum II: The Good Son

His eyes drifted to Jewels, who seemed content now that he had gotten to spill a little blood. When they'd set out on their little mission, he was unsure if Jewels would rise to the occasion, but Jewels had proven himself more than capable and willing. Despite his big mouth and inability to take anything seriously, he stood tall when his number was called and there was no doubt in Tech's mind that he would do so again. He would make a welcomed addition to the Dog Pound. Now all he had to do was convince Animal of this, but first he would have to find him.

CHAPTER 19

Animal stepped from the shadows of the subway station and took in a healthy chest full of the evening air. It stank of old fish, trash and exhaust fumes, but it beat the smell of death and mildew that seemed to cling to everything inside The Below, which is where he spent most of the day, checking on the children to make sure they had enough supplies to last them for a few weeks and that there was money in their stash. He made sure they were properly equipped before undertaking a dangerous task. In his line of work, you never knew which day at the office might be your last, and he dreaded the thought of leaving them underprepared in the event that he didn't return.

When the one they called "Duffy" ventured into The Below with the offer from Tommy Clark, he was tempted to send his response in the way of cutting out Duffy's tongue and mailing it back to the Clark Estate. That was until Duffy explained the situation in detail. Animal didn't particularly care for any of the Clarks, with the exception of their late father, but he cared for

Hoodlum II: The Good Son

child molesters even less, and that was whom they paid him to hunt. Tommy had promised Animal ten grand for his services, which was hardly chump change. But for the honor of killing a pedophile, he'd have done it for free.

For reasons only known to a few, Animal fashioned himself a champion of the broken, those too weak to protect themselves. This was especially true when it came to children, and was why he had become the surrogate guardian for the wayward kids who dwelled in The Below. Much like him, they were abandoned by society and left to fend for themselves. For the most part they were good kids; a bit rough around the edges, but not yet corrupted by the evil. In the children of The Below, he saw what he once was, and did what he could do to protect him from what he was becoming.

Animal came from a less than favorable upbringing with a junkie for a mother, a father he didn't know and a step-dad who showed him what true evil was for the first time. Eddie was his name. He was a musician and a closet junkie who Animal's mother had foolishly trusted to be their salvation, but all Eddie did was drag them further into hell. When Eddie wasn't out trying to score drugs, one of his favorite past times was kicking the shit out of everyone in the house who wasn't strong enough to fight him back. When Animal's older brother was around, things weren't so bad because he was able to protect him. Animal still caught the occasional beating, but there was only so far Eddie would go because he knew Justice would kill him. He was a gangster and Eddie was afraid of Justice, but whenever he would go away to jail or be gone in the streets for weeks at a time, Eddie would make up for lost time. Animal suffered through everything from busted lips to broken bones. The physical abuse he could take, but it was the psychological trauma that left him permanently scarred. One of Eddie's favorite methods of torturing Animal was to lock him in a dog cage for days at a time without food or water. He would even sometimes bring his junkie friends by to witness the spectacle. Sometimes Animal's mother would try and intervene, but most days she was too high to care or notice that her son was being abused. Many nights, Animal would lay on the floor of the cage, soiled in his own urine and feces, praying for death to come and do something to finally end his suffering. It would be years

Hoodlum II: The Good Son

before death finally came, not as his salvation, but as his guide on the path he now walked.

Animal had finally escaped his abusive home and was now living on the streets. He survived mostly by stealing or at the mercies of others, but it was a hard life, especially for someone as young as him. He tried his hands at drug dealing, which ended up leading to the death of his first true love, a girl named Noki. There was also a period of time when he was taken under the wing of a man called Gladiator, who would teach him the art of murder. Halfway through his education, Gladiator was killed by the police. Not long after, he'd gotten the word that his mother was dying. In addition to giving her a drug habit, Eddie had also given his mother HIV. Everywhere he went, death was present, taking away pieces of his life. It wasn't until Animal hit rock bottom that it finally gave him something in return. This is how he met Tech.

Animal had been out hunting two knuckleheads who were giving him grief on the streets and found them in the process of attempting to rob and kill the young dealer. He and Tech didn't know each other at the time, but their mutual enemies made them allies in the coming battle. In the end, four of them had entered the alley, but only two had come out. In return for saving Tech's life, he took the homeless teen in and given him a warm and safe place to stay. Over time their friendship grew, and Tech would become more of a brother to him than Justice. Though it had been Gladiator who taught Animal how to kill, it was Tech who taught him how to survive.

Next to Justice, Tech was the closest thing to a brother that Animal had. He had pulled him out of the streets and given him a home and a purpose, which is why Animal felt so guilty about the way he had been treating him lately. When he saw him walking into his apartment building earlier that day, Animal wanted to call out to him, but he decided against it. He wanted to embrace his friend and tell him what was going on inside him, but he wasn't quite ready, nor was he sure he could articulate it in a way that would make Tech understand.

Animal and Tech were kindred spirits, yet they were as different as day and night when it came to processing right and wrong deeds. Tech was content to assassinate anyone if the price was right, but not Animal. Death was

Hoodlum II: The Good Son

a gift he bestowed on only those he felt were deserving.
This was a rule he tried to live by, but sometimes there
were unfortunate casualties, and such was the case with
Hannah. He and Tech had come for her grandson, a
degenerate piece of shit who had run afoul of the Clarks
and was sentenced to die. They stalked him to his home,
where a firefight had broken out. Animal had been
gunning for the target, but the old woman had gotten in
the way. She survived the injuries, but not without a cost.
Her life had been spared, but she would spend the rest of
her days living in darkness from the bullet that had taken
her sight. Animal had done quite a bit of dirt in his young
life, but never felt remorse about any of it until Hannah,
and he was having trouble processing it. To Tech, what
happened to the old woman was a little more than
collateral damage, but to Animal, the accident snatched
away what little was left of his innocence. The boy that
he once was had died, and now all that remained was the
monster he was becoming. This is why men like Tommy
Clark called on him to do what others lacked the stomach
for.

With this thought in mind, Animal pulled his hood

tightly over his head and slipped inside the apartment building to deliver his gift.

*

Nicholas Bucco, also known as Nicky the Gent, made it into Manhattan from Belleville, New Jersey in record time. His day ran far longer than expected. He'd set out that morning to make his normal Friday collections of protection money from the various businesses that kicked up to the Meloni family, of which he and his crew were a part of. For the most part, things went smoothly, with everyone paying up. It wasn't until the last stop on his route that things took a turn.

There was a guy named Slick who hustled heroin out in Irvington. He was relatively new on the scene, having taken over the spot after his predecessor was busted. Normally Nicholas didn't have a problem with the black guys in Irvington, but Slick was a different breed. Since he'd taken over, he figured he would change the natural order of things, and tried to buck a system that had been in place for nearly five years. Word around town is that

Hoodlum II: The Good Son

he was telling anyone who would listen that they would
no longer be kicking up to the Italians. Nicholas, being
the gentleman that he was, went to see Slick and tried to
have a civil conversation, but found that he couldn't be
civil with a savage. Slick took one look at Nicholas in his
tailored suit and perfectly combed black hair and took
him as soft, and proceeded to tell him to "Fuck off."
Nicholas did fuck off, but when he came back, he brought
a few friends along. Nicholas detested violence and
avoided it when he could, but when he did engage in it,
he was very, very good at it. They spent the better part of
an hour beating Slick to within an inch of his life. Once
Nicholas felt like the dealer learned his lesson, he pushed
him into early retirement with the business end of his
gun. Nicholas left it for those who remained on the block
to choose a successor. Didn't matter to him who ran the
block, so long as they had his weekly envelope.

Handling the mess with Slick had not only been a
headache, but it had also thrown him off schedule. He
had to drive like a maniac through traffic and had even
gotten a ticket outside the Holland Tunnel, but it had all
been worth it for him to be on time for his standing

Friday appointment in Little Italy.

Nicholas parked the car in a garage near the courthouse and walked the rest of the way. It was a nice night and he could use the exercise. As his wife, Judy, pointed out every time she got a chance, he was putting on a few pounds. She was one to talk, considering she was nowhere near the one-hundred-and-fifty-pound looker he married fifteen years prior. It seemed like the older she got, the more bitter she became, and he was about sick of it. The only reasons that he hadn't left her was because of the kids, the fact that divorce was frowned upon in the secret society (which he was a member of) and the fact that her dad, Big Joe Ragotta, was also the head of the family. Big Joe was very protective of his daughters, and Nicholas reasoned that staying in an unhappy marriage was better than being found in the back of a trunk with a bullet in his head.

Pulling his thoughts away from murder, Nicholas focused on his surroundings. He was a long way from home and moving through the territory of a rival mafia family, the Cissaros. There had always been bad blood between the Cissaros and the Melonis, but things got

Hoodlum II: The Good Son

worse when Gee-Gee took over. Unlike his predecessor, who was content to work hand in hand with the Melonis, Gee-Gee showed no such respect. The Cissaros were a bigger family, so he was always trying to flex his muscle. He'd been stretching Cissaro operations so far out that they'd started to press against the walls of Meloni turf. Nicholas and some of the Capos figured maybe it was time to put the Cissaros in their places, but Big Joe wouldn't give them the go-ahead. Big Joe and Gee Gee were tied up in some big business deals together, and he didn't want to risk it over a street beef. His passive stance when it came to the Cissaros didn't sit well with the Capos, but Big Joe was the boss...at least for the moment.

Regardless of Big Joe's stance on the situation with their cousins on the other side of the Hudson, tensions were still running high. The situation was a powder keg waiting to blow once the right match came along. In an effort to help avoid this, Big Joe had cautioned his men to avoid New York when possible, and be vigilant when not. Nicholas fell into the latter. He refused to stay holed up in New Jersey when something sweeter than the Garden State could offer awaited him. The few who knew about Nicholas' secret weekly trips couldn't understand why he would risk his neck every Friday, especially when there was no money involved, but that was because none of them ever had the pleasure of resting between the legs of Carmela Monroe.

Nicholas first met her six months ago at a birthday party in Scores Gentleman's Club in Midtown. Carmela had been one of the bottle girls working their table. Nicholas took one look at those blue eyes and perky tits and fell head over heels. She made Nicholas chase her for a while before finally giving up the goods, but when she did, it was like he had gone to heaven and was knocking on God's door. Two weeks later, he made her quit her job at Scores and set her up in an apartment in Little Italy. He didn't care what she did during the week, but Fridays were his, and every week like clockwork, she took him to a place of pure bliss.

Just thinking about Carmela's sweet pussy added pep to Nicholas' steps. She lived in a five-story walk-up building off Bowery that he'd gotten the hook-up on because the landlord owed him money. He crossed into the lobby and bounded up the stairs two at a time to the third floor. He didn't have to knock because he had a key, but when he went to put it in the lock he realized that the door was open. Fearing the worst, Nicholas drew his gun before slipping inside the apartment. When he crossed the threshold, what he saw surprised him. Candles lined a pathway made of rose pedals leading into the living room. Taped to the wall was a sign that said "Make Me Hot." A smile crossed Nicholas' face, as he could only imagine what she had in store for him.

He followed the path, and near the kitchen found another sign that read "Warm." Crossing into the living room, he found a bowl of strawberries covered in whip cream with another sign that said "Warmer." He placed his gun down and picked up the bowl, headed to the bedroom. Nicholas had already come out of his suit jacket and kicked off his shoes by the time he made it to the bedroom and finally, the sign that read "Hot."

Nicholas pushed the door open and poked his head inside. The bedroom was just as dark as the rest of the house, only lit by the few candles on the nightstand. In the dim light he could see Carmela's silhouette lying across the bed. Even standing across the room, he could smell the sweetness of whatever she had bathed in. His dick swelled so mightily in his pants that he prayed to the saints that he lasted longer than five minutes.

"All this for me, baby?" Nicholas called out. In response, he could hear Carmela moan, and saw her shift on the bed. He planned to ride her like a buck that was being newly broken, after he tasted every inch of her. Nicholas planned to do all this and then some, but first he needed to see her...to lay eyes on the tight young body he'd been longing for over the last two weeks. When he cut on the bedroom light, Nicholas found himself dumbfounded. On the bed was his beloved Carmela, naked as the day she was born, gagged and bound to the bed. It only took Nicholas' brain a split second to process what was wrong with the picture, but by then it was too late.

"The thing that steals the joy from hunting creatures of habit is that you don't have to track them, because you always know where they're going to be," someone to Nicholas' left said. He turned to see a hooded man sitting on a chair, pointing a gun at him.

"What the hell did you do to Carmela?" Nicholas'

Hoodlum II: The Good Son

eyes darted back and forth between his mistress and the intruder. In the light, he could see the fear-stricken look in her eyes and the bruises on her face. She had been worked over before being tied down.

The man removed his hood, revealing a youthful face and a mop of wild curly hair. When he spoke, you could see the gold covering his teeth. "Considering your position, I'd be more concerned about what I'm going to do to you," Animal said as he stood.

"Listen, kid. I don't know what this is about or who sent you, but you're about to make a huge mistake. Do you know who I am?" Nicholas questioned, hoping his status would give the young man second thoughts.

"Sure do," Animal assured him. "Nicholas Bucco, Capo in the Meloni crime family and general piece of shit."

"So if you know who I am, then you know what happens if you kill a Made man..."

"Yes, I do. Killing you means that's one less child who'll be violated tonight." Animal's eyes went to the young girl he had bound to the bed.

"Child? She's twenty-eight!" Nicholas told him.

"This one might be legal, but what about the rest?" Animal inched forward. "I sometimes wonder how the brains of perverts like you work to where you can find children sexually attractive? Is it a genetic defect, or

some learned behavior that you picked up because someone played in your booty as a kid?" Animal pondered it.

What the young man was trying to insinuate finally clicked in Nicholas' head. He was being set up, and considering where the trap was found, he had a good idea of who was behind it. "I'm no more a pedophile than your black ass is the queen of England. Why don't you put that gun down so we can try and sort this all out." He went to take a step, but was clubbed in the head with the gun. The world exploded in stars as Nicholas hit the floor face-first, dropping the bowl he was carrying and shattering it. Before he could right himself, Animal had a fist full of his hair and was pressing his gun against Nicholas' cheek. "Please," he rasped, "I got kids."

Animal sneered. "That's even more of a reason to end you."

Nicholas could tell by the look of rage that there

Hoodlum II: The Good Son

would be no reasoning with the young man, so logic went out the window and his survival instincts kicked in. The gun went off at the same time Nicholas threw himself backward, ripping a batch of his hair out. The bullet skinned his chin, sending a wave of fire through his face, but he was free. Before Animal could fire another shot, Nicholas charged at him, wielding a piece of the broken glass bowl. Had Animal not beenwearing the oversized hoodie, the glass would've gutted him, instead of just opening a nasty wound across his belly.

Nicholas tackled Animal to the ground, sending the gun flying. Animal tried to shove him off, but the older man was much stronger than him. "You little black bastard!" Nicholas punched Animal in the face. "I've never touched a kid in my life!"

He grabbed Animal about the throat and started bouncing his head off the hardwood floor over and over. Spots started dancing before his eyes and he knew he was about to black out. Animal had many plans when he entered the apartment, but dying wasn't one of them.

Just as the darkness came to swallow him, the grip was released from his throat and Animal gasped for air.

He propped himself on his elbow, and saw Nicholas locked in a struggle with a new opponent. A one-eyed man with a shaved head was behind him, choking Nicholas with what looked like a prayer rosary. Nicholas grasped at his throat but could do nothing to free himself. Within seconds the battle was over, and Nicholas fell limply to the floor.

For a time, Animal and the one-eyed man just stared at each other silently from opposite sides of the room. The one-eyed man studied Animal quizzically as if he was trying to decide what to do with him. Animal cast a glance at his abandoned gun on the floor, weighing whether he could reach it before he met a fate similar to that of Nicholas.' The one-eyed man must have been reading his mind, because he let out an amused chuckle.

"I've seen you in action, and though you're fast, I don't think you're quite that fast. But by all means, try it if you like," the one-eyed man challenged. Animal wisely dropped his hands to his sides. "You're smarter than you look," he said as he stepped from the shadows. It was then that Animal noticed for the first time that the one-eyed man was dressed like a priest. "A closed-casket."

Hoodlum II: The Good Son

"Huh?" Animal was confused by the statement.

"A closed-casket funeral," the one-eyed priest repeated. "Those were the instructions you were given, correct?" He picked Animal's discarded gun up from the floor and examined it. Without warning, the man shot Nicholas twice in the face. "Tommy tends to get a little testy when his instructions aren't carried out to the letter."

Carmela's muffled cries reminded both of them that she was in the room. The one-eyed priest raised the gun to finish her, but Animal stopped him.

"No," Animal blurted out, surprising himself and the priest.

"Friend of yours?" the priest asked curiously.

"Nah, I don't know her. She was just in the wrong place at the wrong time. She ain't gotta die," Animal told him, not totally sure of why he was advocating for the girl.

The priest shook his head. "A witness is a loose end, and if it were up to me I'd kill the bitch, but it's your call." He lowered the gun, much to Animal's relief. "One day that tender heart of yours is going to be your undoing." He went to the window and rested on booted foot on the ledge.

"Wait, why did you help me?" Animal wanted to know.

"Who knows? Maybe I'm just trying to assuage an old man's guilt." Priest tossed the gun in Animal's direction.

Animal took his eyes off the priest for only a second to catch the gun, but it was all the time he needed to disappear. The only things left to mark his passing were Nicholas' dead body and several unanswered questions.

*

It took all of Animal's self-control to keep his steps brisk instead of running like his brain was screaming for him to do when he came out of the building. The sooner he got away from Nicholas' corpse and the crime scene, the better he would feel. Animal was no stranger to dead bodies, but it was the one-eyed priest that had him rattled. The man moved as swiftly and silently as the wind. Watching him kill was like watching an artist paint a

Hoodlum II: The Good Son

beautiful portrait. Animal was almost envious at of the man's skills, and only hoped to be that lethal if he lived long enough to reach adulthood.

Something else that troubled him about the whole situation was Nicholas' response when he was informed of the charges levied against him. He seemed genuinely clueless as to what he was talking about. It's possible that he was lying in an attempt to save his life, but Animal didn't feel like he was. That was a question that would have to wait for a later date. All that was left to do was meet Tommy's guy and pick up his money. Animal was so busy mentally ticking off all the things he would spend his ten grand on that he never noticed the man perched in the window across the street snapping pictures of him.

CHAPTER 20

After they left Daddy's House, Shai let Swann talk him into hitting up a local bar. Shai's good mind told him to take his ass home, but after about twenty-minutes of Swann giving him grief over it, he relented. He told himself that he was only going to have one drink and spend no more than an hour out with the fellas, but a half bottle of tequila and three hours later, he was still perched on the same bar stool.

Just hanging around the bar, drinking and trading war stories was no big deal to Swann, but to Shai it represented the most fun he had in months. Over the last few years, he had spent so much time trying to figure out how to be a good and fair king, that he had forgotten how to be just a regular kid. If only for a few hours it felt good to not be a boss, but just an average twenty-something-year-old getting drunk at a bar.

He looked around the room curiously, watching the people in the spot. The crowd had damn near doubled since from the time they walked in. At a table near the back, he noticed some guys sitting with their girls. One in

Hoodlum II: The Good Son

particular, a brown-skinned girl in a blue dress, was slyly watching Shai for most of the night. He shook his head sadly. Even though she was obviously with someone, she was still checking Shai out. It just went to show how trifling some women were. This made him thankful that he had a good one at home.

"Slim, I'm glad you decided to come out with us tonight," Swann said as he draped his arm around Shai's shoulder. From the way his words were beginning to slur, he was obviously drunk. "I miss this kinda shit."

"Me too," Shai said honestly.

"Yo, from here I'm gonna shoot to this spot in Midtown. My homegirl is the bartender so we can drink for free all night," Swann told him.

Shai looked at his watch. "Nah, it's getting late. I should probably be getting home."

"Shai, it ain't even midnight. Come fuck with me, bro!" Swann tried to convince him.

"Another time, Swann. I'm still in the doghouse for the shit I pulled at the baby shower. Best I get back before it gets too late."

Swann wasn't happy, but he understood. "Aight. I

gotta go take a leak before we jet."

"Cool, I'll meet you outside." Shai slid off the barstool. "I need to get some air before I jump on the road to take that drive back to Jersey."

"I'll be out in a second." Swann staggered off to the bathroom while Shai walked out.

The night air helped to clear some of the fog from Shai's head. He was buzzed but not quite drunk, which is why he decided to quit while he was ahead. The last thing he needed was a DUI on his record. All he wanted to do was get home and snuggle up under his lady. Thinking of Honey made him remember that he hadn't spoken to her since he'd left the house. He'd been so caught up with his boys that it had slipped his mind. He whipped out his cell phone and hit speed dial.

"Oh, so you finally remembered you had a woman at home?" Honey started right in.

"My fault, babe. I was caught up handling business," Shai told her.

"Seems like you're caught up a lot these days," she said with an attitude.

"Look, I didn't call to argue. I was just trying to see if

Hoodlum II: The Good Son

you needed anything when I come in?"

"What I need is my man to start spending more time at home than in the streets, chasing pussy with his dumb ass friends," Honey barked.

"First of all, I ain't chasing no pussy. And second of all, when is the last time I hung out? That pregnancy got you bugging the fuck out lately." Shai was starting to get frustrated. He was having a good night and she was blowing his mood.

"How am I bugging because I want you to be more attentive to me than your friends?" she asked.

As Honey was going in on him, Shai noticed the girl in the blue dress come out of the bar with one of her friends. From the way they were giggling, he could tell they were tipsy. Blue Dress' eyes landed on Shai, and she whispered something to her friend before heading in his direction. He could smell trouble coming.

"You got a light, handsome?" Blue Dress asked. She had a joint pinched between her painted lips.

"Who the fuck was that?" Honey demanded to know on the other end of the phone.

"Nobody...just some girl. I don't know..." Shai tried to

explain.

"Shai, you are so full of shit." She didn't believe him. "You know what, I hope that bitch has got somewhere for you to lay your head tonight, because your ass ain't welcomed here!"

"Honey? Honey?" Shai spoke into the phone, but she had already ended the call. "Fuck!"

"I'm sorry, I didn't mean to get you into trouble." Blue Dress said.

"It ain't your fault." Shai fished a lighter from his pocket and lit the cigarette for her.

"I know you from somewhere, don't I?" Blue Dress exhaled a cloud of smoke.

"Nah, baby. I don't think so."

"I'm pretty sure I do." She studied his face. "Didn't you used to play ball for N.C. State?"

"Yeah, how'd you know?" Shai was surprised.

"I'm an alum; graduated last year," she told him. "Nice to bump into a fellow Wolf." She extended the joint to Shai.

"Nice indeed," he said as he accepted it.

Shai and Blue Dress hadn't even been chatting for two

minutes when the dudes her and her girls had been sitting with came spilling out of the bar. They were drunk and rowdy. The loudest of them was a short, squat dude rocking his hair in cornrows. When he saw that Blue Dress wasn't amongst the girls, a scowl came over his face.

"I think your boyfriend is looking for you," Shai told her.

Blue Dress sucked her teeth. "He ain't my boyfriend, just a nigga who was buying me drinks thinking it would help him get into my panties."

"Still, maybe it's best we part ways." Shai handed her the joint back.

"Yo, what the fuck?" the squat man cursed. Shai had been right when he smelled trouble earlier. "Who this nigga you all over here all cozy with?" he questioned as he walked over.

"Ain't nobody getting cozy, we just talking," Blue Dress said with an attitude.

"I'm in there blowing my cash on drinks and you trying to slide with this nigga?" The squat man was becoming hostile.

"And so what if I was? It's my pussy and I can give it to whoever I want." Blue Dress snaked her neck.

"Dig this, my man - I ain't trying to step on your toes. As a matter of fact, I'm gonna leave y'all to work out your issues." Shai tried to walk off, but Blue Dress grabbed his arm.

"You ain't gotta leave, baby. This nigga is just talking. He ain't gonna do shit," Blue Dress taunted her date.

"Damn, he stole ya bitch, kid!" one of the squat man's friends instigated from the sidelines.

"What? You trying to play me?" the squat man took the bait and got in Shai's face.

"I don't want any trouble." Shai told him.

"Too bad, because you got it," the squat man replied, before punching Shai in the face.

Shai staggered from the blow, with spots dancing in front of his eyes. He touched his hand to his lip and his fingers came away bloody.

"Yeah, pretty boy. Do something!" the squat man challenged. Shai happily accepted.

Shai had never been much of a fighter, but that didn't mean he was incapable of defending himself. He fired off

Hoodlum II: The Good Son

a lightning fast combination, tagging the squat man in his face several times. The squat man tried to retaliate, but Shai moved like the wind, raining blows on his face. The squat man went down, and Shai moved in to finish him off when someone sucker punched him. Instead of a one-on-one fight, it was now a three-on-one. Shai slipped on something and lost his balance, falling on his hands and knees. Before he could get up, the three men were on him, punching and kicking him. Shai thought it was over for him until he heard the unmistakable BOOM of a gun being fired. The attackers hurriedly backed away from Shai, allowing him to regain his wits. When he looked up, he saw Swann holding a smoking pistol.

"You good?" Swann asked Shai.

"Yeah, I'm straight." Shai picked himself up off the ground and assessed the damage. He had a busted lip and his knuckles were scraped, but he was otherwise unharmed.

When Swann saw the blood on Shai, he became irate. "Oh, you niggas is going night-night for this shit!" He drew on the terrified attackers, intending to kill all three of them, but Shai stopped him.

"I said I'm good!" Shai assured him. "Let's just get out of here."

"Only reason niggas talking tough is because they strapped," Shai heard someone mumble as they were walking away, followed by a chorus of snickers. They were only words, but they hit Shai in the back like a physical shove. He had always been Poppa's good son, the one who always turned the other cheek, but he was getting tired of trying to be diplomatic in a society of people who only understood one thing. A storm began to build in Shai's gut and pushed its way into his heart. Without warning, he snatched the gun from Swann and turned back.

"One of y'all got something you need to say?" Shai approached the three men, who were no longer snickering. No one said anything, but the squat man was glaring at Shai like he wanted to keep the issue going. "You a tough guy, huh?"

"You got it." The squat man raised his hands in surrender.

"You know what? I don't want it," Shai said, before cracking him in the head with the gun. When the squat

Hoodlum II: The Good Son

man hit the ground, Shai straddled his chest. "I'm sick of muthafuckas like you thinking shit sweet!" He began hitting him over and over. "I ain't no fucking sucka!" he kept repeating while bashing the squat man in the face. Long after he had stopped moving, Shai continued to hit him.

Swann was on the sidelines laughing at the whole scene. It wasn't until he realized that Shai intended to kill the man that he stepped in. "Aight, that's enough. He's learned his lesson," he said as he pulled Shai off him.

Shai stood over the fallen man, chest heaving and heart full of rage, the squat man's smug face now a mess of bruises and blood. Though he was no longer moving, Shai still wanted to keep pummeling him. Shai had never lost control like that, and much to his surprise, it felt good. He could have very well killed the man and doubted he'd have lost a wink of sleep over it. Something about this unexplored side of his brain he'd just tapped into filled him with something that made his heart swell with a feeling that strangely felt like joy. He turned to Blue Dress, and the look of adoration she'd been giving him earlier was gone, replaced by one of fear.

"Come on before we catch a case." Swann pulled Shai down the block towards where the car was parked. "What was that all about?" he asked when they reached the Lexus.

"Nothing," Shai said, hitting the door locks. "That was more than nothing, Shai. You checked out back there."

"Them fools tried to kick my ass, what the fuck was I supposed to do?" Shai snapped.

Swann raised his hands in surrender. "Hey man, I ain't complaining. I'm just a little shocked, that's all."

"Sometimes you just gotta get it out of your system," Shai said, opening the driver's side door. "I'm sorry for fucking the night up."

"You didn't fuck it up, Slim, just made it more interesting. So what's up, we gonna keep the party going or what? We still got time to catch my homegirl's spot downtown."

"Nah, I don't too much feel like it. I'm gonna go for a drive and clear my head," Shai told him.

"You need me to roll with you?" Swann asked.

"I'm cool. Do ya thing. You need me to drop you off at your car?" Shai slid behind the wheel.

Hoodlum II: The Good Son

"Nah, I'm too drunk to be driving all the way back from Jersey. I'll jump in a cab and pick my whip up in the morning. Call me when you get home." Swann tapped the hood of the car.

*

Shai rode around New York for a while, windows down and music blasting. He wasn't sure where he was headed, but he felt like he just had to keep moving. All the adrenaline from the fight had burned through the alcohol, so he wasn't drunk anymore; just wired and frustrated. He thought about going home, then remembered that Honey was on some bullshit. The last thing he needed was to walk into her bullshit after all he'd been through, so he just kept coasting until a better idea struck him.

He pulled over at a bodega and hopped out to get a bottle of water, and as he was patting his pockets for his money, he came across Monet's business card.

PART IV
"DIRTY TRUTHS"

CHAPTER 21

Bustelos was a coffee house on the Upper East Side of Manhattan that was so non-descript, you'd likely miss it unless someone pointed it out. Unlike some of the more modern places that were popping up all over the city, they kept their menu simple - coffee, espresso and pastries. It wasn't the most inviting establishment, yet its doors had managed to remain open for the past ten years. Bustelos flew under the radar, and the people who frequented it most preferred it that way. If you tried to search for the owner of Bustelos on paper, you'd find yourself chasing your tail through a bunch of shell companies and probably still couldn't say for sure who held the deed.

There weren't many people in the coffee shop, save for some of its regulars and the two yuppie-looking guys, wearing sports coats and jeans that didn't quite hit their ankles over designer sneakers. They were unfamiliar faces, which meant they were either cops or had just wandered into the wrong spot to get their dose of

Hoodlum II: The Good Son

caffeine.

The old man behind the counter taking orders was a surely-looking character, with thinning white hair and hateful eyes that hid behind thick black glasses. He looked the two backpackers up and down as if they were hobos who just wandered in to beg for some change.

The tallest of the two pranced up to the counter and flashed his sixty-thousand dollar grin. "Two Cinnamon Dolce light fraps," he said in a tone that seemed to irk the old timer.

"Two what?" the old man asked in his thick New York accent.

The yuppies exchanged glances.

"Coffee, ya know? A little syrup, cinnamon," the second yuppie explained as if the old man was an imbecile. "And only two-percent. Whole milk doesn't agree with my stomach," he added for good measure.

"Does this look like Paris to you?" the old man grumbled.

"Excuse me?" The first yuppie was confused.

The old man rested his withered knuckles on the

counter. "Yous two seem like educated fellas, so how come you didn't read the sign?" he said, nodding at the white poster-board sitting in the window that read "Coffee & Snacks." "See a frap or any other of that sissy shit you just asked for on my menu?"

"There's no need to be an asshole about it!" the second yuppie snapped, clearly taking offense at the statement.

"And I'll bet yous know a thing or three about assholes, huh?" the old man taunted.

Before the argument could go any further, the yuppies noticed all of the light shining through the front window. They initially thought it was overcast, but when they turned toward it, they saw that it wasn't a shift in the weather, but a man. He stood a hair over six feet tall, and weighing at least four hundred pounds. His jogging suit looked like it was stitched together from pieces of a tent. High black hair sat on his sloped forehead, so slick with gel that it resembled a polished tile floor.

"Problem here, Sally?" Jimmy the Whale asked, glaring at the two yuppies. Clutched in his meaty fist was

Hoodlum II: The Good Son

a fiber bar that he desperately wished was a piece of fried chicken. The doctors told him he needed to lose some weight, but it was a struggle.

"I was just explaining the menu to our whimsical friends here," Sal said with a devilish grin.

The second yuppie pursed his angry lips to fire off a nasty retort, but the first yuppie touched his arm and gave him pause. "C'mon, I think there's a Starbucks two blocks from here," he said as he tugged at his friend's arm.

The second yuppie gave Sal one last dirty look before allowing his friend to nudge him towards the door. As an afterthought, he knocked down the poster board sign and flipped Sal the bird. "Eat shit you fucking homophobe!" he spat before running out the door.

"Beat it, you damn fairies!" Sal yelled, tossing a sugar shaker at the door.

"How do you expect this shithole to make any money if you keep chasing the customers away?" Jimmy asked.

"I don't chase all the customers away, just the undesirables," Sal capped.

The front door opened again, and both men's heads turned, thinking the yuppies might have found their balls and came back. In walked three men, laughing heartily as if one of them had just told the funniest joke in the world. They barely made it across the threshold before Jimmy moved to intercept them.

"Hey Jim, what's the word?" Mel greeted him with a smile.

"It's Jimmy, you smart ass. What are you hoods doing on this side of town - looking for a liquor store to knock over?" Jimmy glared at him. He didn't care for Mel and made no secret of it. Jimmy was old-school and from an era where rules meant something, while Mel represented the new age Mafiosos who didn't care whose toes they had to step on to get ahead.

Mel found himself at a loss, not quite sure how to reply to the hostile reception. Thankfully Louie cut the tension.

"He's only busting your balls, Mel," Louie said as he stepped forward and shook Jimmy's hand. "Why you always rousting my guys, huh?"

Hoodlum II: The Good Son

"He looked like he was ready to shit his pants!"
Jimmy laughed, slapping Louie on the back good-
naturedly.

Mel didn't say anything, but inwardly he fumed. It
seemed like every time he was in Jimmy's company, the
big man was mocking him for laughs or saying
something disrespectful. Had it been anyone else, Mel
would have put a bullet, or at least a fist, in Jimmy's
mouth by now. But Jimmy the Whale was a Made man,
and until that changed, he had no choice but to suck it up.
Mel hoped that if he played Frankie close for long
enough, his reckoning with Jimmy would come sooner
than later.

"I'm here to see Frankie," Louie said, getting back to
business.

Jimmy looked over his shoulder at a man who was
occupying a table in the back, pretending to read the
paper, but had been watching the whole exchange. Sitting
next to him was a woman dressed in all black. The man
told Jimmy that it was okay to let them pass. With a
smile, Louie started forward, but was stopped by the

Whale for a second time.

"You know the routine." Jimmy motioned for Louie to raise his hands to be searched. Louie complied. Jimmy kept his searches of Louie and Bruno brief, but took his time when it came to Mel. He patted under his arms, his legs and gave him a light shot to the nuts before letting him join his companions.

"You guys hang out over here at the counter while I straighten this out," Louie told his buddies before crossing the room to pay his respects to the Cissaro Capo.

Franklin Donatello, known as Frankie the Fish to his friends, did not fit any stereotypes of a typical mobster. He was tall and well-built with a head full of beautiful black hair, and had a smile that could light up a room. In secret, some joked that he looked more like a model than a gangster, but they wouldn't dare say it to his face, even in jest. He had gotten the name "The Fish" for his fondness of dumping the bodies of his victims in the ocean to feed the things that dwelled beneath the water. Despite his dashing good looks, Frankie was a stone-cold killer.

Hoodlum II: The Good Son

"Well, if it isn't my favorite of the three stooges," Frankie said as he flashed his signature smile. He folded his newspaper and placed it on the table.

"How you doing, Frankie?" Louie shook his hand, then kissed him once on each cheek.

"That all depends on what news you've brought me." Frankie motioned for Louie to take the chair across from him. "So, did you take care of that thing?" He noticed that Louie was hesitant to speak in front of the woman.

"Yeah, we took care of it. The ball is in play," Louie said proudly.

"Good," Frankie nodded in approval. "How did the kid take it? Did he balk, or jump at the chance to give Gee-Gee a hand-job?"

Louie fell silent. His face said he wanted to say something, but couldn't figure out how to word it. "What?" Frankie pressed.

"That's the thing," Louie began timidly, "I didn't speak to Shai. He wasn't available, so I sat down with Tommy."

Frankie couldn't hide the surprise on his face.

"Tommy Clark? Last I heard, ain't he a vegetable or some shit?"

"A vegetable with a set of nuts you wouldn't believe," Louie said. "You should've heard the way that jig was talking. You'd think he'd taken the oath or something."

"I asked you to present this to Shai specifically."

"I know, Frankie, and trust me I tried, but the kid wasn't available. He got called away on some urgent matter right before we got there," Louie explained. "You said it was important that this get done, so I figure it was better to broker it with the gimp rather than having to come back to you with nothing. I'm sorry."

"Indeed you are, but what's done is done at this point," Frankie said, sliding a large envelope from the folds of the newspaper.

"Frankie, can I ask you a question?"

"Sure, Louie. What's on that tiny little mind of yours?"

"Well, I didn't know Nicky too good, but near as I can tell he was a stand-up guy. I never would've figured him for a child molester." Louie said.

Hoodlum II: The Good Son

"That's because he wasn't," the woman spoke for the first time.

Seeing that Louie looked totally confused, Frankie decided to enlighten him. "Louie, I'd like to introduce you to a friend of mine, Constance Tessio."

Louie's face turned as white as a ghost when he heard the name of Fat Mike's widow.

"Maybe now you understand why it was so important for Shai to greenlight this assassination personally? When the shit hits the fan and the Melonis come across the water to claim their pound of flesh, it's taken out of Clarks' asses and not ours."

"But why would Gee-Gee..." Louie began, but stopped short when all the pieces fell into place. "This was never a favor for Gee-Gee, was it?"

Frankie didn't have to answer. The triumphant smirk on his face said it all.

Two quick chirping sounds to his rear caused Louie to spin in his chair. He was just in time to see both Bruno and Mel fall to the ground with gaping holes in their heads. Standing over them was a tanned young man with slick black hair. In both his gloved hands he held two smoking Berettas. Without bothering to even look at the bodies, he hit them twice more before continuing towards the table they were sitting at. Louie's brain told him to run, but the fear that gripped his heart wouldn't let him. The young man loomed over him like a storm cloud, both guns pressed to the top of his head.

"Right on time as always, Enzo," Frankie greeted the killer.

Louie swallowed. The only part of his body he dared move were his eyes. "Frankie, what the hell is this all about?"

Frankie took his time pulling photos from the envelope and placing them on the table in front of the shocked Louie. In the pictures was a wild-haired man coming out of the building where Nicky was killed. "Restoring the natural order of things."

CHAPTER 22

When Shai woke up the next morning, he felt like he died twice. His head was spinning and damn near every muscle in his body ached. He figured that was the price he had to pay for spending his night boozing and brawling, and some other things he wasn't quite sure where to classify just yet.

Instinctively, he reached over to the other side of the bed and found it was empty. He looked over at the clock and saw it was already passed noon. Honey was likely up and about her day already, which was fine by him. This would give him enough time to think up a good excuse as to why he hadn't made it home until just before sun up. Shai was generally very honest with Honey about his comings and goings, but this was one of those situations where the truth just wouldn't do… unless he wanted to get his head knocked off.

He wasn't exactly sure why he had dialed Lady Monet's number that night, or what he would say to her when she picked up. There was a part of him that hoped

she wouldn't, but she did. She didn't seem
surprised that Shai had called, or at least that's how she
came off. She told him that she and some friends were in
the city getting drinks and invited him to come and join
them. Still not ready to go home and having nothing
better to do, Shai agreed. And this is when his night
really got interesting.

When he'd arrived at the address Monet had given
him, he'd expected it to be a bar or restaurant, but instead
it was a strip club. It wasn't hard to find her once he got
inside. She was sitting at a table in the corner, tossing
dollars at a big-booty dancer while the other girls from
her group, Genie and Lisa, cheered her on. When she
spotted Shai, she dismissed the fifty-inch ass that was in
her face and waved him over.

"Well, well, if it isn't Mr. Chicken Grease," Monet
greeted him. "Glad you could make it."

"I ain't staying long. Just figured I'd pop through to
get a drink and see what's up with you," Shai said coolly.

"As you can see, everything is up on this side."

Monet tossed some singles in the air and watched the

strippers who had been circling her table scramble for them. From the glassy look in her eyes, Shai could tell she was tipsy. "Well don't just stand there looking like a love-struck puppy! Sit your fine ass down," she said, patting the seat next to her. "What you drinking? It's on me tonight," she told him once he was seated.

"Oh, you rolling like that, huh?" Shai asked.

"It ain't on me, it's on Big Dawg," Monet replied as she flashed the company credit card.

"In that case, I'll take a shot of Henny."

"Yo ma," Monet grabbed a passing waitress, "bring us a bottle of Henny, and some more ice. Don't take all day this time!" she ordered as she slapped the waitress on the ass.

"You wild shorty," Shai laughed at her antics.

"So says the man with blood on his shirt." She poked him in the chest. "What's that all about?"

"Nothing," Shai said, noticing the blood for the first time. "My night just started out really rough."

"Well, I hope you checked your troubles at the door. From here on out, nothing but good vibes," Monet promised, and she was right.

Monet's girls hung around until about 1A.M. before calling it a night, leaving Shai and Monet to continue the festivities. They smoked, drank and slapped asses all through the night. Monet was way more fun than he expected her to be, and after a while, he had forgotten about the fight with the dudes outside the bar and his argument with Honey, and was totally focused on her. The club shut down at about 3A.M., but neither of them wanted to go home, so they drove up the West Side Highway and parked in a little cove off of 96th street that gave them a view of the Hudson. Shai rolled up some more weed and the two of them sat and talked, getting to know each other better.

Monet's story was just as interesting as her personality. She was the product of a black mother who worked as a maid, and her white employer, who was involved in all sorts of criminal activities. Eventually the man's wife found out about her husband's indiscretions and fired Monet's mother. Her dad could never claim Monet openly due to the closed-minded circles he ran in

Hoodlum II: The Good Son

and the scandal it would create for his family, but he remained in her life as best he could. He sent money every month faithfully, and even visited a few times per year. Things changed a few years ago when her father was killed in a car accident. With the checks no longer coming, things got tight for Monet and her mother so the young girl had to take it to the streets to help make ends meet. Monet dabbled in different hustles, but after getting arrested for possession, she decided the life wasn't for her, so she turned to what she was passionate about - singing. Monet started doing shit gigs in bars, lounges and even street corners when she had to; anything to help keep food on the table. This was how she was discovered by Don B., and her life would be forever changed.

Shai was almost moved to tears by the end of Monet's story. He knew better than most what it was like to carry that kind of weight on your shoulders at such a young age. That night he felt closer to Monet than he had any other woman, even Honey. He couldn't say that he was in love with Lady Monet, but he felt her on a different level.

At some point, they must have fallen sleep in the car.

Shai was awakened by a cop tapping on his window. He looked for Monet, but there was no sign of her. She had vanished, leaving him to wonder if it had been real or all a dream?

*

Shai pulled himself out of bed and stood. His legs were shaky and his stomach lurched, but he was functional, which was the best he could ask for. It took him roughly a half hour to shower and dress to tackle what was sure to be an incredibly long day. The prior night he had spent with Monet, watching her move, left him feeling inspired. Their talk had also put several things into perspective that he had been on the fence about. It was time for him to boss up, and put his house in order.

His first call was to Sol to have him set some things in motion that would grease the wheels of fate. Next he got their lawyer, Scotty, on the line. He was more skeptical of Shai's plan than Sol had been, but reluctantly agreed to do as he was asked. Last but not least, he had Angelo go out and meet with Chance King. The message would be short, sweet and to the point.

The dominos had fallen, and now all that was left for Shai to do was sit back and watch how they fell.

On his way out of the bedroom, he snatched his pants off the floor and proceeded to empty his pockets. There wasn't much in there except his wallet, some loose weed flakes and a wad of singles he had totally forgotten about. He shoved them in the pocket of the pants he was wearing, making a note to swap them out for some tens and twenties when he passed a store. Honey would take one look at the loose bills and know he'd been in the strip club. It wasn't that she forbade Shai from going to strip clubs, but she wasn't exactly a big fan of the outings either, and he could always expect some type of grief on those rare occasions he did go. This was no doubt due to how they'd met.

When Honey and Shai first hooked up, she was still dancing among, among other things he cared not to speculate on. In the beginning, neither of them expected the relationship to get serious. They were just having fun with each other, but as Shai began to peel back the layers and see more than just a fine ass dancer, he fell hopelessly in love with the person he discovered underneath it all. He plucked her from her from the hustle and made a square of her, and Honey secretly feared that history would repeat itself. The girls he tossed money at and occasionally fucked were fun and nothing more, but from time to time he did have moments of weakness, such as what happened during his night with Monet. They hadn't done anything more than talk, but he still felt guilty about it; probably because he wanted to do more. Had she not vanished, there was no telling how far he would have gone with the girl. He was weak for her, and that rattled him. This had him now more determined to take the meeting with Don B.; not because he wanted to finish what he started, but because he needed some type of closure.

According to Devil, Don B. was trying to add owning a franchise of nightclubs to his already-extensive resume. He had Code Red up and running, which was quickly

Hoodlum II: The Good Son

becoming a hot spot for the younger hip-hop crowd. Don B., being a visionary, saw the potential profit in monopolizing on that success and wanted to spread his wings. Opening one club and getting it running smoothly was one thing, but creating

a franchise was an animal Don B. wasn't prepared to handle; at least not on his own. The outline of the plan was supposed to be enough to wet his beak, but if Shai wanted to hear the rest, it would have to be in person at the memorial celebration. By agreeing to attend, Shai could kill two birds with one stone; hearing Don B's proposal and seeing Monet again. If for nothing else, he needed to see if the hold she had on him was real or a lapse in judgment

Shai finally made his way downstairs, and found the house surprisingly still for that hour of the day. He rolled towards the kitchen, stomach growling and starving, and ready to grub. He was sure he had slept though breakfast, but by then Elsa should have been preparing lunch. He pushed through the double doors, expecting his nose to be greeted by the smell of whatever was on the lunch menu.

To his surprise, there was nothing but the scent of Pine and dish soap. The kitchen was sparkling as if it had just been wiped down, and there were no signs of his staff or his family.

He walked through the first floor, peeking inside different rooms for signs of life, but found none. As he crossed the living room en route to his man cave, Shai picked up on the sounds of muffled whispers coming from behind the door. He immediately thought the worst. What if someone breached the estate's defenses and the place was under siege?

He tapped on the edge of the fireplace, exposing a hidden panel on the side and the small gun hidden inside. Now armed, Shai stormed into his Man Cave. What he saw made his jaw drop; the mystery of the missing maid had been solved. Elsa was inside Shai's private room, bent over his pool table with her uniform skirt hiked up. Behind her, pumping away like a dog in heat, was Swann.

"What the fuck?" Shai's voice startled them.

Elsa's head whipped around so fast it was a wonder it

Hoodlum II: The Good Son

didn't fall off her shoulders. "Mr. Clark!" she hurriedly
pushed her skirt down. Her yellow face was now a deep
shade of red from embarrassment.

"I pay you to wax my floors, not my homies!" Shai
snarled.

"Mr. Clark, I...I... "

"Yo, don't say shit. Just go get yourself together
before Star sees you," Shai dismissed her. He turned to
Swann, who was sitting on the edge of the pool table,
fixing his pants with an amused look on his face. "Please
tell me what the fuck is funny about this?"

"I seen your face when you walked in. I wasn't sure if
you were gonna knock her head off, or join in," Swann
laughed. "But it ain't her fault, Slim. I conned her into
giving me a quickie. After all you went through last
night, I figured it'd be at least another hour before you
rose from the dead."

"What do you mean by that?" Shai asked defensively,
wondering if Swann knew about his secret rendezvous.

"The scuffle, remember? Man, I still think you
should've let me blast on them niggas," Swann told him.

"Nah, one murder is hard enough to clean up. Three would've been too much of a headache. Now getting back to the subject at hand, where's your sense of respect? You know how crazy that shit would've made both of you look if Honey had caught you?"

"Relax, Slim; Honey been gone since this morning. Elsa told me before I deflowered her," Swann told him.

"Where'd she go?"

"Does it look like I bothered to ask? Say, man, I hope you don't plan on firing shorty. She got a way better shot of pussy than the girl you had decorate this place," Swann boasted.

"Swann, how many of my employees have you fucked on my furniture?"

Swann held up his right hand as if he was being sworn in. "I refuse to answer that question on the grounds that it may incriminate me further."

"Fucking dick!" Shai laughed.

"On another note, I got something that you might not find so funny. You read the paper today?" Swann grabbed the copy he'd brought in with him from the pool

Hoodlum II: The Good Son

table and handed it to Shai.

Shai scanned the headline on the page Swann had folded over. "Mafioso Found Murdered..." Shai continued to read the article that detailed the execution-style killing of Nicholas "Nicky The Gent" Bucco, Capo in the Meloni crime family. "Damn, they strangled and shot him? That sounds more like a hate crime than an execution."

"Tell me about it. I heard they had to identify him by his prints and dental records," Swann recalled what his informant at the department told him.

"A tragedy to be sure, but why should I give a shit that some guinea got his wig split?" Shai tossed the newspaper back onto the pool table. "We didn't clip him, nor are we involved with any business deals with the Melonis."

"But we're in bed with the Cissaros," Swann pointed out. Seeing that Shai still wasn't following his line of thinking, he elaborated. "Nicky was killed on Cissaro turf. There's already been tensions brewing between their two families and having Big Joe's son-in-law turn up

323

dead in their backyard is likely gonna kick off a very nasty war. The blow-back is going to be serious, and it could hit us smack in the face because of our relationship with the Cissaros."

Shai hadn't thought about it like that. "Hit Angelo and Big Doc. Have them put the soldiers on yellow alert just to be on the safe side."

"Two steps ahead of you. I did that as soon as I found out what happened. Everybody from the corner boys to the street bosses will be armed at all times. If them Jersey wops so much as take a piss in Harlem, we're cutting their dicks off," Swann assured him.

"That's why you're the eyes in back of my head," Shai said as he patted Swann on the shoulder reassuringly. "Now let's get our day started. It's gonna be a long one," he said, and headed out of the Man Cave.

"Shai," Swann said as he fell in step behind him, "in light of this new development, maybe we should cancel that thing with Don B. later. Until we find out exactly where everyone stands with this Nicky murder, maybe having you in a club full of gangsters isn't such a good

Hoodlum II: The Good Son

idea."

"That's all the more reason for us to take this meeting with Don B.," Shai said, much to Swann's surprise. "Wars are time and money. If this thing goes down with the Melonis, the Cissaros are going to have their hands too full with survival to concentrate on our business interests. We need to start exploring alternative avenues of income to offset those losses."

"And you think investing with Don B. is going to be the difference maker?" Swann asked suspiciously.

Shai shrugged. "Never hurts to hear him out."

Swann still wasn't convinced. "Shai, please tell me this ain't about that broad."

"C'mon, Swann, you know me better than that." "I do, which is why I asked," Swann shot back. "Did you check on that thing with our guy in N.C.?"

Shai changed the subject.

"Yeah, the truck left Charlotte this morning and should make it to Port Amboy sometime tonight where Big Doc and a few of the boys will liberate the driver of his goods. You know, I gotta admit that when you first came up with the idea of jacking cigarette trucks, I thought it would be a waste of time, but I was wrong. We're making damn near as much money off tobacco as we do drugs."

"Everybody smokes, baby boy," Shai said with a wink.

"You be sure to tell Big Doc to check and double check the details. I got something else lined up and I can only make the play in cash," Shai told him before heading out of the room.

"So what's the plan for the day, boss?" Swann fell in step behind him. "I know you didn't have me come out here two days in a row at the crack of dawn for nothing."

"Of course not. We've got places to go and people to see. Today is the day we set the wheels in motion to usher this family into a new era," Shai said proudly. He was about to elaborate further, when something in the window caught his attention. Shai moved closer and peered out. Hope was out on the front lawn, but she wasn't alone. There was a young man snapping pictures, while she struck various poses. Upon closer inspection,

Hoodlum II: The Good Son

Shai realized that he recognized the photographer.

"I swear if this girl ain't got the hardest fucking head," he huffed before storming out the front door.

*

When Hope saw Shai come out of the house, she cut her photo shoot short and moved to intercept him before he could reach her guest. "Shai..." she began, but she was cut off.

"Shai shit! Didn't we go over this yesterday?" Shai looked passed her at Snake, who was standing there looking awkward.

"You said don't bring him to the house, and I didn't. We're on the lawn," Hope tried to joke, but Shai wasn't in joking mood.

"Don't be cute, Hope. You graduated at the top of your class, so I know you ain't stupid, even though your actions say otherwise."

"Hey, Shai..." Snake tried to interject.

"That's Mr. Clark to you, lil' nigga!" Shai said

327

sharply. "Now the only reasons I can see you coming back around here after my brother told you to stay away is you're plum fucking stupid, or you really don't understand what kind of family your little girlfriend comes from."

Snake tensed as Swann moved forward. It wasn't a hostile gesture, but he planted himself close enough into the young man's space that he had a clear shot of his jaw. Snake ignored Swann and spoke directly to Shai.

"I know who you are, Mr. Clark, and that's the reason I came back. I owe you an apology for yesterday. Not because I'm trying to score points, but because as someone who claims to care about your little sister, I shouldn't have let her get that drunk, let alone brought her to the baby shower in that condition. Still, I don't think one lapse in judgment gives you or anyone else the right to treat me like shit whenever I come around. As a man, I can't accept that," he said with a straight face.

"Well, I guess you just volunteered yourself for the first broken jaw of the day." Swann stepped forward, but Shai stopped him.

Hoodlum II: The Good Son

"I got this," Shai ensured him, eyes locked on Snake. "Take Hope with you."

"Wait a second! Let me talk to you, Shai," Hope tried to intervene, but Swann placed a firm arm around her waist.

"Let the grown folks talk, sweetie. C'mon, I'll show you the secret stash of weed Tommy doesn't know that I know he's growing around the back," Swann said as he steered her away from the confrontation.

"Your mama drop you on your head or something when you were a kid?" Shai asked him seriously.

Snake chuckled. "Nah, man. I just ain't never been big on holding my tongue. I know you don't know anything about me and I understand why you and your brother are dealing with me from a distance, but honestly I ain't trying to get close to you or anything you got going on. I'm just trying to get to know Hope a little better. I hope you don't feel like I'm being out of line, but I got too much respect for your family name to be anything but straight up with you."

Shai measured the young man's words. He still didn't like Snake, but respected his honesty. "My sister is a good kid and on the right track, and the last thing I need is somebody else's bad habits rubbing off on her and derailing this life we've laid out."

"Mr. Clark, I don't drink and I only smoke once in a blue. I'm a second-year accounting major, with a 3.6 GPA, who likes to take pictures of pretty things," he said, hoisting the camera for Shai to see. "I ain't nothing to worry about."

"That remains to be seen, but until such time, just know that I've got my eye on you."

Snake gave him a smug grin. "I wouldn't expect anything less."

*

Shai rolled back around to the front of the house to find Swann and Hope having a heated debate. When she spotted Shai walking up alone, a look of dread crossed her face. She breathed a deep sigh of relief when she finally noticed Snake bringing up the rear. She rushed passed her brother and hugged Snake tightly.

"Damn, Hope. What did you think I was going to kill him and burry him in the yard?" Shai asked sarcastically.

"Wouldn't be the first time," Hope mumbled. "Watch that shit," Swann warned.

"Look, I'm gonna leave you good people to it and take my ass back to the city," Snake announced.

"What?" Hope was surprised. "I thought we were gonna have lunch today?"

"I know, and I'm sorry to disappoint you, ma, but I think it's best for all parties involved if I take a rain check," Snake said as he cut his eyes at Shai. "I'll call you later." He kissed Hope on the cheek and walked towards his bike, which was near the foot of the driveway.

"You be careful riding that thing on the highway! I'd hate to hear you mysteriously got hit by a truck!" Swann called after him mockingly.

Hope stood there, watching sadly as Snake rode off. When she turned back to Shai she was furious. "Are you happy now? You ran him off!"

"Hope, I did you a favor. You're lucky it was me instead of Tommy, because he doesn't make it a practice to warn people about shit twice," Shai told her.

"Amen to that." Swann added.

"You mind your business, Swann! And Shai, I keep telling you and your asshole brother that I'm not a little girl anymore. I can make my own decisions!"

"Then make them wisely," Shai replied. "Hope, I don't know why you're so head-over-heels for this slum ass nigga, but you need to knock it off. Now I'm not judging Snake, because I don't know him well enough to form an opinion about his character, but I know he's not right for my sister. You represent the Clarks, and anybody you choose to lay with is a reflection on this family."

"So says the man who wife'd a stripper!" Hope snapped. The words were sharp, but she was angry and emotional.

"Hope, you're about to cross a line," Swann warned her, seeing where the argument was headed.

Hoodlum II: The Good Son

"Nah, this conversation is long overdue," Shai said. "Let me tell you something, little miss. I'm about sick of you running around with your nose in the air, like you're better than everybody else in this family. You always got some slick shit to say about what and how I do things, but I didn't see you balking when I paid the whole four years of your tuition in advance, nor do I recall you returning any of those checks I send you once per month so you can stunt with your dizzy ass friends."

"You know what? Fuck you and this!" Hope rolled her eyes and tried to walk away, but Shai grabbed her arm. When she looked into his eyes she saw something that she had never seen in them before: rage.

"You ungrateful little bitch, how dare you give me your back!" Shai rained spittle in her face. "Do you have any idea what I had to sacrifice to keep this family together when they killed Daddy? I live every day of my life as a walking target and an indictment waiting to come down, and I do it with a smile because I love my family, even if they're too damn dumb to realize it!" Tears danced in the corner of his eyes. "Hope, I understand that

333

you don't like some of the decisions I make, just like I didn't like some of the stuff Daddy did, but you have to understand that I do these things from a place of love. I don't want you pissing away your formative years and end up having to play whatever life has left to offer you."

"You mean like you did?" Hope jerked loose of his grip. "Shai, we might share the same genes, but we are nothing alike." She stormed back into the house. Shai attempted to go after her, but Swann stopped him.

"Let her be, Slim. Give her some space and revisit the conversation when cooler heads can prevail," Swann told him.

Shai's shoulders sagged like he was carrying the weight of the world on them. "I just want Hope to have a shot at being something better in life, Swann. Why doesn't she understand that?"

"They never do until it's too late."

*

Shai and Swann were just about to pull out when they

Hoodlum II: The Good Son

saw Honey's SUV turn into the driveway. Brutus got out from behind the wheel, dressed in his black suit. He gave a nod in greeting to Shai and Swann, before walking around to the passenger's side to help Honey out. Shai took one look at her face and knew that he was about to deal with another angry woman.

"Give me a sec," Shai told Swann, before walking to meet Honey. "Sup, babe?" he asked as he kissed her. Her lips were flat and passionless. "Damn, who kicked your dog?"

"Nobody, I'm just tired. I've been running around all morning and I need a nap," Honey told him.

"Yeah, I see you were up and out early. Where you been, Penny?" Shai did his best Chip Fields impersonation.

"In Woodlawn. I had Brutus take me to the gun range."

The revelation stole the mirth from Shai's voice. "What you need to go to the range for? I pay Brutus to catch the bodies."

"I know, and Brutus is exceptional at his job, but there

may come a point when he's not around and I gotta
handle a situation on my own."

From the tone of her voice, Shai knew there was
something she wasn't saying.

"Honey, what's going on?" Shai asked. She looked to
Brutus as if she was waiting for him to give her the
greenlight to answer. "What the fuck are you looking at
him for when I'm the one talking to you?"

"Your cousin Hammer paid us a visit," Brutus
answered for her.

"What? When? What did that nigga do to you?" Shai
fired off questions.

"He didn't do anything. We were at the mall shopping
and he showed up at the store we were in. He told me to
tell you that it was urgent that the two of you spoke," she
said, replaying the conversation between her and
Hammer.

"I'm gonna kill that nigga!" Shai began pacing back
and forth.

"Shai, it wasn't that serious. He wasn't rude or
threatening; just a little creepy," Honey explained.

Hoodlum II: The Good Son

"And where were you when this bitch ass nigga was having my woman play messenger?" Shai spun on Brutus.

"I sent him to get coffee," Honey answered for him.

"Coffee? Nigga, do I pay you to get coffee or keep my wife safe?" Shai was angry.

"Shai, I was only gone for five minutes," Brutus explained.

"And it only takes half a second to pull a trigger!" Shai shot back. He invaded Brutus' space. "Let me tell you something, and please be clear on this; you've got one job and that's to keep Honey out of harm's way. Now if you don't feel like you're capable of doing that, speak now and I'll get a more qualified soldier to replace you. Do you understand me?"

Brutus didn't trust himself to speak for fear of what might have come out of his mouth, so he simply nodded.

"Don't blame him because the men in your gangster ass family don't know their places. Maybe if you hadn't been so busy with your new little friend, I wouldn't have had to depend on the next man." Honey pulled Monet's business card from her purse and flicked it at Shai.

Shai was stunned and his face said it.

"Honey, it isn't what you think," he said honestly.

"Oh, that's painfully obvious. You just can't keep your dick from straying can you? This shit with you is getting old, Shai...real old. The bitches, the late nights," she shook her head. "I don't even know why I continue to get mad at you. A leopard never changes its spots. I knew you was a dog when I got with you, but I chose to stay. That's my fault, but I got a trick for your slick ass, Slim."

"And what's that supposed to mean?"

"You'll find out right after I drop my load," Honey said slyly, and started towards the house.

Shai grabbed her by the arm and spun her to face him. "Don't walk away from me when I'm talking to you!"

"Get your fucking hands off me!" Honey yelled as she jerked loose of his grip. "While you out here trying to get all buster bad ass on me, you need to put some of that same aggression into them niggas who are in the streets pissing on your name like you soft. On his worst day, a nigga would have never had the balls to get next to

Hoodlum II: The Good Son

anything Tommy Clark held dear, but I forgot - you ain't
Tommy, you the little brother!" Honey had only been
talking shit to get under Shai's skin, but she wasn't ready
for what would happen next.

"What the fuck did you just say to me?" Shai's voice
was calm...too calm.

"What? You got some frog in you?" She pressed,
seeing that she now had his attention. "Jump, lil' nigga. I
dare you."

Shai took her up on her offer. He reached for her, not
quite sure what his intentions were. Honey wisely moved
back, but when she did, her feet got crossed up and she
fell hard to the concrete. Quicker than she
should have been able to move in her condition,
Honey was back up and on Shai's ass like a wild woman.

"Nigga, you think I'm soft?" she questioned as she
started raining punches on him.

"Honey, chill out!" Shai tried to restrain her, but she
was too far gone. She managed to get one hand free and
clocked him in the lip, busting it. Shai looked from the

blood dripping into his sneaker to Honey. "Bitch, you must have lost your mind!" He raised his hand, but Brutus grabbing him about the wrist stopped the blow from falling.

"I'm going to need you to calm down, Shai," Brutus said. His tone was soft, but his eyes were hard.

"You sure about this?" Shai challenged. Before Brutus could answer, Swann's shadow loomed behind us.

"I'm gonna need all three of y'all to chill the fuck out before we make a mess out here that nobody wants to clean up," Swann said. It wasn't a threat, but there was no misunderstanding about what he meant.

Brutus waited until he was sure Shai wasn't going to take a swing at him, before releasing him. "We good?" Shai didn't reply, and simply walked away; too stunned to speak. It was a bad sign and Brutus knew it.

Swann stood there, and watched his friend walk to the car seemingly in a daze over what happened. He waited until he was out of earshot before addressing Honey and Brutus. "You good, sis?" he asked Honey.

Hoodlum II: The Good Son

"Yeah, but something is wrong with your boy," Honey replied as she brushed herself off.

"That we can agree on; something is definitely not right in this equation," Swann said as if he knew something they didn't. "Why don't you go in the house and get yourself cleaned up." He waited until Honey was gone before turning to Brutus.

"Swann, I..."

"Whatever you were about to say, why don't you hold onto it until I've spoken my piece," Swann cut him off. "I'm going to say some things that you're probably not going to like, and after I'm done, you're welcome to react to them however you feel the need. You, my friend, are a snake. When we got busted for selling weed in high school, and I know for a fact that it was you who told, Shai wouldn't let me put hands on you. When you fucked the girl you knew he was sweet on, he gave you another pass, and let's not forget one of my personal favorites; when you allegedly saved his life when old man Miller ran up on y'all shooting. But I think you and I both know who that bullet was meant for and who orchestrated the whole thing."

Brutus' eyes went wide.

"Don't look so surprised. I know the whole story. You were fucking the bitch too, but when the shit hit the fan and she wound up pregnant, the two of you concocted that lame ass plan to blame Shai because you thought nobody would be stupid enough to try and lay hands on Poppa Clark's kid. I guess old man Miller proved the both of you wrong, huh? If it'll make you feel any better, I killed old man Miller not long after that. Took me a little longer to track his whore of a daughter, but she eventually got what she deserved too. They always do in the end."

"You gonna tell Shai?" Brutus asked.

"I'd thought about it for a long time, but Shai has had a rough enough go of things. Better to let sleeping dogs lay than heap more heartache on him. I don't like you, Brutus. I never have and probably never will, but right now you're in Shai's good graces, which is why I'm expressing myself with words instead of the business end of my strap. But your slip is starting to show, my friend.

Hoodlum II: The Good Son

Sometime real soon, that hold you got over Shai is going to waver, and when that time comes, I'm going to take extreme pleasure in erasing you from existence. Tick-tock, my nigga, tick-tock," Swann warned as he ambled off.

"You good?" Swann asked once he was in the car with Shai.

"Yeah, I'm straight," Shai said, but it was a weak lie. It wasn't the first time that Honey said some fly shit to Shai, but it was the first time he let her words cut deep enough to pull him out of character. Besides Swann, he had never confided in anyone else about his insecurities about not being as good a leader as Tommy, and she had thrown it in his face. "I need you to do something for me."

"Anything, Shai. You know that," Swann said, hoping he was finally going to give him the green light to off Brutus.

"Get somebody in the streets and have them track down my cousin Hammer."

From the tone of Shai's voice, Swann knew something

343

was wrong. "Everything okay?"

"It will be once I put this nigga in his place. I want him standing in front of me before the day is over."

"You got it," Swann agreed. "Speaking of niggas being put in their place, what you wanna do about Brutus?"

"Nothing."

"What you mean nothing? That cat was out of pocket."

"Nah, it ain't his fault. I brought it on myself. I shouldn't have raised my hand to Honey."

"That we can agree on. You played yourself, bro, but who the fuck is this nigga to get in the middle of family business? That cat is forgetting his place and needs a reminder," he said as he brandished his gun.

Shai shook his head. "Whether he overstepped or not, I owe that man my life."

Swann looked at Shai in disbelief. "Shai, you've paid that debt a hundred times over. How long you gonna carry that? I promise, I can go in and get it done and over before Honey even knows what's going on."

Hoodlum II: The Good Son

"I said leave him!" Shai's tone was stern.

"Fuck it." Swann put the gun away. "So what's up with this master plan you were telling me about earlier?" he asked, changing the subject. "You gonna keep an asshole in suspense or what?"

Shai let the faintest hint of a smile touch his lips. "For that, I can show you better than I can tell you. Head over to Newark."

As Shai and Swann were pulling away from the estate, Shai noticed a car sitting right outside the gate. Behind the wheel was a white girl with blonde hair. She was turned away talking to someone, so he couldn't see her face. Swann was going too fast for Shai to get a good look at who was in the car with her, but if he didn't know any better, he would have sworn it was his brother, Tommy.

CHAPTER 23

"Man, this has got to be the fanciest whore house I have ever seen!" Jewels said, giving the three-story house the once over. It was a big white house in Long Island in a beautiful residential neighborhood. It was hardly the type of place where you would find a den of criminals, which is probably why the owner selected the location.

"Nigga, would you please shut the fuck up? And for the love of God, please try not to embarrass me while we're in there. You only get once chance to make a first impression," Tech told him. He was trying to appear the picture of calm, but his stomach was doing flip-flops.

"Let me ask you something, T. What you think that old woman really called you out here for?" Jewels asked.

"I told you; Belle says she wants me to court her the right way if I plan to kick it with her," Tech repeated what he'd already explained the day before.

"And you believed her? Listen, all I'm saying is that this old bag is as big a gangster as Shai. Half these bitches in here sell pussy or steal, so why is she all of a sudden concerned with etiquette when it comes to you?" Jewels questioned. He didn't like the setup and felt like there was more to Tech being summoned all the way to Long Island.

"My nigga, you being paranoid. Let's just go in here and humor this old lady, so we can get back into the streets," Tech told him before ringing the doorbell.

After a few moments, he could hear the locks being undone and took a second to make sure that he looked presentable. He smiled when the door opened, expecting to be greeted by one of the girls, but instead found himself looking up at a hard-faced man wearing a tee-shirt and jeans.

"Fuck you want?" He glared down at Tech.

"Uh, I'm here to see Lulabelle," Tech told him.

"Why?" the man asked. It was an unexpected question that he wasn't quite sure how to answer. Thankfully, he didn't have to.

"Who is that?" Belle came from behind the man. She was wearing a sundress and sandals. When she noticed Tech and Jewels standing there looking awkward, she frowned up at the doorman. "Rick, why are you harassing my guests?"

"Ah, I'm just having a little fun with them. You niggas can take a joke, right?"

"Sure man," Tech said dryly.

"Move, so they can come in!" Belle nudged Rick out of the way so that the men could enter. "Sorry about that. Rick is like our caretaker-slash-pain in the ass. He can be kind of a dick sometimes."

"So I've noticed," Tech mumbled, falling in step behind her.

The inside of the house wasn't as impressive as the outside, but it was nice. Long couches formed a horseshoe around the living room and there was a big television mounted on the wall. Several of the girls who weren't at the party were sitting around watching videos. When they saw Belle come in with Tech and Jewels, they exchanged giggles.

"I done died and gone to heaven," Jewels said, eyeing the different flavors of women.

"Hi, Tech-Nine," one of them greeted him playfully.

Hoodlum II: The Good Son

Obviously, he had been the topic of conversation before they arrived.

"Sandy, don't let me come out of this dress and handle you," Belle warned.

"Chill out, Belle. I was only joking," Sandy said, but didn't sound believable.

"Well, my name is Jewels in case anybody is wondering," Jewels said.

"C'mon, let's go sit outside. Ms. Ruby is waiting for us in the backyard," Belle said as she grabbed Tech by the hand. She was marking her territory.

Belle led her guests across the living room, under the watchful gaze of her roommates. Tech couldn't help but to feel like a piece of meat from the way they were looking at him. Through the kitchen was a glass door leading to the backyard. He could see Ms. Ruby sitting on a lawn chair, but she wasn't alone. She was chatting with a brutish-looking white man with a shaved head. Tech's radar immediately went off and he hesitated.

"What's this?" Tech asked Belle suspiciously.

"Relax, Tech. That's just Natalia's brother, Pietro."

"I feel a little underdressed for a party. Maybe I should go back home and change."

"Stop being so paranoid and just come on. Everything will make sense in a second and please try to keep an open mind before you form an opinion," Belle said as she pulled him by the hand through the doors.

When they stepped out into the yard, Ms. Ruby and the white guy immediately stopped talking; another bad sign.

"Welcome to our home, Tech," Ms. Ruby greeted him with a crocodile smile.

"Thank you for having us, ma'am. You remember my buddy Jewels from the baby shower," Tech said in way of an introduction.

"Indeed I do. Hello, Jewels," Ms. Ruby spoke to him. She craned her neck and looked beyond them as if she was expecting someone else to be coming out of the house.

"Something wrong?" Tech asked, not feeling the setup.

"I was half-expecting you to be traveling with your

Hoodlum II: The Good Son

little shadow. What is it they call him?" Ms. Ruby
searched her memory. "The Animal, right?"

Tech's face couldn't hide his shock. If he wasn't sure
about this being a setup before, her mentioning Animal's
name confirmed it. Instinctively his hand dropped to his
side, where he had his gun shoved in his pocket, covered
by his shirt.

"Relax, Tech. I didn't ask you out here to hurt you. I
brought you hear to offer you an opportunity to make
some money," Ms. Ruby said in an attempt to put him at
ease.

"I'll pass, thanks. We outta here, Jewels." Tech turned
to leave, but found Ricky standing in the doorway
blocking his path. Slung over his shoulder was a shotgun.
Tech cut his eyes at Belle, who looked nervous. "This
how you do all the niggas who come by here to date
you?"

"It ain't her fault. Belle had no idea what this was
about until right before you arrived," Ms. Ruby said.
"Tech, I assure you that if I wanted you dead I wouldn't
have you killed where my girls lay their

heads, nor would I have allowed you and Jewels to keep your guns. I just need a few minutes of your time. If at any point you find yourself uncomfortable or not interested in my proposition, you are free to leave. Now please, sit down."

Grudgingly, Tech and Jewels did as they were asked.

"That's better." Ms. Ruby was smiling again. "Can I get you something to drink?"

"Nah, just get to the point," Tech said angrily.

"Very well then." Ms. Ruby was now serious. "What Belle told you before was true; anyone who wants to court one of my girls is expected to present themselves like a proper gentleman, but before you crossed my threshold I wanted to know a little more about you, so I did some digging. I found myself quite surprised that for someone so young, you have quite the resume; murder, extortion... It seems you dabble in a little bit of everything, but you seem quite good at taking things that don't belong to you. I've even heard stories about dealers in the city who pay you not to rob them. That's impressive."

Hoodlum II: The Good Son

"Your point?"

"My point being that I have found myself in need of a man like you for a piece of business that Pietro and Natalia have brought to us." Ms. Ruby motioned to the white man, who was just glaring at them with his cold blue eyes. "Problem is, we've found ourselves shorthanded and are in need of some capable young men to help us take off this score."

"Sorry, I'm not interested," Tech said as he stood. "Now that you've spoken your piece, I'm leaving. Let's go, Jewels." He headed for the door leading back to the kitchen.

"You must be doing pretty well for yourself to turn your back on twenty-thousand dollars!" Ms. Ruby called after him.

This stopped Tech dead in his tracks.

CHAPTER 24

When Swann arrived at their destination, he found himself more confused than when they had set out. Shai directed him into Newark's industrial district, which consisted of mostly warehouses and buildings that looked like they had seen better days. It was also the area where Poppa had once planned to build his dream casino.

A feeling of nostalgia swept over Shai as they got out and took in the unfinished landscape. He could remember coming out there with his father before he died and listening to him talk for hours on end about how he was going to bring big business back to Newark. Shai thought it was a bad idea to try and build a casino in Newark, but his father wouldn't be swayed. For as passionate as he was when he spoke about it, you'd have thought he owed the city a debt. Whatever the debt was, the secret died with Poppa Clark.

"What the hell are we doing here?" Swann asked, stepping over a broken beer bottle.

Hoodlum II: The Good Son

"You'll see," Shai told him, and ventured deeper into the rubble.

Sol was already there. He was deep in conversation with an older white man who wore a bewildered expression on his face. His shadow, Jacob, loomed not too far away, looking at the place in disgust. When Sol spotted Shai, a broad smile crossed his face and he waved him over.

"Morning gentlemen," Shai greeted them.

"More like late afternoon, but who am I to judge?" Sol joked. "Shai, I'd like you to meet someone. This is Allen White. He's one of Chance's guys."

"Thanks for agreeing to meet us on such short notice," Shai said as he shook his hand.

"No problem. It isn't too often that Chancellor King calls in a personal favor. I figured you were somebody important," Allen told him.

"Nah, just a kid with a dream. I trust that my partner has filled you in on the specifics of what I'll need. My question is, can you do it?"

Allen looked over the property. "I mean...we can do

anything, it's just that this seems like a strange place for what you're planning. I was telling Sol that I have a guy who can show you some other properties which may fit the mold a little better."

"No, it has to be here."

Allen looked at Sol, who just shrugged. "Ah, okay. I'll come out with my crew Monday morning so we can get a better idea of what needs to be done and what we need to do it, and we'll follow up with an estimate. We'll be in touch." He shook Shai and Sol's hands respectively before leaving.

Shai just stood there for a minute, looking at the mess of trash rubble and unfinished buildings, smiling like he was watching a beautiful sunset. "Amazing," he whispered as the vision came together in his head.

"You know this is not gonna be an easy task, right?" Sol stood next to him.

"Nothing worth having ever is," Shai responded. "Would either of you like to clue me in on what you're looking at?" Swann was confused.

"Our future," Shai told him.

Hoodlum II: The Good Son

"You gonna move forward with Poppa's casino?" Swann asked.

"Nah, that was his dream, but this one will be mine."

Swann looked back and forth between Shai and the rubble. Either his best friend was playing a prank on him, or he just wasn't getting it.

"Low-income housing," Sol filled in the blanks.

"That's what you plan to build here? Fucking projects?" Swann was dumbfounded.

"Nah, man. These ain't gonna be no crummy ass projects. They'll be more like affordable condos, geared towards working-class people. This is just the first step to us helping to undo some of the harm the Clarks have done to urban communities over the years. This is my way of paying it forward."

"Nigga, you must be out your mind. First of all, in case you hadn't noticed, this is an industrial district!" Swann pointed out. "Let's say for the sake of argument that building condos in this shithole was a good idea, which it isn't; how do you expect to get residential building permits for it?"

"Already taken care of. Our good friend Bill O'Connor is going to see to that," Shai informed him.

"Bullshit! There's no way you're going to get him to try and push this through. They'll laugh him out of office," Swann said.

"I'm not giving him a choice. As we speak, Scotty is in his office making him an offer he can't refuse."

*

With each step Scotty took down the hallway, the more foolish he felt. Shai had come up with some off-the-wall ideas, but this one took the cake. He figured one of two things were going to come of this meeting; he would be thrown out on his ass or arrested. Neither prospect appealed to him. Still, if this is what Shai required of him, he'd do it.

At the end of the hall, a chubby brunette sat behind a desk chatting on the phone. From the way she would bust out laughing every so often at whatever the person on the other end was saying, he figured it was a personal call.

Hoodlum II: The Good Son

When she looked up and saw the young black man standing there, she made a face as if she had smelled something foul. "I'll call you back," she said before ending the call. "Can I help you?"

"Martin Scott to see Bill O'Connor," Scotty said in a clear and professional voice.

"Are you on the calendar for today?"

"No, but I'm sure he'll see me."

The girl glared at Scotty for a while as if she was trying to decide whether she should call security or not. "Give me a second," she said as she picked up the phone and punched in an extension. "I'm sorry to bother you, sir, but you have a Scott Martin..."

"Martin Scott," He corrected her.

"A Martin Scott to see you," she said as she rolled her eyes. Whatever O'Conner said to her on the other end completely changed her attitude by the time she hung up. "My apologies, Mr. Scott. Please go right in."

Scotty strolled in to find Bill chatting on his cell phone and typing on his computer at the same time. From his disheveled hair to the half-empty bottle of scotch on his table, he looked like a man who was having a bad day. Little did he know, it was about to get worse. He motioned for Scotty to have a seat while he finished up what he was doing.

"Sorry about that," Bill apologized once he had finished up his call. "This has been the day from hell. Of all the cities I could've chased office in, why the fuck did I pick Newark?" he asked as he flopped back in his chair. "I'm sorry, Scotty. How have you been?"

"I'm good, Bill. I could complain, but who'd listen?" Scott joked.

"When you're right, you're right. Listen, I don't wanna seem like I'm rushing you, but I've got a ton of shit to do. When I leave here, I've got to run out to Union. A friend of mine lost his son-in-law last night and his daughter is all broken up. I gotta go over to pay my respects."

"My condolences, and I totally understand. I see you've got your hands full so I'll make this short and sweet. I trust either Shai or Sol has reached out already?"

"Yes, I spoke to Sol. To be honest, I thought he was

Hoodlum II: The Good Son

pulling my leg when he told me what Shai wanted."

"Afraid not. He's very serious about building these condos, but needs a little help on your end before he can break ground," Scotty explained.

"Right... about that. I spoke to a few people and it's a no-go. Doing something like that will require a lot of moving parts. Building a low-income housing area that close to the goods housed in that area would mean

we'd have to hire additional police to make sure nothing gets out of hand."

"What you really mean is to keep the niggers in line?" Scotty read between the lines. "No worries, Bill. We plan to hire private armed security to prevent such things. It won't be yours or the city's problem."

"Even still, I'd have to bring it before the city council to get it approved and who knows how long that could take. Shai could have his money tied up in that for years."

"Then get it done quicker," Scotty shot back. "Let's talk turkey here, Bill. Neither one of us wants me to leave this office telling Shai you didn't wanna play nice, so let's stop yanking each other's dicks. I kinda like you and would hate for something bad to happen to you."

"Is that a threat?"

"Not at all, just me giving you some friendly advice."

"Well look here, friend, the bottom line is I can't do it; at least not in that area. Now if Shai wants to try and build his fantasy sand castle somewhere else, but it's not going to happen on that site. He might as well sell it off and move on."

Scotty shook his head sadly. "I was hoping I wouldn't have to go there, but you forced my hand," he said as he reached into his pocket, causing Bill to jump back nervously. "Relax, I'm a lawyer not a gangster," he said as he tossed something wrapped in plastic on the desk. "That look familiar?"

"What the fuck is this?" Bill looked down at it nervously.

"The mirror you and that dead girl were snorting coke off. I'll bet if they run it through ballistics they'll find your prints all over it. Care to see what else we got tucked away for a rainy day?"

Hoodlum II: The Good Son

"But...but Shai said I wouldn't have to worry about this anymore. He said he would take care of it!" Bill was almost in tears.

"Provided that you play ball," Scotty told him. "That sneaky little black motherfucker!" Bill slammed his fists on the table.

"Bill, slinging insults isn't gonna get us anywhere. You know I don't like doing this kinda shit any more than you do, but it doesn't change the fact that we both find ourselves in a very, very sensitive position with only two possible outcomes."

"So, this is how the Clarks treat their friends?"

"Bill, you and I both know we ain't never been friends nor will we be," Scotty said as he got up and straightened his suit jacket. "If we don't hear from you by morning, trust and believe we'll see you on the news by afternoon. Oh, and you can keep the mirror. Good day, sir," he capped, and headed for the door. The last thing he heard before closing it behind him was Bill's sobbing.

CHAPTER 25

"This is bad idea...a real bad idea," Louie said from the backseat of the Cadillac. He had been shaking like a hooker in church the whole ride to New Jersey.

"Would you shut the fuck up already?" Frankie snapped from the passenger seat. "The only reason I let you live instead of sending you along for the ride with your friends is because I think you can be useful to me. Now if I made a bad decision, let me know and I can have Jimmy end our business relationship right now."

Louie looked up at the fat man who was glaring at him through the rearview. "No, I'm with you Frankie. I'm with you."

"Then act like it."

"You need me to go in with you?" Jimmy asked. He wasn't comfortable with Frankie rolling into a nest of vipers with only Louie to watch his back.

"No need, I bought insurance," Frankie replied as he held up a yellow envelope. "Now let me go in here and pay my respects." He grabbed the bouquet of flowers

Hoodlum II: The Good Son

from the dash and slid out of the car.

The front lawn of the house was crawling with Meloni soldiers and associates. All eyes turned to them when Frankie and Louie approached. Louie looked like he was ready to shit himself, but Frankie was as cool as the other side of the pillow when he walked up to the door and rang the bell. There was a commotion on the other side of the door before it finally swung open, and a woman who could only be described as robust greeted them. Behind her were several hard-looking men wearing uninviting scowls. When she saw who it was, her eyes narrowed to slits.

"Good afternoon, Mrs. Ragotta. My name is..."

"I know who you are. What do you want?" Mrs. Ragotta said in a voice that was far deeper than Frankie expected.

"Simply to offer my condolences and pay my respects," Frankie said in his silver tone, offering her the flowers.

Mrs. Ragotta looked at the flowers for a while like she was trying to figure out if they were poison or not.

"Thank you," she said as she accepted the flowers and stepped aside to let him in. "Little Joe," she called to one of the men, a thin Italian with brown hair and eyes to match, "show our guest to the study where your father and the other guys are."

"I'll cut his stinking Cissaro throat is what I'll do!" Little Joe snapped, which got him a slap to the back of his head with one of his mother's meaty hands.

"We've had enough craziness today and I won't have any more of it upsetting your sister. Now I don't know what business you boys have going on in the streets, but while he's under this roof, he is a guest. Do you understand?"

"Yes, Mama," Little Joe said in a low tone. "C'mon," he said as he motioned for them to follow him inside.

After Frankie and Louie were checked for weapons, Little Joe escorted through the house. If looks could kill Frankie, would have surely dropped dead on the spot from all the murderous eyes that turned to him. One soldier even went as far as spitting on the floor in their path.

Hoodlum II: The Good Son

"When we get inside, shut the fuck up and let me do the talking," Frankie whispered to Louie when they reached the study door.

Inside there were about a half dozen men, smoking and talking amongst themselves. Sitting on a sofa, in all of his bulky glory, was Big Joe. His eyes were rimmed red like he had been crying and a young girl of about twenty was rubbing his back trying to console him. From the striking resemblance, Frankie reasoned that it was one of his daughters. Little Joe motioned for them to stay put while he went and whispered something in his father's ear. When Big Joe's eyes landed on Frankie, a chill ran through his body, and he wondered if he should have have listened to Louie.

When Big Joe rose to his full height, which was about 6'5", he seemed to dwarf everyone in the room. One of his Capos opened his mouth to say something, but a look from Big Joe silenced him. The huge man took his time walking across the room and came to stand directly in front of Frankie. Frankie was a tall man, but he looked like a child standing in Big Joe's shadow.

"Frankie the Fish," Big Joe said his name, as it was something vile.

"My condolences on your loss, Big Joe," Frankie said, trying to keep his voice steady. When he leaned in to kiss Big Joe's cheek, a massive hand wrapped around his neck.

"You and yours kiss my son-in-law and now you further insult me by fouling my home with your Cissaro stink during our time of grief?" Big Joe snarled, shaking him like a rag doll.

"Break his neck, Dad!" Little Joe cheered his father on.

"I didn't..." Frankie croaked but Big Joe's grip made it near impossible to breathe let alone speak.

"Didn't what? Didn't have anything to do with it? Is that what you were gonna say?" Big Joe cackled. "I'm going to crush your throat and then I'm going to roll into Manhattan with every able body I can muster up and wipe you back-stabbing Cissaros off the map once and for all."

"If you kill Frankie, then you'll never find out what

Hoodlum II: The Good Son

happened to Nicky!" Louie blurted out, turning all the attention to him.

"What did you say?" Big Joe turned his murderous stare to Louie.

Louie took a step forward, but several guns being aimed at him made him pause. "The envelope," he said, pointing to the parcel clutched in Frankie's hand.

Little Joe snatched it and began thumbing through the pictures inside. "What the fuck is this?"

"Killer," was the only word Frankie was able to get out. Thankfully, it was enough to get Big Joe to release his grip and allow him to fall to the ground.

Big Joe took the pictures from his son and started looking at them. "Who is this?" he asked as he held one of the pictures up for Frankie to see.

"The man responsible for Nicky's death," Frankie said, massaging his throat. "Those pictures were taken outside the building where they found Nicky moments after his death."

One of the younger street bosses came over and peered over Joe's shoulder at the pictures. "I think I've seen this guy around before. Isn't he with the Clarks?"

"Yes, he's one of their young hitters," Frankie told him.

"Bullshit!" Big Joe balled the picture up and hit Frankie in the face with it. "There's no way you can convince me that a bunch of second-rate thugs had the balls to kill a Made man. Doesn't make any sense. Drag this piece of shit out back and off him."

Several sets of hands grabbed Frankie and Louie and began dragging them away.

"It makes sense if Gee-Gee promised them your territory after they pushed you out of Jersey!" Frankie said in a last ditch attempt to save his life.

Big Joe raised his hand and the men stopped. "Okay, Frankie. I'm gonna let you humor me. You've got thirty seconds to convince me not to bury you in my backyard."

"Big Joe, there's no secret that our two families have never quite seen eye to eye, but I've always had a lot of respect for you. You're one of the few who still play this thing by the rules, which is more than I can say about the man who now sits at the head of our table. Ever

Hoodlum II: The Good Son

since Gee-Gee took over, things haven't been good over on our side, and they got worse when he gave those black sons of bitches seats at our table." He paused to make sure Big Joe was still following. "Gee-Gee is willing to break bread with anyone to put coins in his pockets, even niggers."

"You've burned through twenty of your thirty seconds and I'm still not convinced," Big Joe told him. "Were the Cissaros responsible for Nicky's death or not?"

"Yes."

"That's good enough for me. Let's do this fuck, then ride into Manhattan and kill the rest," Little Joe suggested.

"But it wasn't a family decision," Frankie added. "To kill a Made man would've meant all-out war. We all knew it, which is why Gee-Gee couldn't get the full support of his captains and had to go to his new black friends to carry out the hit."

"Let's say that I did buy this load of horse shit you're shoveling, which I don't. Why would you risk Gee-Gee's wrath by coming to me with it?" Big Joe asked.

"To be perfectly honest with you, it's because I'd rather die old and rich than young and foolishly, and I'm not the only one who feels this way. Gee-Gee is running our family into the ground and I can't just sit by and watch anymore." Frankie's voice was heavy with emotion. "If you don't believe me, have one of your people check it out."

Big Joe handed one of the remaining pictures to one of his Capos, who went off to verify the story.

The minutes seemed to drip past while they waited for Big Joe's man to verify the story. Frankie glanced over his shoulder at Louie, who looked like he would faint at any moment. It had been an Oscar-worthy performance, and he hoped that it would be enough.

Finally, Joe's man came back, and they held their collective breaths waiting for him to deliver the news.

"It checks out. They call him The Animal and he indeed works with the Clark family," The man informed them.

Frankie wanted to drop to his knees and thank God,

but he had to keep his composure. They weren't out of the woods yet. For a long while, Big Joe paced back and forth looking at the picture as if he was trying to commit it to memory.

"So," Big Joe finally broke his silence, "where can I find this Animal?"

CHAPTER 26

Animal had been in good spirits when he woke up that morning. As promised, Tommy sent his man to meet him the night before to drop off the ten grand. For a long while, he just sat with it sitting on his bed, staring at it in wonder. It wasn't the first time he had ever laid eyes on ten grand in a lump sum, but it was the first time he didn't have to split it up amongst the Dog Pound.

After stashing the bulk of the money in his hiding place in his apartment, he hit the streets. His first stop was to go by Brasco's crib. His best friend was currently in jail, again, and he wanted to make sure he had something on his books. Animal would have loved to go see him and drop it on his friend personally, but he wasn't yet old enough to be allowed in prison without an adult. He had to settle for the next best thing, which was dropping it off with one of his uncles. There were three of them, Bizzle, Pop-Top and Vernon. Pop-Top was in jail and Vernon was a notorious thief and addict, so he trusted the thousand dollars to Bizzle to make sure

Hoodlum II: The Good Son

Brasco got it. He and Bizzle chopped it up for a few hours while catching up on Animal's life since he had moved out of their crowded apartment, before he had to move onto his next destination.

Animal jumped on the bus and headed across town to Pathmark to go grocery shopping. Some of the stuff was for his place, but the bulk of it was for the kids in The Below. He raided the aisles, grabbing hordes of their favorite snacks, five loaves of bread and spent two hundred dollars at the deli counter getting fresh turkey, ham and roast beef. There would be no bologna sandwiches for his little ones that night. He couldn't wait to see their dirty little faces when he popped up with all the stuff, but first he had to make a quick stop back by his place.

By the time the taxi pulled up in front of Animal's building, it was almost nightfall. He told the driver to wait for him while he ran to take some of the bags up to his apartment. As he fished around in his pocket for his keys, an eerie feeling settled in the pit of his gut. Putting the bags down, Animal ran his fingers along the edges of the door. Sure enough, the small piece of tape he always left on it had been tampered with. Drawing his gun, he slipped into his apartment.

Moving on the balls of his feet, he crept down the hall. He could hear the sounds of music coming from the living room, "The Lizard King" by The Doors, which filled him with rage. Not only had someone been foolish enough to break into his place, but they had fucked with his record collection. They were going to die, but he would take his time killing them. Ready to deliver the gift of death, Animal jumped out into the living room, gun drawn and finger on the trigger. He was quite surprised when he realized that he knew the intruder.

"You always did have strange tastes in music," Tech said. He was standing by the window, smoking a blunt and reading the back of an album cover.

"Are you crazy? I could've killed you!" Animal barked.

"Doubt it. You always hesitate for a second before you pull the trigger," Tech said as he exhaled the smoke. "That's a habit you're going to have to learn to break before it breaks you. Besides, sneaking in here seems like the only way I can get an audience with the high lord of abandoned buildings. You been avoiding me?"

"No."

"Feels like it. You don't return my calls and whenever I swing by, you always seem to be out. Knowing you the way I do, you probably watch me from the roof until I leave before slipping back in here." Tech tossed the album cover onto the table. "How you been?"

Animal shrugged. "I'm hanging in."

"I see you've done some shopping. I saw you with the bags when you jumped out of the cab." Tech nodded to the window.

"Oh, yeah. I had to grab some stuff for the kids," Animal told him.

"Since you needed a cab to get it here, must've been quite a bit of stuff."

"What are you, my fucking parole officer?" Animal asked defensively.

"Calm yo' little ass down. I'm just trying to figure out what's going on with you. You've been moving real funny lately, and I'm starting to worry. That's all."

"You wouldn't understand."

"That's never stopped me from listening to your problems before and trying to help you figure them out before, now has it? Talk to your big homie, blood."

Animal searched for the words. "I don't know, Tech. I just been feeling different lately, starting to question a lot of shit. What we do, how we live..."

"You thinking about hanging up your guns?" Tech asked.

"It's the opposite actually. Ever since that shit happened with the old lady, I feel like I lose a little more of myself every time I do some dirt."

"Ah, I see. That's your soul dying off a little bit at a time," Tech told him.

"Nigga, I'm trying to have a deep conversation and you're making fun of me?" Animal's voice flashed hurt.

"Not at all. I'm being serious. Look here, man, let me try and put this into perspective for you. Deep down we're good people, but we do bad shit. I'd think something was wrong with you if you didn't at least feel

a little guilt. Ain't no shame in that. What there is
shame in, is you letting this shit eat away at you so deep
that one day you're sitting on the edge of that bed
contemplating eating a bullet. Take it from someone who
knows first-hand."

"Get the fuck outta here!" Animal said in disbelief.
For as long as he had known Tech, he always seemed so
emotionally removed that Animal wondered if he was
capable of feeling anything at all.

"Real shit, man. After Jah got killed, I went through a
very dark period in my life. I didn't have anyone around
me to explain what was going on, so I had to figure it all
out on my own. I was fighting the battle of my life
between light and dark."

"Which side won?" Animal asked.

Tech looked at him. "Do you really not know the
answer to that question?"

"So, you're telling me that I should give into these
urges?"

"I can't tell you which way to jump, because it's your
life. What I can tell you is that I've seen a lot of dudes try

379

and straddle both sides of the fence and it never ends well. You have to either embrace that little monster whispering sweet nothings in your ear, or put him in a box and don't ever look back. No matter which way you go, you'll always be my friend, feel me?"

"Yeah, I think so," Animal said as he nodded. Outside, the cab driver honked his horn. "Shit, I forgot I had him waiting. Why don't you come with me to The Below to drop this stuff off?"

"You know I don't fuck with them creepy ass kids," Tech laughed.

"Blood, I don't know why you're so hard on them kids and they're just like we were a few years ago," Animal said.

"Nah, ain't too many like us, baby bro. We're the last of a dying breed."

"You're right about that. Well I'll be done with them in a few hours, so let's hook up tonight and do something."

Tech was about to agree, but then remembered he had to meet Jewels and Pietro. "Nah, tonight is no good."

Hoodlum II: The Good Son

"What's more important than kicking it with your dawg?" Animal wanted to know.

"I kinda got a date," Tech half-lied.

This caught Animal by surprise, as he had never known Tech for anything but one-night stands. "Damn, this must be some special broad."

"I ain't sure yet, but I'd like to find out. Tell you what; how about we meet in the morning for breakfast and I'll tell you all about her?" Tech suggested.

"Sounds like a plan," Animal agreed.

The taxi horn blared again.

"Let me get out of here before I have to shoot this nigga," Animal said as he headed for the door. "Oh and Tech, thanks for the talk."

"We all we got." Tech saluted him.

"Indeed," Animal said as he returned the gesture before heading out.

Neither of them knew it at the time, but when their paths would next cross, nothing would be the same.

The taxi Animal was riding in hit an unexpected wall of traffic. It seemed to be backed up for blocks and it was starting to irritate him. "Damn, man, can't you go around this shit?" He was thinking about the ice cream in the bag, which was surely starting to melt by that point.

"I wish I could. Looks like there's something going on down there," the taxi driver said, beating his horn.

"Fuck it. I'm only a few blocks away. I can walk from here." Animal paid the driver and got out with his bags.

Now that Animal was on the sidewalk, he had a better view of what was going on. In the distance, he could see the flashing lights of police and fire trucks and smell the smoke. One of the buildings appeared to be on fire. As he got closer he realized it wasn't just any building, but his building! Dropping the bags, Animal ran as fast as his little legs could carry him. People stood around spectating as the fire fighters fought to put out the blaze. "Move! Move!" he yelled as he shoved his way through the crowd. He had just broken the ring of people when a cop grabbed him.

"Stay back, please!" the cop instructed as he shoved him.

"But you don't understand..."Animal tried to explain,

Hoodlum II: The Good Son

but the cop cut him off.

"No, you don't understand. This is a dangerous situation and I need you to get back!"

"Fuck this shit!" Animal slipped passed the cop and made the mad dash for the police tape.

"Hey!" the cop called after him, but Animal kept going.

"Please God," Animal prayed under his breath, but when he made it through the tape, he knew that God hadn't heard him. "No!" Animal dropped to his knees as he saw one of the EMT's bring out a body bag and place it on the ground next to the half dozen or so already lining the sidewalk. Animal was so overcome with grief that he was dizzy. When he thought of the children who had been inside and how horribly they died, his heart shattered into a million pieces

"Big homie?" he heard a voice behind him. He turned around hopefully and saw Ashanti sitting on the back of one of the ambulances with an oxygen mask over his face.

Animal rushed over to Ashanti and hugged him as tight as he could. He had never in his life been so happy to see his mischievous little friend. His eyes were red and his body covered with soot. "What happened?"

"I don't even know, man. I went to the store to get some candy and while I was walking back I seen some white dudes come running out. That was right before the explosion knocked my ass out," Ashanti recalled. "When I woke up, I was in the back of this ambulance."

"Damn," Animal lowered his head. "How many made it out?"

"None that I can tell," Ashanti began sobbing. "This shit is fucked up, man. Who would do something like this to a bunch of kids?"

Ashanti continued speaking, but Animal had checked out. He replayed Ashanti's account of what happened over in his head and one phrase kept jumping out at him - "Some white guys." What were the chances that less than twenty-four hours after Tommy had sent him to kill Nicky, that a group of white men would venture into Harlem and burn down a building that held no meaning to

Hoodlum II: The Good Son

anyone except Animal? This was no coincidence. As
Animal stood there watching the paramedics zipping bags
over the charred remains of his children, he couldn't help
but to feel like it was all his fault. He may not have lit the
match, but he poured the gasoline. It was then that Tech's
words came back to him - "Either embrace that monster
whispering in your ear, or put it back in the cage and
never look back." Animal would indeed embrace his
monster, and then he would unleash it on those
responsible for this.

CHAPTER 27

By the time Shai and his team made their way to the event at Don B.'s spot, he was in better spirits than he had been earlier. Chance had finally sent a response and it was a favorable one. The deal was that Shai would allow him to expand his street operations, provided he did him a favor in return. Chance would have one of his building crews complete the work on his housing development at half cost. Chance wasn't happy at having to give him such a huge discount, but it was the cost of doing business with the Clark family.

As expected, Bill came to his senses and agreed to pull some strings to get him the building permits. Of course, it would cost Shai a hefty sum in bribes, but this is where the cash from the cigarettes would come in. He needed the transaction to be totally untraceable. It wouldn't cover the total cost for the palms that needed greasing, but it would get the ball rolling. A part of him felt guilty about blackmailing the Deputy Mayor, but he reasoned he had it coming. It was payback for Bill shitting on his father's

Hoodlum II: The Good Son

dream after his death. His was only one name on a list of people Shai would revisit before it was all said and done. He was a man who could forgive, but never forget. In due time, they would all kneel before the one true king.

Shai's business in the streets was running smooth, but his family life was a mess. He had gone back to the house to get dressed and try and make things right with Honey, but got home to find her gone, along with some of her clothes. Shai tried calling her, but she sent him to voicemail every time. She was still in her feelings, so he would allow her some space to get over it.

Brutus was also absent from the house. Tre said he had to leave to take care of some personal business, but it sounded like bullshit. He was either embarrassed about what happened earlier, or afraid of what might happen to him because of it…and rightfully so. After having time to reflect on Brutus' strange behavior lately, Shai had begun to question where his head was at. Giving his high school friend the position as head of his security team said that Shai had a lot of trust in him, but what if that trust was misplaced? Maybe Swann was right and Brutus was forgetting his position and needed a reminder.

"You good, Slim?" Angelo nudged him. He was one of several men who were riding in the limo with Shai.

"Yeah, I'm straight."

"Still no word from Honey?" Angelo asked. Shai had confided in him about the argument and her leaving.

"Not yet."

"I wouldn't worry about it too much. She's mad now, but when she calms down, she'll be back," Angelo assured him.

Shai wanted to believe his friend, but in his heart, he wasn't so sure. Though he hadn't done much other than talk with Lady Monet that night, he might as well have fucked her, because to Honey it was the same difference. Shai had a history of sleeping around, so it made sense that the one time he was telling the truth, it didn't help.

"Man, you gonna spend the whole night pouting or try and have some fun?" Swann sat in the seat across from them, sipping a glass of Hennessey and smoking a blunt. "I plan on taking advantage of all the free liquor and pussy in this joint, as you should!"

Hoodlum II: The Good Son

Shai shook his head at Swann's one-track mind. "Did Big Doc check in yet?" he asked, changing the subject.

"I spoke to him a while ago. Him and his boys are already in position; they're just waiting for the truck to get there. We're all set," Angelo informed him.

"We're arriving now," the driver informed them.

"Look alive," Angelo addressed the two young shooters who were riding with them, brushing imaginary lint off of his suit jacket. "Now it's gonna be all kinds of unsavory muthafuckas in here, so stay on your toes. Most importantly, you are not to let Shai out of your sight. Do you understand?"

"I don't need no babysitters, Angelo. Ain't nobody dumb enough to try nothing with all these people out here. Besides, I'm sure Don B. got plenty of security inside tho joint," Shai said, looking out the window at the crowd gathered in front of Code Red. The line to get in stretched at least a block. One thing he could give the Big Dawg CEO credit for was he knew how to bring people out.

"Outside of Devil, I wouldn't trust none of those cats

with my life, so I'm sure as hell not gonna trust them with yours," Angelo told him. "Besides, with all this shit going on with that other situation, we don't wanna take any chances."

What Angelo wouldn't say in front of the shooters was that he was talking about the fallout from Nicky's murder. Word on the streets was that the Melonis were arming up to come across the Hudson and make a mess of the Cissaros and anybody unfortunate enough to get in the middle.

"Nigga, you finished with your pep-talk?" Swann asked sarcastically, to which Angelo flipped him off. "Good, now everybody get a glass. I wanna propose a toast." Swann waited until everyone had liquor in their cups before continuing. "Shai, I know how important it was to you to finish your father's work in making us a legitimate family, and today I watched you lay the foundation that we're going to build that on. I'm proud of you. So here's to the future, and whatever it may hold for us!" He raised his glass.

"To the future!" the men said in unison.

Hoodlum II: The Good Son

Swann threw his drink back, then slammed the glass down on the mini-bar. "Now let's go in here and show these rap niggas how to ball the fuck out!"

*

The minute the driver opened the limo door, they were immediately swarmed by thirsty paparazzi, hoping to capture the star-studded event. There were so many cameras flicking at one time that Shai had to shield his eyes against the flash.

"Get back, you fucking vultures!" Angelo said as he shoved a path through them, while Swann and the shooters brought up Shai's rear.

At the door stood a man who was at least 6'6" and wearing a tight black shirt that had "Security" printed across the front. He initially greeted them with a scowl, but when he realized who it was, his face softened.

"Good evening, Mr. Clark. The Don told me you were coming. I have some people waiting to escort you to your table."

"That's what I'm talking about," Swann said excitedly. He was ready to go inside and get the party started. When he tried to step through the doorway, the big man stopped him.

"I'm gonna need to check you guys before you go inside," the bouncer informed them.

"Nigga what?" Swann looked him up and down angrily.

"Sorry, but it's the rules," the bouncer explained.

"Blood, you acting like you don't know who we are? You better go get your boss or whoever is running this circus," Swann told him. There was no way he was going anywhere without his gun.

"We outta here, Shai," Angelo told him.

"What's going on out here?" Devil asked as he appeared in the doorway.

"Red Devil, how you gonna invite us to this joint then have your people treat us like some commoners?" Swann asked.

Devil turned on the bouncer angrily. "What the fuck is wrong with you? Don't you know who this is?"

Hoodlum II: The Good Son

"But you said..." the bouncer started.

"Nigga, I know what I said, but those rules don't apply to Shai and his people. They're guests of the Don. Besides, I know we ain't gonna have no trouble out of them, are we?" he directed the question at Swann.

"You know me; I don't start the drama. I just finish it," Swann told him.

"Well let's hope this is a drama-free night. Now y'all come on inside. Don B. is waiting."

*

If someone had asked Shai to describe the action in Code Red that night using one word, it would have been "zoo." It was standing-room only with people boozing, dancing and engaging in things he was sure was illegal; at least in public. He had been to more than a few clubs in his life, but none quite gave off the energy that was floating in the air that night. It was electric.

The crowd of partygoers parted like the Red Sea as Devil led Shai and his entourage across the room. Shai could feel eyes on him as those not in-the-know were trying to figure out who he was. The fact that he was with Devil said that he was someone important, but wearing a blazer and jeans, he hardly fit the part of the gangsters Don B. was known to associate with. Shai wasn't sure how comfortable he was with all the attention on him. Ever since he became boss of the family, he tried his best to fly under the radar, but that night he felt like he was on display and it made him uneasy.

Shai's eyes drifted toward the small stage where a DJ was setting up some equipment. Behind him was a backdrop that stretched the length of the stage. Painted across it was a mural that depicted a group of young men, throwing up gang signs and rocking heavy jewelry. At the forefront of the group was a fresh-faced youth with a bandana in one hand and a microphone in the other.

"That was True," Swann answered the question in Shai's eyes.

Shai had never been a fan of any of the music Big Dawg made, but he was familiar with the name True. It had been plastered all over the news when he was caught

Hoodlum II: The Good Son

up in a gang-related shooting. Let the streets tell it, he
was supposed to be the next big thing in music.

"Sad," Shai said, thinking of what the young man
could have gone on to be if given the chance.

"That's the game, Slim; die young and leave a good-
looking corpse," Swann laughed before falling in step
behind Devil.

Devil escorted them up a darkened stairwell. He could
feel Angelo and Swann close in on him in case anything
popped off. At the top of the stairs there was

a black curtain, but through it Shai could see a sliver
of light. They'd almost made it to the top when a man
appeared in front of them as if by magic. He glared at
them for a few seconds, but once he recognized Devil
amongst the group, he went back to his post. Don B.
definitely wasn't taking any chances.

Shai thought the scene downstairs was wild, but he
was totally unprepared for what he saw when they
stepped through the curtains. The stairwell let out into
a private balcony that overlooked the crowd. About a half
dozen men were loitering about; members of Don B's

inner circle. Their eyes turned to the newcomers, but no one spoke. Several girls were walking around wearing little more than thongs and heels, pouring bottles and rolling up blunts that they handed out like free candy. The crowd was thicker downstairs, but the balcony was obviously where the real party was going on. Lounging on a sofa was their host, the self-proclaimed Don of all Harlem.

Don B. was wedged between two beautiful young women, sipping champagne straight from the bottle. His eyes were covered by his signature mirrored sunglasses. As usual, he was dressed in black from head to toe, with the exception of the red Gucci belt he was wearing. Around his neck hung a thick link-chain, with a diamond-flooded Rottweiler pendant swinging from the end of it.

If you weren't familiar with Don B., then you had to have been living under a rock for the last five years. It was rare that you could turn on a television and not see him, or pick up a magazine and his name not be mentioned. The acts on his roster at Big Dawg Entertainment had collectively sold millions of records

Hoodlum II: The Good Son

around the world, and made him a very rich man. Don B. was like the ghetto Clive Davis, but it hadn't always been like that.

Don B. had literally come from nothing, growing up dirt poor on the streets of Harlem. When he was of age, he jumped into the drug game and excelled in a very short period of time. Seeing most of his friends either killed off or sent to prison for the rest of their lives, Don B. soon realized that he would need to find an alternative source of income, so he started taking the money he was making from selling crack and dumping it into starting his own record label. In under a year, Don B. was able to leave the streets, and he took those closest with him along for the ride.

Sitting beside Don B. on the couch was Lady Monet. Shai felt his breath catch in his throat when he saw her. She wasn't dressed like a hood rat that night, instead wearing a tasteful, yet revealing black dress that stretched to her ankles, but had a high slit showing off her healthy thighs. She had taken the braids out and was now wearing her black hair straight. Shai tried to give her a greeting

397

smile, but the look she gave him in return was vacant of all the mirth she'd been spilling over with less than twenty-four hours before. It was as if she had never seen him a day in her life.

"Is that my nigga Swann?" Don B. turned to greet him with a grin, but didn't bother to stand.

"What up wit ya, blood? Been a minute." Swann gave him dap.

"Indeed, it has. Too long, my G... too long."

"Oh, you remember Shai right?" Swann said in way of an introduction.

Don B. dipped his sunglasses and peered at Shai over the top of them like he was trying to place him. "Of course, man. Yo, thanks for coming though, Shai. I know you a busy dude."

"No problem. Your partner said you had a proposal to lay out so I'm here to listen," Shai told him. He was speaking to Don B., but his eyes were on Lady Monet, who was nestled deep into the crook of his arm.

"Straight to the paper. I can respect that." Don B. nodded in approval. "Oh, where are my manners? This

Hoodlum II: The Good Son

fine piece of candy here is Lady Monet. Ma, you know
Shai Clark, right?" he asked her.

Lady Monet studied Shai for a second. "Oh yeah, the
guy from the chicken shack," she said, as if they hadn't
just spent the previous night together.

"Shai slings more than just chicken, baby. But that's a
conversation for another time," Don B. said as he stroked
her hair. "Shai, you and ya peeps ain't gotta stand around
all stiff. Grab a seat and a drink. You're guests of the
Don, so it's all on me."

"We can pay our own way, but thanks," Angelo
interjected. "Your guy said we'd have our own section
tonight."

"Yeah, I got a table set up downstairs that I was gonna
seat you guys at, but to be honest, this is the best section
in the house," he said as he motioned around the balcony.
"What's good for the Don, is good for the Don's friends,
and I expect we'll be great friends before the night is
over."

"That's all well and good, but we kinda like to do our
own thing," Angelo told him.

Don B. frowned. "This ain't Burger King, but you know how the slogan goes. I'll have my people set you up right away."

"Nah, we're cool sitting up here. Thanks for the hospitality," Shai said, much to Angelo's displeasure.

"Then it's settled." Don B. clapped his hands to get the attention of the bottle girls, and a light-skinned woman with big breasts and a weave that looked like it needed a comb ran through it came over. "Bring these boys some bottles, and not none of that cheap shit that you been serving the goons all night, either. Shai is an honored guess, and he should be treated with the same respect you would show your Don."

"Yes, Don," she said submissively, and went off to do as she was told.

"You've got quite a way with the ladies," Shai said sarcastically.

"I do, don't I?" Don B. pulled Lady Monet closer. "That's just one of my super powers. My other one is knowing how to flip a dollar, which is what I plan to convince you of before the night is over. Grab a seat,

Hoodlum II: The Good Son

King Clark, so I can run down to you how I'm about to
make us richer than we already are."

CHAPTER 28

For the next twenty minutes, Shai drank Hennessey like it was going out of style, and listed to Don B. run down his plan of starting a franchise of Code Reds. He had to admit, Don B. had come correct with his proposal with everything from project venture capital, to mapping out what they stood to make in the first three years. He even had one of the girls bring out a miniature model of the next location he wanted to open up. From what Shai had heard so far, it was a pretty solid plan, but he was too distracted to really digest it.

He watched Lady Monet move around the room and work it like the budding superstar that she was. Hanging with her in the strip club was a totally different experience than seeing her in her element. The way she held the attention of everyone she chatted with, Shai could understand why Don B. signed her; she was beautiful and had a magnetic presence about her. A few times Shai caught her looking in his direction, but she refused to make eye contact. She was toying with him,

Hoodlum II: The Good Son

and it started irritating Shai. Usually he was the one
pulling those kinds of stunts on women, and he wasn't
used to having the tables turned on him.

"So, I thought you guys had some live performances
set up for the night?" Shai changed the subject, hoping to
get some insight as to what was going on with Lady
Monet.

"Yeah, but we had to switch some shit around. This
dizzy broad," Don B. thumbed in Lady Monet's
direction, "decided it was a good idea to hang out
drinking and smoking blunts on the night before her
performance, so now her voice is shot." He shook his
head in disappointment. "Of all my artists, she's the
hardest to work because she still got that street shit in her.
I could make a big star out of Monet, if she'd only get out
of her own fucking way. It's like this shit is all a game to
her, smell me?"

"Yeah, I can definitely dig that," Shai said, thinking of
her treatment of him that night.

"But enough about her; what do you think of my
idea?" Don B. got back to business.

"Well, I think it has potential, but ultimately I'd have to bounce it off my lawyers and my business partner before I could commit," Shai told him. His eyes drifted over Don B.'s shoulder to Lady Monet. She was in the middle of the room, drinking Hennessy out of the bottle and twerking. When she went to drop it low, she lost her balance and crashed into the lap of one of Don B.'s minions.

Don B. looked over his shoulder and frowned. "This drunk bitch," he mumbled. "Excuse me for a second, Shai. I need to handle this." He got up and went over to Monet.

Shai watched as Don B. grabbed her roughly by the arm and snatched her to her feet. He barked something at her, to which she responded by laughing in his face. This only angered him further, which was evident by the way he began shaking her. Monet tried to pull away, but Don B. held fast. The situation was going south quickly, and Shai could smell the threat of violence lingering. Before he had even realized it, he was on his feet. He'd have gone over and intervened,

Hoodlum II: The Good Son

had it not been for Swann appearing and cutting his path off.

"Looks like you could use a drink," Swann said, brandishing a glass of Hennessey.

"I ain't thirsty," Shai told him, trying to peer around Swann to see what was going on between Don B. and Monet.

"Drink it anyway." Swann forced the glass into his hand. "That ain't for you, Slim."

"What you talking about, Swann?" Shai faked ignorance.

"I'm talking about that look in your eye that says you're ready to do something stupid over a bitch who don't belong to you," Swann told him.

"Whatever, man." Shai handed Swann the drink back and turned for the exit.

"Where you going, Shai?"

"To take a leak, if that's okay with you?"

"Hold on, I'll walk with you," Swann offered. "Swann, right now I don't need a shadow, I need to piss this alcohol out. Now unless you plan on holding my dick, fall back and give me a little space." Shai walked out before giving him a chance to argue.

*

Shai bumped his way through the crowd downstairs, trying to get control of the drunken rage that was trying to settle over him. He found himself at the bar in the main level. It wasn't that he needed another drink, but he was trying to put some distance between himself and the temptress. He had come dangerously close to playing himself by intervening in what was going on between Don B. and Lady Monet, and he had a sneaking suspicion that it was her intention to goad him into getting involved. She had been fucking with his head all night, and his dumb ass was letting her.

Shai ordered a bottle of water, which he proceeded to guzzle. The cool drink was helping to clear some of the cobwebs from his head. By his second bottle, he had begun to sober up and was seeing things slightly clearer. He was no longer feeling the scene at Code

Hoodlum II: The Good Son

Red and was about ready to go. He was in the middle of ordering a third bottle of water when he felt a presence behind him. He turned and found himself confronted with the object of his anger, Lady Monet.

"Who drinks water in a club?" Monet squeezed next to him at the bar. "Give him a shot of Henny," she told the bartender.

"The last thing I need is another shot. I might end up doing something I'll regret," Shai told her.

"What's eating you?" she asked, as if she didn't already know.

"Are you fucking serious?" Shai gave her a disbelieving look. "Listen, shorty, I don't know what kind of games you're playing in here tonight, but I'm not the one for them." He attempted to leave, but she grabbed him by the hand.

"Don't be like that, Slim," she said as she attempted to touch his face, but he grabbed her by the wrist.

"Knock it off."

"What? You upset about that little show with Don B.? Let me find out you're jealous," Monet said as she gave

407

him a sly smile. "That is so cute."

"I'm glad you think fucking with niggas emotions is funny, because I don't."

"I'm not playing with your emotions, Shai. It's just that..." her words trailed off. "Look, can we go somewhere where I don't have to scream over the music for you to hear me? It's loud as hell in here."

"I'm cool. I'm actually about to call it a night," he told her.

"C'mon, Shai. Let's go talk outside. Give me five minutes to explain." She took him by the hand and began leading him toward one of the exits.

"Hold on, let me tell my people."

"Do you need to clear everything you do with your entourage?" she teased him. "I'll have you back before they even notice you're gone." She pushed open the side door and walked outside. Shai reluctantly followed.

"What the fuck is wrong with you?" he asked once they were outside in the alley.

"I'm just having a bad night," she told him with a sigh.

Hoodlum II: The Good Son

"I kinda get the impression you brought it on yourself. You were up there showing your ass in front of Don B."

"Fuck him!" Monet spat. "That arrogant bastard thinks the fact that he's invested in my career gives him ownership papers over me. The only reason he was even acting like that is because he knows I'm feeling you."

"Well you've got a funny way of showing it. First you slide off without so much as saying goodbye, and then you spend half the night acting like you don't know me. You've got a funny way of showing a guy you like them."

"Because I usually don't," she said honestly. "Understand something, Shai; I came up different. All the shit with my dad kinda fucked me up, so I try not to get too attached to guys. When you came along that changed."

"Because I'm just that special, huh?" Shai asked sarcastically.

When Monet looked up at him, he was surprised to find her eyes rimmed with tears. "Here I am trying to keep it real with you and you're making fun of me? You know what? Fuck you!" She started back for the door.

"Wait, don't go!" Shai grabbed her arm. "Look, I'm sorry. It's just kinda hard to tell when you're serious and when you're playing games."

"This isn't a game for me, Shai...at least not with you." Monet wiped her eyes with the back of her hand. "I didn't intend to fall for you, Shai Clark. I know you got a girl, and in the beginning I was just flirting with you to see how far I could get you to go, but after spending last night getting to know the man behind the myth, I realized that there was more to you. I felt myself slipping and it scared me. The reason I left while you were in the car sleeping is because I felt like I was about to cross a line that we wouldn't be able to come back from. When I saw you again tonight, it just stirred up old feelings, and that's why I got so drunk. I feel guilty because I'm falling for another woman's man," she said, lowering her head in shame.

Shai nudged her chin with his finger, so that she had to look at him. He was lost in her moist hazel

410

Hoodlum II: The Good Son

eyes.

"Would you believe me if I said I was falling for you too?" He kissed her. He knew it was wrong, but it felt so right.

"Shai, don't start something you can't finish." She ran her hand down his chest and let it come to rest on his dick, which was damn near bursting through his pants.

"I never do," he whispered as he slipped his hand under her dress and began playing with her wet pussy.

Shai pressed Monet against the wall of the alley, and kissed her deeper. His tongue tasted like spearmint and Hennessey. "From the moment I saw you, I felt like I had been looking for you all my life," she said between kisses. "I need you inside me. Please give it to me, baby." She began undoing his belt.

Shai wanted to resist, but he couldn't. He was like putty in Lady Monet's hands to do with as she would. He felt the cool night air run over his penis as it was freed from his pants. Lady Monet played with it for a while, getting it hard enough to her liking before slipping him inside her. Her pussy felt like warm silk, and it closed

411

around Shai's dick as snuggly as a glove.

It was as if they had been made specifically for each other. He started pumping in her slowly at first, but it seemed the deeper he went, the tighter she got. The next thing Shai knew, he was humping and grunting like a dog. Monet's pussy was so good that Shai felt a tear spring to his eye, but he refused to let it fall. He lasted all of five minutes before he exploded inside her.

"Damn," he cursed, resting his head on the wall behind her. He was still inside Monet, emptying the last of his juices.

"I kinda expected you to last a little longer than that," Monet teased him.

"I'm sorry, baby. It was just so good," Shai said, trying to hide his embarrassment.

"Don't worry, the next round will be better. Let me get you back to where you need to be," she said as she pushed his pants down around his ankles and got on her knees.

Shai's body went rigid when Monet took him in her mouth. Sweat began to pour down his face as she took

Hoodlum II: The Good Son

him in and out of her throat expertly. If he wasn't sure before, he was absolutely sure then that he was in love.

"Shai," she said, popping him out of her mouth and running her tongue around the head of his dick, "I left a few things out when I was telling you the story about my father."

"Tell me later, baby. Just keep going." Shai grabbed her by the back of her head, but she resisted.

"No, it's important that you know the truth... the whole truth." She ran her tongue across his nuts. "My father didn't die in a car accident. He was murdered."

"I'm sorry to hear it," Shai said, only half-listening.

"I promised that if I ever crossed paths with the man responsible that I would set things right. That man was you," Monet hissed.

Before Shai could even process what she said, he felt a pinprick in his thigh. He looked down and saw a hypodermic needle sticking out of his thigh. "What the fuck?" He pushed her away and stumbled back. He suddenly felt nauseous and the alley began to spin. Through blurred vision, he watched Monet stand up and wipe her mouth. "What are you doing?"

"Settling an old score for my father. I believe you two knew each other very well. His name was Michael Tessio."

The name hit Shai like a slap in the face. "You rotten bitch!" He stumbled forward trying to grab her, but whatever drug she had stuck him with was starting to kick in and he had trouble keeping his balance. A pair of strong hands grabbed Shai from behind and threw him to the ground. He focused as best he could and was able to make out a man. From the long handle, he first thought it was a baseball bat, until he noticed the steel hammer at the end.

"You!" Shai spat when he was able to make out his cousin Hammer's grinning face.

"I tried to tell your lady that I had something to talk to you about," Hammer sneered. "There's been a bag dropped on your head, and I was contracted to do the job."

"You double-crossing piece of shit!" Shai spat at his cousin. He knew from the time that Hammer walked into

Hoodlum II: The Good Son

his house that he was snake, but no one would listen.

"Where's Enzo?" Monet asked.

"Around the corner waiting in the car with a few of the boys. They're going to help me get rid of the body," Hammer told her, twirling his weapon like a baton.

"Hurry up and finish it. I have to get back inside before anyone gets suspicious, but first I want to watch the man who caused my father's death bleed," Monet said wickedly.

"You paid for blood, and I aim to please." Hammer raised the sledgehammer high above his head.

"Tommy will see you hunted like a dog and killed for this," Shai promised.

"I highly doubt that," Hammer said, before swinging his hammer.

Shai's eyes snapped closed, waiting for the end. There was a rush of wind and them something warm splattered across his face. When he opened his eyes, he saw Monet's body laying a few feet away from him. Her skull had been crushed like a rotten watermelon. His eyes couldn't hide his shock. "But I thought... "

"On your feet," Hammer instructed as he pulled him up. Shai was unable to stand, so Hammer tossed him over his shoulder like a sack of potatoes. In a minute, Enzo and the rest of those cock-suckers are gonna realize something isn't right and come in this alley with guns blazing. We'll be long gone before that happens."

"But I thought... "

"That I'd cross my blood over a few dollars?" Hammer finished the sentence for him. "You've got a lot to learn about your cousin Hammer, kid. There's a war coming to your doorstep and I'm gonna make sure my family is good and ready by the time it arrives," he told Shai before he lost consciousness.

CHAPTER 29

"Fuck do you mean you lost him?" Tommy raged. The entourage that had set out for Code Red earlier that night had returned, but they were missing a man... his little brother Shai. His right-hand man, Duffy, was at his side. They were in the pool house, so the staff wouldn't hear what they were talking about.

"T, the kid said he was going to the bathroom. I guess he slipped out with the broad," Swann said.

Tommy turned his angry eyes to Swann. "And you let him? I'd expect this kinda stupidity from someone else, but not from the man who I raised up."

"We'll find him, T," Swann promised.

"Fucking right you will, or I'm hanging all you niggas out to dry!" Tommy promised.

"Maybe him and the broad slid off and are shacked up in a hotel," one of the shooters suggested.

Tommy looked at him as if it was the dumbest thing he'd ever heard. "My brother, your boss goes missing in a party full of gangsters and that's your theory? Duffy, can

417

you tell this nigga what I think of that idea?"

Duffy whipped his pistol out and shot the shooter in the leg. He dropped to the floor howling in pain.

"Anybody else got any dumb theories they wanna share?" Tommy addressed all the men. No one spoke. "That's what I thought."

"Well I hate to add insult to injury, but we've got another problem," Angelo spoke up. He had been on his cell phone while Tommy was barking on Swann and the others. "That was Big Doc. The truck got jacked."

"Of course the truck got jacked. That's what we sent him down there to do," Tommy said.

"I know. What I mean is someone jacked it before they could," Angelo explained. "They were waiting at the usual spot for the shipment. When the truck never showed, Big Doc thought something might have been wrong, so they backtracked the route. They found the driver walking up the side of the highway. Apparently, he stopped for gas in Delaware and somebody stuck him up and took the shipment."

Hoodlum II: The Good Son

"You have got to be shitting me," Swann said as he slapped his forehead. He knew Shai needed the money they'd get from the cigarettes to bribe the officials for the building permits. "First Shai and now our truck?"

"I need everybody we got in the streets. Our first priority is to find my brother and our next is to find the truck. Anybody and everybody involved in taking our shit is going to sleep!" Tommy declared. The men nodded in agreement, but nobody moved. "Fuck are you all standing around for, get to it!" he roared. "And somebody get this idiot to a hospital."

Angelo helped the remaining shooter pick his bleeding friend up off the floor. As they were carrying him to the door, someone was coming in. It was Hammer.

"Is this a private party or can anyone crash?" Hammer joked.

"Fuck are you doing here?" Angelo asked.

"Just came to deliver a bit of news to my family. You can call off the manhunt. I know where Shai is," Hammer told them.

"You dirty muthafucka. If you've done anything to

my friend I'll..." Swann began.

"You'll thank me," Hammer cut him off. "Shai is outside in my car. He's a little doped up, but he's alive."

"How did you end up with him?" Angelo asked suspiciously.

"That's a long story, and it can wait for another time. I suggest you get Shai in the house and maybe call a doctor. I'm not sure what she dosed him with, but he's out of it," Hammer told them.

The men scurried off to do as they were told, leaving Hammer, Tommy and Duffy in the pool house.

"What the fuck is going on, Duffy?" Tommy asked.

"You boys have got yourselves a little problem. A while back I was contracted by some white broad, an Italian, to hit somebody in New York. I didn't know who the mark was going to be until yesterday. It was Shai," Hammer explained.

"That don't make no sense. Why would some broad want Shai whacked?" Duffy wondered.

"Apparently, she holds him responsible for the death of her husband." Hammer went on to tell them how he

Hoodlum II: The Good Son

had been contracted by Constance Tessio to avenge the death of her husband.

"Even from the grave, Fat Mike is still a pain in my ass," Tommy said, shaking his head. "Well, we'll take care of that bitch and anybody else who wants to dance."

"You know I'm with you, T," Hammer assured him.

"Thanks for your support, cousin, and for saving my little brother's life," Tommy told him.

"Ain't nothing man. I told you when I showed up, I'm here for y'all."

"And you've proven it."

"If it's okay with you guys, I'd rather not drive back into New York tonight. Especially in light of everything going on." Hammer knew that by then the Italians realized he double-crossed them. For that and what he had done to Monet, he was surely a marked man and nowhere in New York would be safe for him.

"No problem. I'll have one of the maids make up one of the guest rooms for you. Go on to the house, I'll be right behind you. I need to holla at Duffy for a second," Tommy told him.

"This shit is crazy," Duffy said after Hammer was gone.

"Crazy ain't the word, but I tried to tell Shai this was coming. Them Italians ain't to be trusted. Now maybe he'll listen," Tommy said.

"So what now? You want me to get in the streets with the guys to try and track down the truck?" Duffy asked.

"Nah, don't waste your time. I already know who took it."

This caught Duffy by surprise. "How?"

"Because I set it up."

Hoodlum II: The Good Son

EPILOGUE

Tech rode shotgun in the truck, with Pietro behind the wheel. For the millionth time, he asked himself if he had made the right decision.

They had an inside tip on a truck coming into New Jersey that would be carrying a shipment of cigarettes. Natalia's job was to get the route it would be taking. She knew that it would have to stop for gas at a station in Delaware, and that's where they would make their move. The driver barely put up a fight when Tech and Jewels drew down on him and forced him to get out of the truck, and Pietro jumped behind the wheel. Jewels, Belle and Ricky followed them in an unmarked passenger van as they tore ass up the highway. It took them less than five minutes. Just as Ms. Ruby promised, it had been an easy score...almost too easy.

They pulled into the warehouse, where Ms. Ruby, Ricky and Natalia were waiting for them. As usual, Ms. Ruby was wearing a church hat, a dress and gloves, but this time they were all black. She flashed him her crocodile grin as they climbed out of the truck.

"Behold the conquering heroes. You boys did good, real good."

"Man, this shit was so easy we could've pulled it off in our sleep," Jewels boasted, as he got out of the unmarked van.

Belle followed him. She tried to make eye contact with Tech, but he avoided her gaze. He was still mad at her for setting him up for the meeting with Ms. Ruby.

"It's just like I promised, easy work." Ms. Ruby kissed Jewels on the cheek. "Now, I have something for you boys," she said as she reached in her purse and pulled out two envelopes. One she handed to Tech, and the other went to Jewels. "There's ten grand a piece in there for both of you. Come around my house in a few days and I'll settle up what I owe you."

"Thanks," Tech said, stuffing the thick envelope into his pocket. There was a questioning look on his face.

"Something wrong, sweetie?" Ms. Ruby asked.

"I don't mean to sound ungrateful, and I damn sure ain't looking no gift horse in the mouth, but why so much

Hoodlum II: The Good Son

money just to rip off some cigarettes?" Tech asked. The question had been eating at him ever since he found out what they would be stealing.

"Pietro, would you like to do the honors?" Ms. Ruby asked.

"Follow me, boys," Pietro led them around to the back of the truck. Tech and Jewels watched curiously as Pietro used a pair of bolt cutters to clip the lock away and opened the trailer. Inside were dozens of boxes of cigarettes, but there was something else. He slid one of several wooden crates out, and popped it open before stepping to the side for Tech and Jewels to see what was in it.

"Holy shit! Are those machine guns?" Jewels' eyes got big when he examined the contents.

"Not just any guns," Ms. Ruby said as she hoisted one of the weapons and handled it expertly, "the finest quality Russian AK47s."

"But you said we were jacking cigarettes," Tech reminded her.

"No, I said you would be jacking a cigarette truck,"

she corrected him. "The cigarettes were just cover for the real prize. There's a very important man who went

through a great deal of trouble to get these guns into the tri-state. Couldn't have happened without you boys. You should be proud."

"This is some bullshit." Tech cursed, realizing he had been duped...again.

"No, this is big business. Ms. Ruby don't deal in no nickel and dime shits" she told him. "Now if your conscience is bothering you, you're free to give back the money."

"Hell no," Jewels chimed in.

"That's what I like to hear. Now you boys go home and get some rest," Ms. Ruby dismissed him. Tech and Jewels started for the exit, but Ms. Ruby called after him. "Tech, if you got the stomach for it, I got some more work that needs doing. Ms. Ruby can always use able-body souls like you and your boys."

"Thanks, but this was a one-time thing," Tech told her. He was done with Ms. Ruby and her double talk.

"Suit yourself, but if you change your mind, it's a

standing offer."

"Do you think we can trust them to keep their mouths closed?" Pietro asked after the two men had left.

"I don't know about Jewels, but Tech don't strike me as the chatty type." Ms. Ruby replied. "Besides, I seriously doubt either of them want word getting out that they just robbed Shai Clark."